Mona Lisa's Seduction

Mona Lisa's Seduction
(Two Teaspoons of Soul)

Kim Rogers

∞
b'Evolutionary books
New York

Copyright © 2006 by Kim Rogers

All rights reserved. No part of this publication may be reproduced or transmitted in any form or by any means, electronic or mechanical, including photocopy, recording, or any information storage and retrieval system, without permission in writing from the publisher.

Requests for permission to make copies of any part of the work should be made through www.kimrogers.org

This is a work of fiction. All names, characters, organizations, and events portrayed in this book are either products of the author's imagination or are used fictitiously for verisimilitude. Any resemblance to any organization or to any actual person, living or dead, is unintended.

ISBN 0-9774437-0-1

Text set in Garamond
Designed by Joanne Asala
www.compassrose.com

Dedication

Francesca Marinone Carnevale. My Noni. Now that you're gone, your life beats inside my heart. I pray that when my life ends, I walked as gracefully and lovingly as you did.

Biography

Kim Rogers graduated Brown University in 2000 with a degree in psychology. Upon graduation, she drove across America alone in her Toyota Echo and back again. She has lived in San Francisco, Montgomery, Italy, Provincetown, and currently resides in Manhattan. She has been a waitress, a receptionist, a radio dee-jay, a teacher in a behavior special needs classroom, a stage manager in a theater, and a field hockey coach. Her heart has been inspired by love, broken by love, lonely in love, and healed through love. Her passionate experiences led her to create her first novel, *Mona Lisa's Seduction*.

Besides writing, Kim is a lover of John Coltrane's *Sentimental Mood*, Tabasco sauce, oysters on the half shell, ocean waves, yoga, exuberant laughter, talking with strangers, the wisdom of children and the elderly, Starbuck's venti vanilla skim lattes, helping people, dancing with reckless abandon, shoe shopping, asking the question "Why?", the scent of lilacs, Ray Charles, U2, the Rolling Stones, Ella Fitzgerald, the color red, the saxophone, full moons, *Sex in the City*, butterflies, helium balloons, eyes that speak the words "I love you," Karaoke, strong hugs, self-awareness, Italian culture, and people that have the courage to expose vulnerability in spite of how others may react.

Please Note: Kim despises the sound of people shouting at one another, people in pain, people driving fast in the slow lane or slow in the fast lane, abuse of power, people that slam into you in the subway and don't say sorry, purposefully hurting others for personal gain, and egos.

In her spare time, Kim is currently attempting to develop a scientific definition of love. She admits it's rather tricky. Until then, you can follow her soulful, amusing, and often embarrassing escapades through New York City at *www.kimrogers.blogspot.com*, and learn more about upcoming projects at *www.kimrogers.org*. She's very grateful that you've taken the time and resources to invest in *Mona Lisa's Seduction*.

Prologue

"Come out. Come out. Wherever you are!" My older sister Neely shouts from the hard wood floor in our living room. Our dad isn't home from work yet, so we're allowed to play hide-and-go-seek in the house. After work my father needs his rest. We know not to wake him during his nap time or else he roars at our mother to tell "us" kids to "shut the fuck up." That's when "us" kids find a quiet activity, real quick. But for now, we can be silly.

"Angelina?" Neely asks, but I don't want her to find me. This is my special hiding place, stuffed in a small crack between a dresser drawer and the sidewall of my bedroom closet. The space allows me to fold my stubby legs Indian Style without my knees touching the walls. That's why it's good to be only four-years-old. Neely would never fit in here.

"You know I'm going to get you eventually. And, when I do, you're going to get a tickle torture."

I'm definitely not coming out on my own, but I secretly hope Neely finds me. From the wooden slits in my closet door, my eyes peer out to watch her run into my parents' bedroom. Her frizzy black ponytail sways like a horse's mane. I could stay silent forever. Once I stayed inside the closet from daylight straight through, until I heard crickets chirping in the darkness outside. My dad was calling my mommy bad names. She cried. He threw stuff. Right here, in this secret place, I was lulled to sleep.

"Girls, I'm home." I strain my ears to recognize the gentle voice. The footsteps tap delicately down on the firm oak floor. Loose change jingles at the bottom of her black suede purse just like when I shake my piggy bank. I'm saving up to buy my dad a new red tie. My mom put it in the washing machine and ruined it. He was real mad.

"Mommy!" I scramble from my hide-out and cling to my mother's thigh. She brushes my forehead with her lips.

"Gina-girl, what's up?" She asks.

"The sky."

"And the birds?"

"Yeah, and the birds."

"And tell me about the sun?"

"Shining real bright."

"Brightly. Brightly shining."

"Yeah. Brightly shining."

"Good. Keep your head up, Gina-girl."

We do this everyday. It's our thing.

"Neely, how was school?" My mother places her briefcase down on an antique trunk at the base of the stairs and sifts through a pile of bills.

"Fine."

"Did you do your homework?"

"No."

"How was soccer practice?"

"Okay."

"Did your father call?"

"Why would he? You told him to get out." Without glancing up from the collection of white envelopes, my mother's forehead wrinkles. She sighs heavily.

"Please, Neely, don't start this now. I've had a long day."

"Yeah, well, being a big time lawyer must wear you out. You don't even have time to love Dad anymore."

"Did he tell you that?" My mom raises her chin and widens her eyes. Ignoring her, Neely stampedes up the stairs, purposely stomping right on top of my silver slinky. "Gina, get your crap off the stairs," she shouts.

My eyes fill with tears and I spring up into my mother's arms. I'm her little bumble bee. Neely peers down at me from the top of the stairs.

"Jesus, Gina, you're such a baby." My mom and I sway together and wait for Neely to slam her bedroom door.

I whisper in my mom's ear, "She said a swear word."

֍

A few hours pass and the tension in the air tightens. The television rambles in the background to make up for us not having anything to say. My mom and I sit at the dinner table, prettily lit with two cranberry scented candles. She makes sure everything looks normal, whether my father comes home for dinner or not. I shift through cubes of cut up steak with my fingers, arranging them in order by size. Through the silent pauses, when the news shifts into commercial breaks, the two empty place settings do the talking. If my dad were here, Neely would never have the courage to skip dinner. That's for sure.

"Mom, watch this." I zoom a french fry into the sky like a rocket ship.

"Don't play with your food, honey."

I release my grasp of the rocket ship and yell, "Kaboom!" The french fry free falls onto my plate. My mother is not impressed when the ketchup splatters onto my white turtleneck. She shakes her head, reaches for a large green bottle, and pours a blood red drink into a glass with a long stem. Neely and I can't drink out of the large green bottles. It's just for my mom and dad.

"That's your fourth glass, mommy. That's four, like me." She cocks her head to the side and half smiles, but she doesn't look so happy. When my mother laughs she is the prettiest lady I know, even prettier than my teacher Ms. Ketchum. Her milk chocolate eyes open real wide and burst like firecrackers. Bam. Bam. Just like that. She has thick and curly ebony hair (like me) and a crescent moon scar carved into the temple near her left eye; I don't know how she got it, but it dissolves when she laughs. I miss her laugh. I know that for sure.

The front door rushes open and the footsteps bang like a marching band drum. I know it's him. All my secret hoping pays off.

"Daddy!" I run to greet him and lay my feet on top of his brown loafers smooth as apple skin. He carries a single red rose with a sparkly heart-shaped necklace dangled around the thorns.

"Hi, Angel." I hold onto his waist as he dances me into the kitchen, but a pain I want to spin out of him pulls his lips down.

They glare at one another. My mom covers her thick burgundy-painted lips with her long thin fingers. Once I asked her why she wasn't a piano player like Moses. Ms. Ketchum said that he was a world famous musician a long, long time ago and had long fingers to reach all those white keys. My mom told me that Grampy M said that she should be a lawyer. So that's what she did. She became a lawyer just like her dad. A tear popped up in her eye when she told me that story, the same way a tear pops up in her eye now. She freezes in position, hardened by the sight of him.

"Hi, Nancy," he says softly.

She pauses before saying, "Hello, Jim." She greets him the way she does when she talks to her work people on the telephone. He walks to her and holds her head in between his sturdy hands, using his thumbs as windshield wipers across her cheeks. She knows that he is sorry. He didn't mean it. He never means it.

"There's a filet mignon in the oven," she says, taking another sip of her red drink before crossing her arms. He kneels down, pushing his torso between her legs.

"I'm sorry," he says and with his face in her lap, he unfolds her closed arms and places them around his shoulders. They have already forgotten that I am in the room.

She slowly sifts her fingers through his straw blond hair, "There's mashed potatoes on the stove."

"Filet? And mashed potatoes? Wow, honey." His head still rests in her lap, so he doesn't see her tender grin. When he looks up, her lips quickly fall to a straight line.

"Yeah, well, don't get too excited. The mashed potatoes are instant," she says and he chuckles.

"Tell me. How's the meat?" He places the necklace around her neck and closes the clasp on the back.

"I didn't eat. I wasn't in the mood." She smiles slyly.

"Oh, really. Well, are you feeling hungry now?"

"I'm afraid it may be a bit too dry."

He kisses the hollow space at the base of her neck, where the rainbows twinkle from her new necklace. My mom laughs. I cover both my hands over my mouth, so they won't hear me giggle. He tugs her blouse loose from her black suit skirt and he slides his hands around her back. She closes her eyes, takes a short breath, and suddenly breaks from the moment, "Jim. Stop." She remembers me. "Angelina!"

"See ya', wouldn't want to be ya'," I shout out the saying that I stole from my big sister and slide around the corner in my thick purple socks, across the smooth floor, grabbing a hold of the banister just in time. I scurry up the stairs like a jungle monkey on all fours. I can't wait to tell Neely the news. Daddy's home!

PART ONE

❧

"And the day came when
the risk it took to remain tight
in the bud was more painful
than the risk it took
to blossom."

—Anaïs Nin

Chapter One

My feet pounded against the cement, moving fast in the center of Harvard's campus green; a young girl facing an oak tree trunk and cupping her chubby hands over her eyes, shouted, "Come out. Come out. Wherever you are!" My kneecaps reached high into the air with perfect runner's form. In an instant, she had disappeared from my view, but her words had followed me. Come out. Come out. Wherever you are. I had thought of them then—Neely, my mother, dad. My lungs ached. I ran faster.

I had just graduated from Harvard at twenty-four, a bit older than the average college graduate because my mother held me back from kindergarten, hoping to give me an "academic edge" over my peers. A third grade teacher had decided to do the same three years later based on my "poor socialization skills." "Academically superb." "Isolates herself from peers."

I burst through an iron gate and hooked a sharp right, nearly crashing into a student walking with his head bowed as he flipped through index cards. "I'm so sorry," I yelled, looking back. With the Charles River in sight, I was almost finished with my daily running route and within hours I would be headed to New York City. My diploma received with honors in both history and psychology, and stamped with a golden seal of approval, proved that I, Angelina Moreau, was officially ready for the "real world."

My name has always aggravated me. It was just plain weird, worse than weird. It was a contradiction within itself. Moreau, meaning "little dark," signified the regal French fifty percent of my birthright; Angelina rounded out the sassy Sicilian in me. In Italian it meant "little angel." And I was: vice president of my graduating class, head coordinator for an abused women's crisis center, captain of the soccer team for three years, and volunteer mentor at Boston Latin Elementary School. My parents envisioned my next move to the Big Apple, living in a high-rise, wearing a tailored pinstriped suit, collecting a six-figure salary within four years. My destiny was set, my bags packed in my reliable Toyota Camry.

Except, I had a funny feeling that morning. My Honey Nut Cheerios hadn't crunched the way they usually did. I had eaten the same breakfast for almost fifteen years, but that morning I was uneasy, itchy in my mind. I had thought the run would clear out the scratchiness. An hour later, I ended up where I always did, Starbucks.

After purchasing my vanilla double skim latte, I snuggled into a violet velvet chair to watch the worker bees begin their daily ritual. Through a large glass windowpane, I observed them crisscross on the sidewalk at DSL connection speed. Left. Left. Left. Right. Left. They marched with confidence, but the quickness of their steps could not cover their blank stares. Amid the buzz of Starbucks, the classified section of the *Boston Globe* slipped from underneath a gentleman's arm. He checked his watch and flipped open his vibrating cell phone.

"Sir, your paper," I said as he passed. He didn't have time for a sullen girl in a hooded sweatshirt casually drinking a vanilla double skim latte on a Monday morning. If my sweatshirt were silk-screened with the distinguished word "HARVARD," then he probably wouldn't have dismissed me.

I glanced through the employment section of the classifieds

even though Morgan Stanley had already offered me a decent entry-level position in the mergers, acquisitions, and restructuring department.

> **Wanted:** *Mona Lisa's Seduction. Wait staff position offered in a fast-paced tourist restaurant. Provincetown. No experience required.*

Just for fun, I pulled my cell phone out of the fanny pack wrapped around my waist and I dialed the restaurant's number.

"Mona Lisa's Seduction. Dylan speaking. What can I do for you." His words escaped without the intonation of a question, the statement seemed to indicate I needed him to fix something (a leak in my kitchen faucet or a squeal in my car engine perhaps).

"Uh. Hi. I'm wondering if you still have any positions available for this summer?" I asked.

"What sort of position?" His squeaky voice suggested a harmless mouse behind the receiver, so it was safe to tease.

"What sort of position would you like to place me in?" I fidgeted with the rim of my sweaty tee-shirt and rested my fingertips on my collarbone.

"Well, why don't you stop in at noon, fill out an application, I'll see what you have to offer, and we'll get right down to business."

My cheekbones heated. I checked my watch. 9:00 AM on the dot. Considering the potential traffic, I had two and a half hours to drive to Cape Cod. Two and a half hours was the exact amount of time required to breach the one hundred and twenty miles that lay between Boston and the peaceful retreat of Provincetown. I imagined a community of artists and writers, saxophonists and jazz guitarists, the ghosts of Eugene O'Neill and Ella Fitzgerald. I dreamt of the magical electricity I had read about in books.

A black leather briefcase dropped and the brass latches clicked open, knocking scalding coffee onto my gray spandex shorts.

"Darn it." I leapt up to grab napkins, still holding my connection to Dylan.

A young woman in her late twenties (too young for the two thick frown lines adorning the corners of her mouth) shouted, "Jesus-f'in-Christ. My CRM reports!" She bent over to gather her scattered papers, carefully aligning the edges into a perfectly symmetrical stack.

Her pulsating temples, her grinding jaw, and her combination of the words "f'in" and "Jesus Christ" to characterize a less than traumatic event disturbed me. Coffee stains on a couple of sheets of paper. That was the situation at hand. At the same time, I understood. Just last week, before my final exams ended, I whined to a college roommate from behind my computer desk, "I'm going to flunk this psych paper. I'm totally freakin' dead!"

"So, you're coming, right?" Dylan sensed my hesitation. I watched the hysterical woman while his question burned inside my brain. I flashed my life forward eight years. She was not the person I wanted to become.

She spoke loudly into her industrious Blackberry. "We must. And, I repeat, must, restructure the creative department to ensure maximum revenue for the division. If you have to fire Louis, just do it. I don't care who you need to lay off. Figure it out."

Was this lady serious? And, what about my burned knee? Where are your priorities? I stifled my reaction. I did not want to initiate conflict. I didn't want anything to do with her. I didn't want her tight bun and her pursed lips and her robotic mannerisms and her business suit and her anger. I didn't want her anger.

"Hey, what's your name?" Dylan asked, remaining patient and slightly flirtatious.

Mona Lisa's Seduction

"Angelina. But, uh, you can call me Gina. That's what my friends call me."

"Alright, Angel. See you at twelve."

"The name's Gina."

"Well, that's what your friends call you. We're not friends."

"Yet," I stated, clicking off my cell phone with a nervous certainty, but I knew that I presented myself with a false confidence. It reminded me of the one time that I lied to my father in high school, telling him that I slept over Molly's house. Really my boyfriend and I had spent the night camping in the woods. The secret I kept from my father was to maintain my post on the pedestal, to remain untouchable. In a way, the secret was reassurance that the charming hypocrite didn't know me at all.

I sprinted back to my apartment, quickly showered, pulled on my crisp white button-down-collar shirt and gray pants, straightened my long curly hair with the flat-iron—pulling it tightly back in a low ponytail, and hopped in my already packed Camry. My car drove to the point of decision. 95 South or Route 3 to Cape Cod? Vehicles crammed together like crayons in a box, horns beeping and directionals blinking at a standstill on 95 South. My car chose the path of least resistance. On the road, I bit the white tips of my fingernails down to the pink edges. I gnawed on all twenty corners of my cuticles, chomping off a hangnail until blood pooled in the crack of my pinky, and the rush was churning in my insides.

When I approached the steel bridge linking Cape Cod to the rest of America, I knew it was time. I dialed Morgan Stanley in New York and told a woman in the HR department, I was sorry for any inconvenience I may have caused, but I had changed my mind. As my car tires touched the pavement on the other side of the canal, I glanced back in the rearview mirror. The gray steel bridge glistened against the sun's midmorning glow; I was looking for a place to put my past behind me and that's how Provincetown found me.

～

The longer I gripped the steering wheel, the safer I felt. Inside my metal bubble on wheels, the past and future dissolved. My finger flipped through the radio stations to find something local. Monday morning's tribute to "Old Blue Eyes" blared on WOMR, "Outermost Community Radio." Frank Sinatra had always been a favorite of mine, information I never admitted to people my age. My shoulders swayed to his oily voice and I imagined myself in a dark, smoky lounge. A big brass band moving men in crisp shirts to flirt with women wrapped in satin; a wrist peeking out from a sleeve's end and a glove's beginning. A stage set by the seduction of the minds and the haunting curiosity of what lay beneath the modesty. I had never been in love.

My car slowed on a slight incline, weighed down by boxes packed from the floor to the ceiling with the precise organization of an engineer. Feeble scrub pines with golden needles passed by in a flurry, weathered by the forceful N'oreasters that often threatened to tear them down. Tiny white cottages with cobalt blue shutters lined straight in a row on the bay's edge; the chipped paint exposed patches of gray wood to display their individual personalities. I could easily forgo skyscrapers and traffic jams for this simplicity, for cottages and single lane highways, for the sight of live trees (even if they were battered, runt-sized scrub pines). Who said I needed to become a New York City hot shot?

As the car turned a bend in the roadway, a tall granite tower with evenly spaced rectangular windows rose up into the wispy clouds, conspicuously out of place among the purity of the natural environment that surrounded it. The structure belonged in the middle of a piazza hovering over elderly Italian gentlemen, sipping cappuccinos and debating the latest *calcio* match. Yet, something about the fortress's dominance over the territory stated the fixture belonged, for it had observed decades of history unfold.

The single lane highway changed into two. Finally I had space to let go. My foot bore down on the gas pedal, but I carefully monitored the dashboard to make certain to let up when the meter reached more than seven miles over the speed limit. My father had taught me to drive when I was only fourteen. It was our "little secret," because my mother would have had a brain aneurysm if she knew.

After church, he drops Neely and my mother at home, then he drives his Bentley to Sherwood Island Park in Westport. We switch positions. I pull the seat up, grip the wheel in the eleven and two o'clock positions, and gingerly touch the gas pedal. My father encourages me to speed up, saying, "C'mon Angel. Let it fly." I do what I'm told and drive down a road that runs parallel to the ocean, taking the lead ahead of a flock of seagulls. After a half hour, he tells me to reverse into a parking space. I hold my breath and inch backward into the spot. "Perfect," he says, "we should get back before your mother puts out a search warrant and blows our covert operation. Hit it, Kiddo." Forgetting the clutch is still in reverse, I press the gas pedal. We fly backwards over a curb and into a patch of sand. I quickly push the clutch into drive and rev the engine, but the tires spin and kick sand into the air. I place my hands in my lap and wait for my father to shout. He starts to laugh so I laugh with him. "O'well. I always wanted a boat," he says. "But, I'm not sure…should we tell your mother the truth about this little debacle? I think it's best if I say it was me."

I look at him, smiling, "Either way, Dad…"

"I know," he says, "she's going to ground us both for at least two months."

Thoughts flashed like lightening bolts through my mental circuits, temporarily obscuring the picturesque scenery around me. A seagull soared steadily above a rolling sand dune. He was a lonely creature with a grotesque beauty that I admired. Far from the flock, a seagull's course was a solitary journey. He dipped down onto an inlet of water at the base of the sand dune, grazing his claws against the still surface and launching upward to return to his haven in the azure sky. How had I come to appreciate a bird that chewed on scraps of barbeque ribs and orange peels inside torn garbage bags at the dump? At any rate, he was to be trusted, not a surprising feature associated with a creature that relied on autonomy. The seagull guided me directly to Commercial Street, the main drag.

Tourists sauntered in the middle of the one-way street. A man stopped to tie a shoelace. A woman glanced back, waiting for him to catch up. In the meantime, cars inched along at two miles per hour, paving a path through the lagoon of bodies. The atmosphere devoured the senses like a casino; cigarette smoke competed with the scent of hazelnut coffee, salt from the sea, dog dung, and fried dough sizzling in oil from a Portuguese bakery. In anticipation of locating Mona Lisa's Seduction, I slightly revved the engine to remind people of my vehicle's presence. Heads turned to locate the source of the racket, but they disregarded my warning and continued to stroll in the middle of the street. Only one father dragged his young daughter to safety while scowling at me. "Sorry," I mouthed. After all, they were tourists and this was their vacation. They fled to Provincetown to get away from people like me, and in a way to get away from themselves, to escape the predictable pattern of their lives.

Mona Lisa's Seduction

I passed by Town Hall, a quaint white building with eighteenth century old New England architecture that stood out among the renovated clothing shops and restaurants that tightly sat up and down Commercial Street. A green bell on the rooftop rung out the time of day, although tourists continued to meander, browse, or sit together on green park benches spaced along the brick sidewalk. Some speedily licked ice cream cones before the sizzling sun melted their treats, others drank coffee or smoked cigarettes, and all clutched shopping bags in their spare hands. They rested on the sidelines to observe the game being played out before them. They watched local boys in baggy tee shirts hung over their kneecaps and cargo pants practice skateboard stunts on the sidewalk curb. A buggy parked near the sidewalk and two young girls hesitantly petted the horse's white mane. Meanwhile, two dogs engaged in a vicious argument. A poodle barked ferociously at a Pitt Bull who could care less and a Rottweiler hid behind a black trash barrel to pee.

Commercial Street conversed like a drunken person in a slurred, speedy, and nonsensical manner. A shirtless man strutted down the road in a pair of leather pants with two holes cut out to reveal the bare skin of his butt cheeks. Interesting. Two women—one wearing a baseball cap and the other sporting a hockey-style mullet haircut fondled one another outside a bar named The Pixie that was lit up with a purple neon sign. Yes, Yes. Very interesting. I investigated through my mind's magnifying lens like Sherlock Holmes. A splendid woman in a turquoise sequined gown, balanced on spiked high heels, cat-walking in the middle of the street as if she were a supermodel. Her calves were two tight period marks at the end of pencil thin thighs. She passed me a flyer though my open window and winked. "Darling, I hope to see you tonight." Her rich raspy voice startled me. This wasn't a Misses, or a Ms., or a M'aam. Nope. This was a dude in a dress. I begrudged her for having more perky (if phony) breasts than my 34Bs and for elegantly carrying herself in a way that challenged my femininity, but I always gave credit when credit was due. I read the flyer; her drag name was Thirsty Burlington. Very clever, indeed.

After approximately fifteen minutes in Provincetown, I encountered bare butt cheeks, two lesbians necking, and a woman with a penis, all in broad daylight. Suddenly Boston didn't seem so diverse. In Boston, a Republican wearing a pair of jeans on "Dress Down Friday" was considered risky behavior.

I imagined what my parents would say about my new home. My mother would finally possess the evidence that I was "one of those homosexual types." She questioned my sexuality when I broke up with John. He would be attending Stanford Law in the fall. Law school! She exclaimed. How could I possibly cut him loose? I explained how the correctly aligned and color coded dress socks drawer really got to me. She had waited with an open mouth, shaking her head and staring at me. So, I took it a step further and told her that John also had separate drawers for his socks and underwear, which he actually labeled. "So?" She asked, not understanding the profundity of my frustration, because she was one of them. Perfectly organized, compartmentalized, and prioritized. She only purchased Ralph Lauren embossed cashmere sweaters. Three Christmas's ago, I presented her with a sweater without a designer label. Never saw it. Sometime later, I noticed the sleeves cut up and pulled over Neely's calves like legwarmers. "Success comes at a high cost," my mother said.

She infused this value into me at a young age, when she had forced me to copy forty capital letter E's before I could go bike riding with Molly on a Saturday afternoon. I drew them with four horizontal lines instead of three, but couldn't she have just cut me some slack? I was only in kindergarten. My mother had trained me to succeed the way a master trains a dog to give its paw for a biscuit. And, she trained me well. I never wrote a capital E with four lines after that day.

However, last April Fools Day, I pondered my achievements. Neely phoned me from Logan airport. She wanted to meet me for coffee before she left for London. I told her I couldn't rearrange my schedule because my essay on the Vietnam War was due the following day. Later that night, alone in the cubicle at the library, I wondered how two hours of my day to meet Neely could have caused any harm. How could I be so on track, but feel completely derailed? An A on one college assignment had become a higher priority than my older sister leaving to visit a foreign country. I realized I was becoming one of "them" too. The next evening, I stopped by Spartacus, found John at his barstool, and broke up with him.

As I continued the drive down Commercial Street the concentration of people finally thinned. I approached a stop sign. A white saltbox house faced me with a calico cat curled inside the windowsill, licking his paw. I turned left, traveling slightly faster along the narrowing street and leaving the restaurants and shops behind in exchange for small houses tightly stacked in a row. Cars parked along the brick sidewalk on the right, leaving only inches for my side mirror to pass through. I applied the brakes to allow a muscular man on a bicycle to cross the street. He got off his bike, pulled it up over his shoulder, and walked down a small flight of wood stairs between two homes. Inside the space, I captured a snapshot of the sand and sea, noticing that Commercial Street ran parallel to the bay.

My gaze returned forward. I was there. The rush returned. Mona Lisa's Seduction.

The lemon colored restaurant rested twenty feet from Cape Cod Bay. The navy blue sea danced against the sand, leaving a layer of white foam, and stealing tiny pebbles back into the water. The waves crashed lightly, but slowly they built into a superior sound like violinists just before the orchestral climax. A wooden pier stretched into the sea where a gazebo sat garnished by a mosaic of cracked cherry and gold china across the circular roof. Boats intersected in an intricate spider web on the choppy water and cruised together under the sultry sun. Whale watchers, commercial fishing boats, ferries, yachts, and motor boats, all traveled with separate intentions, but were all united in the sea, secreting rainbows of gasoline that smudged the surface. Across the bay, a lonely lighthouse on a sand bar stared back at the land of activity. An outside patio wrapped around the restaurant in a U shape—from the front of the building, around the left side, and hooked around the back. Customers enjoyed the serene view and servers frantically weaved between the plastic tables, transporting Heinz 57 and trays of martinis and margaritas with military efficiency.

A sign read, "Parking Across the Street." I pulled into the pebble lot and luckily detected the last open parking space. A seagull shat on my windshield, but before my annoyance could set in, a convertible Porsche cut me off, attempting to conquer the spot that was indisputably mine. Before the vehicle could rob my spot, I scooted my Camry into the space, now fully irritated by the Porsche's blatant disregard of one of the ten commandments of the road: Though Shall Not Covet Parking Spaces That Are Not One's Own.

As if that weren't bad enough, the scarlet red convertible parked perpendicular to my car and boxed me in from behind. The speakers blared Miles Davis's "Kind of Blue" loud enough to entertain a stadium of concertgoers. On principle alone, I didn't want to look at the driver, but I couldn't resist the temptation. What egotistical a-hole cruised around thinking he owned the parking lot and the two miles of air space around him? I cautiously stole a peek in his direction. He combed his fingers through his chestnut hair speckled with strands of gray, and secured a Yankees cap on his head. That really did it. The nerve of him to wear a Yankees hat in Massachusetts. A pair of black Ray Ban sunglasses covered his eyes and blocked me from getting the information I was looking for. He noticed me. Noticing him. My scowl evaporated and I rushed across the street toward the restaurant's front door. All the while I felt, through the impenetrable black lenses, his eyes boiling my backside.

"Inside or out?" A woman in her late twenties stood behind a wooden podium, holding a stack of florescent green menus across her chest. She wore a tee shirt silk-screened with the picture of the Mona Lisa with the sleeves rolled up to her armpits and a sapphire blue-stud glinted from her right nostril.

"Excuse me?"

"You wanna' sit inside or out?"

"Actually, I'm not eating. I'm looking to apply for a job." She scanned the back of the restaurant, agitated by my request.

"Lisa!" she screamed. "Another one looking for a job!"

An elderly man, using a walker, feebly crept into the restaurant and stopped to ask me, "Excuse me, Miss. Where are the bathrooms?"

"I'm sorry, sir. I don't work here," I said.

"In the back! To the right!" The waitress snapped, pointing to the sign that read "Restroom in the Back." Before he was safely out of earshot, she declared, "Open your eyes, you senile old fart."

I took a step back from the young woman, scanning the room for a place to remain out of the way, but the booths that ran along the wall and the center tables were filled with customers. In the bar area to my right, I spotted a black upright piano resting against a wall under a painting of a naked woman lying on her side, her dark wavy hair covering her breasts. I pulled out the piano bench and sat down, folding my arms and crossing my legs. I waited.

My watch read ten minutes before twelve and there wasn't even an empty seat at the bar. Two small children chased one another through the tables; a waitress dodged them with five plates of fish and chips stacked on her left arm. One customer in a corner booth shouted to her for a side of mayo and another complained to Lisa because he ordered a tuna sandwich medium rare, not medium. I hid from the confusion with my eye on Lisa as she diplomatically handled the customer. She was a striking woman—her creaseless bronze skin glowed and her lips were elongated, producing a wide and toothy smile.

"You're the girl looking for a job?" Lisa hollered above the overlapping conversations and commotion in the background, pulling her eggplant highlighted hair into a high ponytail. A woman laughed, a child whined, and the hostile waitress with the blue studded nose ring stuffed the menus in the hostess stand, saying, "Man, this job blows," before stomping off and kicking the swinging kitchen door open with her black clog.

"You know, we are actually all set right now, I mean, maybe we could put you in as a bus girl…" Lisa spoke without taking a breath, as if she was running a road race without a finish line.

I stood from the piano bench. "But, just today, I saw an advertise…"

"Except, we actually won't need an extra bus person until the end of June, so actually leave a resume and I'll look over it."

"Well, to be honest, I have never worked in a restaurant before."

"Oh, in that case..." I wasn't going to get the job. She had made up her mind.

"The ad said no experience necessary," I added, gnawing at my thumbnail.

"Good luck finding a job in this town. What ad?" Lisa asked and rambled on before I could respond, "Anyway, it's just going to take too much time to train you, as you can see, we are extremely busy. Table for two?" She looked past me to the two men waiting for a seat at the front door.

"I spoke to Dylan today."

"Dylan? Are you a friend of his?" Lisa's eyebrows raised and her almond shaped eyes returned to me.

"Not exactly. But he told me to meet him today at noon." I continued talking rapidly, hoping to show that I was trustworthy and dependable, "I am a Harvard graduate." I desperately threw out my degree, praying it might carry some weight. Lisa grabbed two menus off the host-stand and took a step toward the two men. I needed someone to stand up to bat for me. Where was Dylan?

The intolerable man from the parking lot entered, abruptly ending his cell phone discussion at the sight of me. His nose was broad and his pronounced forehead enhanced his masculine appearance. Plush, slightly crooked lips softened and sweetened him. I couldn't determine if he leaned more toward nearly handsome or nearly hideous. He stood with his shoulders arched back and his feet spread apart, shifting his weight from one leg to the other like a pendulum, until he settled into the scene. A long metal chain dangled against his faded and cuffed rolled jeans, securing a pack of keys to a loophole in his pants. Ray Bans still sheltered his eyes. He placed his hand on Lisa's back, the blacks of his lenses never shifting away from me.

"Lisa, who's this?"

"I don't know, Caesar. She's looking for a job, but there's no room for her on the schedule." Lisa sighed.

"Hello, Sir. Angelina Moreau." I modestly offered my hand. He received it with a smooth shake, allowing his thumb to slide delicately across the back. A tingling sensation lingered on my skin and I shifted my gaze to Lisa. He placed his sunglasses on top of his head, finally presenting me the opportunity to find out what lay beneath them. The blackness of his dilated pupils shot into mine and I immediately looked down at my feet. His eyes followed me down my lips and my chin and my neck, along the plane in between my small breasts, my belly button, and down to my hips, a bold surveillance considering his age. Who did this cocky man think he was? Men never made me nervous. My lips parted, but unable to formulate a syllable, my teeth bit down on my inner cheek in agitation.

"Make room for her," he said, grinning mischievously.

"Caesar, she doesn't have any restaurant experience. This place is a zoo. You know that…" If Lisa continued to speak, I would lose my only chance.

"Listen. I can handle this. In fact, by the time the summer is over, I will be one of the best waitresses in here," I said. Lisa stared at me, frowning, and Caesar looked pleasantly surprised by my sudden boldness.

"Honey, I bet you will. I bet you will." Caesar faintly pinched my elbow and walked away.

"Well, if you want to train today, I suppose I can set you up with Cara." Lisa stated. My eyes followed Caesar as he replaced his Ray Bans over his eyes and entered the kitchen.

"Uh…. okay…yeah, right, sure……thank you," I said.

Lisa introduced me to Cara, the angry waitress with the blue nose ring, and then quickly headed outside to seat customers.

"Sorry for being so lame before. This job just stresses me out," she said.

"No problem. I could see you were pretty busy."

"Waitressing isn't my gig. You know what I mean? I'm going to be a star someday. After this summer, I'm driving out to LA." Cara framed her face between her hands like a television screen and winked. "I have that innocent All-American look, that director's go for, but I know that I got to can the nose ring." She was right. Her hair was cut in a stylish chin length bob with long bangs swept across her tan forehead, reflecting the light like Caribbean white sand beaches. Her wide-set blue eyes hid under long and thick lashes.

"Are you interested in working in TV or film?"

"What?" She asked.

"Well, I mean, what's your dream? To act in movies or on a sitcom?"

"Frankly, my dear, I don't give a damn," she said. I laughed and Cara beamed, delighted she had amused me.

"C'mon, girl. Time to meet the boys. I'm gonna warn you right now. They look like grown men, but don't let 'em fool ya'. They're just prepubescent fourteen-year-olds. Sort of like the Lost Boys from Peter Pan." She kicked the swinging kitchen door open and I followed close behind. I snuck through a small space between the metal counter where teenage bussers dropped off plastic buckets filled with dirty dishes and the counter where a waitress was preparing a bowl of clam chowder.

"Oh, excuse me. I'm sorry." I had stepped on someone's sneaker.

"No problem, girl," a Jamaican dishwasher with thick dreadlocks smiled warmly at me.

"I say, you lookin' mighty good today."

"Painter don't start flirting with her yet! She hasn't even been here an hour." Cara playfully scolded. She reached for my hand, pulling me closer to her like I was a child.

"Why is he called 'Painter'?" I asked.

"It's not that big a mystery. He paints crap for Caesar. The cement on the patio. Signs. Stuff like that. Don't worry. He's harmless," she paused, adding, "Painter, not Caesar. I mean."

The kitchen was smaller than I would have expected for a restaurant of such high volume. The majority of the workers were from Jamaica or Eastern Europe. The room radiated a cheerful energy despite the turmoil of twenty bodies intersecting at top speed. One young man danced as he chopped onions, another sang the lyrics along with Bob Marley, *'…feel alright,'* and in between scrubbing pots, Painter sipped on a Red Stripe beer. Waitresses charged through the swinging kitchen door with a frenzied determination to pick up their customers' food.

"Turn 'em and burn 'em, ladies." The head chef shouted to the waitresses in a squeaky voice that sounded familiar.

"Burgers, on line." He called out as his eyes scanned a dozen white ticket stubs stuffed in the edge of a steel frame that held stacks of porcelain plates and bowls. He focused on the orders like a hawk on field mice.

"Dylan, baby?" Cara called.

Dylan? The cheery man that I spoke with on the phone?

"Sixteen!" Dylan screamed to a plump cook at the right hand side of the line, who immediately punched the number sixteen into a small black box that lit up with red blinking numerals.

"So…we all have a specific number and a buzzer and that's how we pick up our food?" I asked, wanting to quickly understand the system.

"Dylan?" Cara sighed heavily, tapping her bubble gum pink nails against a cutting board. Dylan wiped droplets of perspiration on his forehead with the shoulder of his tee shirt decorated with the image of a clam shell and the words "Frankly Scallop, I Don't Give A Clam." He turned toward the grill and began flipping burgers with a large silver spatula.

"Where's Nadia? Her food has been sitting here for five minutes. What is she doing? Buzz, number sixteen, again," he demanded.

"Dylan, sugar buns? Are you gonna answer me or am I gonna have to come over there and tickle a response out of you?" Cara shifted her voice as if cooing to an infant in a stroller, but Dylan ignored her, furrowing his brows.

A tall, lean girl jogged over to Dylan, shouting in a European accent, "Sorry, sorry, sorry," as if apologizing for committing treason against the king.

"Nadia, you should know better by now than to leave your food. Look. Your tuna steak is now medium, instead of medium rare. Weren't you the one with the same problem, like ten minutes ago?"

"I know. I know. I know. I'm really, really sorry." She stabbed the white ticket lying on top of the burger bun onto a metal stick, grabbed the tuna sandwich, pushed the blinking sixteen off the machine, and jogged out the kitchen door. A bus boy carrying a bucket of glasses walked the wrong way into the exit door and barreled into Nadia. Her grip on the sandwich slipped and the plate cracked against the floor; the tuna steak landed in black sludge built up from the servers' clogs and spilled tartar sauce that hadn't been cleaned up.

"Uh," Nadia grunted and scurried back to Dylan with a terror-stricken face.

"Dylan, please, please, please may you cook up another medium rare tuna?"

"Nadia!" Dylan shouted, shaking his head.

"It wasn't my fault…"

"Ring it in through the computer, Nadia. You should know that by now!" He snapped.

"Bobby walked through the door wrongly and…"

"Ring it in!" Dylan said and Nadia slowly walked away, defeated.

"Cara, maybe we should talk to him later," I whispered, folding my arms across my chest.

"No, he will answer, eventually. He's just being a control freak, as usual. Besides, you need to meet him sometime, anyways." She accentuated the words "control freak" as if it were a sword drawn against him.

Dylan placed his hands on his hips. The lunch rush appeared to be almost over. He grabbed a pint-sized beer mug and took a long swig. He bent down and raised his eyebrows at Cara to signal that he was ready to talk to her; his upturned lips showcased his dime-sized dimples.

"Dylan, this is Gina. She's new." He surprised me with a genuine, boyish grin.

"Hey. So you made it?" Dylan asked, his wide eyes drooped slightly, making me want to pat his wavy golden hair.

"Yeah. I made it, but to be honest, I'm not so sure if I'll cut it here."

"You'll be fine, Angel. Don't worry." He shifted his gaze and took another swig of beer, twice as long as the first.

"Do you two already know each other?" Cara asked.

"Not really," he said.

"Sort of," we simultaneously answered. Cara frowned.

"So, Cara's training you?" Dylan asked, running his fingers through his hair.

"Yeah."

"Well, you're in very, very good hands. The best." Dylan winked at Cara like a conspirator, and she batted her lengthy eyelashes.

"Oh, Dylan!" She scolded him and tip-toed behind the chef's line to kiss him on the cheek.

In the dining room, Cara explained the table station layout. A string of lilac booths followed along the edges of the walls. Tables and chairs filled the inside floor space. Large sliding glass doors served as a back wall, offering a view of the outdoor back patio and the sea further in the distance. The men and women servers swirled around us like fallen leaves swooped up by a gust of wind. Could I handle the perpetual pandemonium of Mona Lisa's Seduction? My world used to be secure and evenly paced: breakfast, classes, lunch, soccer practice, study, meetings, John, dinner, bed. It was a world I completely understood, a world I successfully mastered. What was I doing in this joint? I could be climbing the corporate ladder at Morgan Stanley with a 401K and health insurance, building a secure future. But, then again, there was the compact cubicle, the eighty-hour work weeks and bland florescent lighting. Morgan Stanley didn't need me, but did I need Mona Lisa's Seduction?

"Dylan seems like a nice guy, but he's awfully stressed out, huh?"

Cara snapped her head to respond, "Dylan is a womanizer. Don't lose sight of that fact."

"I wasn't saying I'm interested. I'm just saying he's a nice guy."

"Good. But keep your shield up and don't let it down. Not for a second, Gina. Or that shit-head will shoot you when you're not looking. Know what I mean?" I laughed at her dramatics, but Cara raised an eyebrow. A grave silence passed between us. She wasn't kidding.

Why had Cara felt it necessary to warn me about Dylan? I had just ended a two-year relationship with John. John and I had made sense. He was the captain of the ice hockey team and an honors student. He grew up in Greenwich, Connecticut, a wealthy community only twenty minutes from my hometown of Westport. I had met him in a bar near campus called Spartacus my sophomore year. A bouncer was attempting to steer the crowd out the door, John tapped me on the shoulder, his eyelids fluttered while he whispered in my ear, "I have a secret to tell you. I've had the biggest crush on you. Ever since last year, when I saw you in the trainer's room before practice." He walked me to my dorm room and he said, "I would really like to kiss you now." I laughed, "Okay." We kissed and he said, "Thank you." He turned away and stumbled down the long hallway, passing the elevator.

"John…the elevator," I yelled.

He turned around, saying, "Right. I thought I'd just give myself a tour of the premises. Nice hallway, you've got here." He pushed the elevator button with his thumb, whistling to himself and waving at me with a mischievous grin. The doors opened and I pulled the dorm key from my purse. "Ms. Moreau," John shouted, with his head peeking out of the elevator and his hand holding the door open. "I'm going to marry you someday." The doors slid shut. I had never thought about dating, marriage, or babies, but after that night, I did start thinking about John Goldman.

He showed up at my soccer game that week, and the Saturday after I returned to Spartacus to meet him and his friends. I drank an Amstel Light and a cranberry and seltzer with lime. John drank six Buds and three tequila shots.

Soon, he started to call me late at night. I would let him come in. He crawled into my twin sized bed. He told me more secrets. His father and mother were divorcing. He didn't even know if he wanted to become a lawyer. He was afraid. He rather become an ice hockey coach. He loved me so much and he didn't want to mess it all up like his parents. We faced one another, holding on tightly.

Mona Lisa's Seduction

The tequila lingered on his breath. Sometimes, when the stench was too much for me to tolerate, I turned on my side and John spooned me. He would ask, "What's wrong?"

"Nothing," I answered. I didn't want to upset him. But I wondered if John could ever say he loved me in the daylight? Could he ever share his secrets soberly?

"Did you get all that?" Cara explained the floor plan and the opening and closing side work requirements: spraying down the computers and glass windows with Windex, filling the olive oils, stocking the coffee and oyster crackers in the kitchen and paper products in the bathrooms located through the right wood door in the back. She clutched two spoons in her hands and banged them against the lavender tablecloth, hitting a coffee mug like a cymbal to a drum set.

"Let's bust out of here. I'm going to tell Lisa that I want to be cut early." She paused for a moment, mulling something over, "Hey, do you have a place to crash yet?"

The question forced me to recognize the recklessness of my decision to come to Provincetown. Me? The person that double checked all electrical appliances before leaving my dorm room.

"No, but I have some money saved. I could stay in a hotel for a little bit. Is it going to be difficult finding a place?"

"Like, duh. It's only the hardest place to find housing in like, the entire universe. You got a better chance at winning Mega-Freakin-Bucks."

"I don't know what I'm doing here, really. Especially without a place to live." I sighed and gazed at the bay through the back sliding glass doors; a seagull glided toward the lighthouse on the sandbar across the harbor. I wished I could be that seagull, knowing exactly where he wanted to be without hesitation.

"You know what? I have an extra room in my apartment. If

you don't mind two Great Danes the size of horses. The dishes are never done. I got carpenter ants running along the walls. And you should probably know I have late night parties and my boyfriend is basically a coke head. Yeah. That's about it. But you are more than welcome to rent the room."

Cocaine? I had only smoked pot twice in college, but each time it made me lazy and unproductive, which led to an overwhelming sense of guilt about wasting my time, and ultimately wasting my life. A butterfly with coral wings speckled with black splotches fluttered through an open window, landing on an arrangement of sunflowers in a teal glass vase.

"Sounds perfect. I'll take it." I said. How bad could it be?

"Cool. I'll be right back. I'll meet you outside in the parking lot," Cara said, beaming.

Cara returned to the kitchen to complete her side work, refilling plastic ketchup bottles and folding dinner napkins. I quickly headed for the exit. I didn't want to be in the way and I wasn't prepared to memorize twenty or so names of my new co-workers. What had I done? As I pushed my palm against the front glass door, a voice from behind shouted above the noisy chatter in the restaurant. "Goodbye, Angelina Moreau." My stomach flipped. The tingle returned. My breath halted for the internal rush. I looked over my shoulder, smiling widely, and with a confident tone to mask my inner chaos, shouted back, "Goodbye. Caesar Riva."

୬

After crossing the street and entering the pebble parking lot, I saw Caesar's Porsche still trapping my car in the space. I returned to the restaurant and found Caesar on the side outdoor patio. He stood with his hands on his hips, talking to a group of customers. I patiently waited until a break in the conversation.

"Excuse me, Mister Riva. You car is boxing me in. Do you mind moving it?"

Caesar eyes glowed and with a smirk he said, "Anything for you, Honey."

I walked rapidly back to the lot, hearing his black boots crunch against the pebbles close behind me. Caesar was suddenly there- leaning against my car.

"If I'm going to move my car, you can't call me 'Mister.' I ain't that old." He said with a faint lisp.

"I'm sorry, Mister…uh…I mean…Caesar." I stuttered.

"Alright, Kid. You started a war." Caesar said, laughing. He opened his car door.

"No war. There's too many already."

"Ah….Angelina Moreau this could be the beginning of a beautiful friendship."

I sat in the driver's seat, smiling to myself. He started his engine and Miles Davis's trumpet played, "All Blues." From the rearview mirror I watched Caesar backing into another parking space.

My cell phone rang and, pulling it from the side compartment of my purse, I checked the caller ID. My mother's office. I allowed two more rings to pass before answering. "Hello, Mom."

"Angelina, are you almost there?"

"Well, there's sort of been a change in plan," I said, thinking it was best to slowly ease her into my decision—like first touching your toes to the ocean, then moving in up to your kneecaps.

The passenger door to my Camry opened and Cara sunk down into the seat. "Sorry babe, I had a wicked ketchup disaster to deal with."

I lifted my index finger to indicate "just a minute." A minute was awfully optimistic of me; after all, my mother was a lawyer and she was bound to present her case with a sharp witted and flawless rationale.

"Angelina who is that that you're with?"

"A new friend. I'm in Provincetown. Not New York. I'm going to stay here for a little bit. Okay?"

"Angelina Phoebe-Francis…" My mother spoke loudly.

I pulled the phone away from my ear and Cara covered her mouth with hands, muffling her laugh. She mouthed "Phoebe-Francis." I cupped the receiver with my hand. "Yeah, that's my middle name," I whispered. "With a hyphen, by the way. My grandmothers got in a battle over who I should be named after when I was born."

"…And, not to mention work. What about work?" I caught the last part of my mother's lecture.

"Don't worry. I have a job."

"What kind of job? You already had a job at Morgan Stanley. What about Morgan Stanley?"

"Morgan Stanley will be okay without me, Mom."

"Angelina, I'm coming down there. This isn't reasonable. What are you doing?"

"I got a job at a restaurant."

"A restaurant!" I imagined my mother standing from her leather chair to shut her office door. I had never disappointed her before now. I had always been somebody. I had always been *her* somebody.

"Mom, I really should go. I'll call you later."

"I don't like this…"

"I know." I said softly and then pushed "end" on my cellphone.

Cara reached for my hand, "You okay?"

I nodded. My throat tightened, filling up with a thick fog, but I didn't cry. I only cried alone.

"You know what you need?" She asked.

"What?"

"A new middle name. Phoebe-Francis? Your parents smoke crack or something?" I looked at her and we exploded into laughter. I started the car and backed out of the spot.

"Alright, babe, hang a left," Cara said and we turned down Commercial Street.

Cara led us to Bradford Street and we passed a large brick building.

"That's Provincetown High. My alma mater. That's what shaped me into the outstanding citizen that I am today. Where did you go to school?"

"Harvard."

"Damn. So you must be pretty smart, huh? I used to be really smart. Well, until like the ninth grade. That's when I started dating this twenty-year-old loser who wanted to become a surfboard champion. So, I stopped the whole "study" thing. Cut class to surf with Marco. Can you believe that? Take a right at the Cumberland Farms and another down Commercial Street."

"You live on Commercial Street?"

"Correction. We live on Commercial Street," Cara said, winking.

We drove past Town Hall, still packed with tourists. An elderly woman, wearing purple platform heels and a short gold skirt stood in the middle of the brick sidewalk with a microphone in hand, belting out Frank Sinatra's "My Way." A cardboard sign taped to her microphone stand read: "Sixty-Eight-Years Young and Living the Dream."

"That's Ella. Transgender. She used to be a minister. Just in case you're wondering. Bet you don't see that at Harvard University."

"What was it like to grow up in this place?"

"Well, it's pretty cool. You can just be who you are. But at the same time, it's like everywhere else. There are always some people who are just dying to learn about your secrets…dying to tear you down for all your mistakes. In high school, when we would travel to other schools for soccer games, some kids would shout out things like 'Faggot' and 'Dyke.'"

"That's awful."

"Yeah. But, it's crazy…because in the summer, I would see those same kids hanging out in front of the Town Hall. Even singing songs with Ella and having a great time. People can be so bizarre."

Cara told me to slow down as we approached a three story Victorian guest house filled with shirtless men dancing on the balcony, listening to techno music and drinking frozen beverages in blue martini glasses.

"Meet your new neighbors." Cara rolled down the window and leaning out with her bottom on the edge, shouted, "Hello, lovers. Did you miss me?"

"Of course, Gracie." One man shouted back. She blew him a kiss and returning into the passenger's seat, said, "He calls me Gracie. Thinks I'm a mini Grace Kelly." Cara pointed to a two-story saltbox home on the left that was painted forest green. My Camry pulled into the cracked shell driveway. Two large lilac bushes sat on either side of the entrance, a good sign, I thought. Lilacs were my favorite flowers. I opened the car door and immediately heard calm waves lapping against the shore. Inhaling the salty air, I said, "Wow, Cara. This is lovely. And, it's on the beach?"

"Yeah. Not bad right?"

"How much is rent?"

"Six hundred bucks between the both of us," she said, walking up the porch steps and opening the screen door to the apartment. A steep staircase led to the second floor.

"There's tenants below. We're on top. Just wait until you see the back deck."

"How could this place be so cheap?" I asked.

"Caesar owns it. He cuts me a deal."

"Oh." I said. That was nice of him, I thought, considering he could make a killing on a rental property on the beach. Cara unlocked the door.

Suddenly, the view shifted. My new apartment was worse than I anticipated. Maxi pad wrappers, empty cartons of Häagen-Dazs ice cream, paper plates crusted with mildewed macaroni and cheese, and about three dozen half-empty Bud bottles piled up between the only furniture in the room—a large black leather sectional couch and glass coffee table. The space rank of stale cigarettes, spilt bong water, and vomit. Even the two Great Danes couldn't take the filth; they sat alert at the front door, waiting for a chance to escape. The apartment needed a serious overhaul.

"If you don't mind, I'm gonna lay down for a bit. I'm beat." Cara said, nodding her chin, "Your bedroom is in there."

I thanked her and when she shut her bedroom door, I immediately rummaged through the hallway closet stacked with terrycloth and paper towels, suitcases, and light bulbs. I found unopened cleaning supplies under a carton of toilet paper. I put on a pair of latex gloves, rolled up my gray pants to my mid thighs and filled a bucket with Lysol and water from the bathroom tub faucet. I bent on my hands and knees on the cracked wood floor and scrubbed the black film with a large brush. I sneezed for a half an hour while I dusted cobwebs from the wooden beams in the ceiling, and I used a full bottle of Windex to wipe splattered spaghetti sauce from the sliding glass doors that led to the back deck. The Great Danes slumped on the leather sectional couch into a lounging position with their long tongues, dripping with slobber and hanging out.

After I mastered the living room, I charged forward with a mop glued to my already blistered palms. I conquered the bathroom, using a knife to scrape the green grime from the white colored tile cracks, and gagged while I wiped the toilet bowl splattered by someone's diarrhea from the night before.

Three hours later, Cara emerged from her bedroom, wearing a pink lace bra and underwear and rubbing her eyes, "Woah. You really didn't have to do all that. I feel like totally bad."

"It's okay. Cleaning is sort of therapeutic," I said.

"Well, then, you certainly came to the right place for therapy," she said, grabbing a hold of my wrist and checking the time. "Why don't you chill out. Come with me downtown to The Claw. The least I can do is buy you a couple drinks." She turned; walking into her bedroom she unclasped her bra and it dropped on the floor. Cara rummaged through her make-up bag. She applied sparkling silver shadow on her eyelids before grabbing a cleavage-revealing halter top from a dirty laundry hamper. She put on a tight hot pink skirt and sniffed her armpits.

"I think I'm going to stay here so I can get a good night of sleep for work tomorrow. Next time," I said.

"I'm gonna hold you to it," she said, sitting on the edge of her unmade queen size bed and zipping up a pair of knee high black boots.

"Alright, I'm off. Don't wait up, sweetie." Cara sprung up and out the door, her high heels clicking down the staircase.

I still had my bedroom to clean. I mopped the floor, wiped down the antique wooden nightstand, dresser, and bookshelf with Pledge, and washed the large sliding glass window. Next, I headed to my car and lugged cardboard boxes and suitcases up the staircase. The hours passed as I unpacked my belongings late into the night. I placed my stereo on top of the bookcase and stacked my

Mona Lisa's Seduction

CDs on a shelf: Miles Davis, John Coltrane, Billie Holiday, Ella Fitzgerald, Nina Simone, Black Sabbath, and Metallica. The last two albums were gifts from John. I had once told him that I wasn't a fan of heavy metal, because the violent and angry music made me feel edgy. He had purchased them for me for my last birthday. I squeezed the rest of the shelves full with my book collection and I tucked a Bible inside the drawer by my nightstand. I hadn't opened it in years, but I couldn't give it away. I hung my Bill Brauer, Scarlet Dancer poster above my bed and my Jack Vettriano print, Road To Nowhere, on the wall next to a large mirror hung over my dresser. As a final touch, I hung white lace curtains over the large sliding glass door. After seven hours, I showered, crawled naked into my bed sheets and watched the shadows from the lace curtains skate over the white feather comforter.

An orange tinted moon beamed through a skylight above my king size bed. I turned on my left side. I hadn't adjusted to sleeping alone. I flipped on my stomach, tucking my hands underneath my pillow. Even though John snored and sometimes farted in bed, he had been there through all my nightmares. I was restless without him and afraid to fall asleep. I shifted onto my right side, pulling my knees to my chest. In the underworld the nightmare came alive. My leg instinctively stretched over to the empty side of the enormous bed; I had always checked in with him by feeling his anklebone with my big toe. I fought the urge to call him, because it wasn't John that I desired; but the comfort of our history.

He was the only person from Harvard that ever visited my home in Westport. I had invited him to my family's New Year's Eve party. I should have known better. Forty or so of my parent's friends and colleagues were there, devouring shrimp cocktail, oysters on the half shell, and sipping Dom Perignon. The lobsters came and there weren't enough. My mother had been four orders short. "Nancy, dear, you're so brilliant, but sometimes you can be an absolute moron," my father said in a flat tone. The jubilant chatter ceased. A few guests exchanged looks and others stared down at their plates. I stood from the table, fighting the tears. I walked outside to my car to cry. After a bit, John entered my Camry, handing me a bouquet of lilacs that he ripped from a bush outside my home. Immediately, I wiped the tears from my cheeks. "You know, it's okay to cry, Angel," he said, pulling me into a hug. My body fell limp into his arms and I rested my head on his shoulder. I didn't cry anymore, but I welcomed his fingers, raking through my long hair. I sniffed the lilacs, saying, "My mother's going to kill you for this." "What is she going to do. Sue me?" John said and we broke into laughter.

When my head hit the pillow at the end of the day, I was not capable of drifting off to sleep like normal people. Normal people closed their eyelids and within twenty minutes, they floated off to sleep while I replayed the day's events. I worried about tomorrow; stressed about world hunger, my 25,000-dollar college loan debt, the potential of our planet's nuclear bombs that could blow up the world, my mother's happiness, the latest impending war, but I was most haunted by the most terrifying question of all, "Did I belong here?" Not until the sun cast a sliver of pale pink light into the morning sky did the constant churning of my thoughts finally wear me out. I sunk into a deep slumber.

༄

"Leave me alone. Just go home," a woman shouted from outside. My eyelids shot open.

"If you would just stop to listen…" a man replied. A car door slammed.

"Get your hands off me," she yelled, before letting out a scream.

I opened the sliding screen door, pulled on my peach silk robe, and stepped onto the wood balcony, asking, "Are you alright?"

"Yeah…yeah…we're fine," the young woman replied, looking down at her feet and smoothing her flip-flop across the cracked shells. They began to whisper and I returned inside, sliding the screen shut and locking the glass doors.

I thought of the nightmare, the same repeating nightmare that disrupted all of my peaceful dreams since I was nine-years-old, a nightmare that I once lived with eyes wide open.

I cautiously turn the knob on my bedroom door and peer out into the hallway. My sister Neely whimpers at the top of the stairs; she is curled in a ball. Peaches, my cat, wails and paces by her side.

"Neely?" I tap her shoulder, but she doesn't move. She can't answer me, but she has to. She has to answer me. She's the big sister. She's fourteen.

"Did he do it again?" I ask, already knowing the answer.

I run into the bathroom in my parent's bedroom. My mother crouches on the brand new tile floor. She quickly stands when she sees me and moves to the sink. In the mirror's reflection, I see a cut along her left eye spewing blood down her cheekbone. There is blood on the white walls, which they told me not to dirty with my fingerprints. There is blood on the new tile floor, which they told me not to soil with my sneakers. I hear him breathing. I turn. There is blood on my Dad's hands.

"Angel, get out of here," he shouts.

I trip over Neely, who still shivers at the top of the stairs. I rush to the phone. I dial 911.

"You shouldn't have allowed me another glass." I hear him, yelling at my mother.

"Angel, who the fuck are you talking to? If you called your

grandmother, I'm going to kill you." His footsteps pound down the stairs, shaking the floor. My heart beats fast and out of synch and I wheeze for air. He rips the phone from my trembling hands and I squat down onto the cold marble holding my knees.

"Who's this?" he asks. "Uh. Hello officer." He shifts into a nice tone. "I'm really sorry about the call. My young daughter just made a prank. Typical kid's stuff."

I belt out a long shriek, as shrill and as long as I can hold it, because I can't do this anymore and I hate him so much and I wish he would just die.

He puts his hand over the receiver and whispers, "You better shut your mouth. Real fucking quick." I bite down hard on my lower lip.

"No, no. Everything's fine here. She's just upset because we won't let her stay up to watch television. I'm sorry again officer." He hangs up.

That's it. Nobody is coming to save us. I have never gone this far. I block my head with my arms, peeking out through the cracks with one eye, and I wait. I wait for his fist.

"You always hide under your mother's skirt and suck up to her cunt. You little bitch," he says, spitting on the floor. I pull my feet back just in time, before his spit lands on my toes. "Clean that mess up." I flip onto my knees, stretch the fabric of my shirt, and wipe up his spit with the bottom my Wonder Woman tank top.

My mother walks down the stairs, dragging an air mattress into the living room. Her eye isn't black and blue yet, but it will be tomorrow. Neely climbs in beside me on her side and her arms wrap around my waist so tight I struggle to take a breath.

"Mom?" I call out into the pitch black.

"Yes. I'm here, Angel. Would you like me to rub your back until you fall asleep?"

Mona Lisa's Seduction

"Uh-huh." The sweet hummingbird song my mother sings to me lulls my sister to sleep. But I haven't even tried to close my eyes. She sings "You are my Sunshine," but her song is weighed down by sadness. I shut my eyes. I see the blood draining down her carved cheekbone and I see the blood all over his hands. I open my eyes.

"Nancy!" My father calls down the stairs. That's her cue. She stands. Her footsteps fade. She returns to their bed, leaving Neely asleep and me alone in the dark.

I hold my breathe until my lungs hurt, to the point that I make myself feel pain, to the point just before I pass out for good. Tomorrow, we'll take a family drive. My mother will sit silently in the passenger's seat, gazing out the window, hiding her black and blue eye with a pair of Gucci sunglasses. My dad will stop at the gas station to buy Neely and I each a pack of watermelon Hubba-Bubba gum. We'll go to church and then out to a fancy dinner in a fancy restaurant with fancy people. My father will tell funny jokes. We'll laugh to cover the shame. We will play pretend. My mom will never take off her sunglasses. And I will want to die.

Chapter Two

It was my first day on the job and I had to be at the restaurant at 7 AM. As usual, I set my alarm two hours ahead; punctuality was crucial. I pulled on a pair of gray running shorts and a black tank top, laced up my sneakers and wrapped my hair back in a low ponytail. I placed my cell phone in my fanny pack and secured it snugly around my waist.

My legs welcomed the pavement, the pounding of my body against the ground. I ran on the balls of my feet, the closest I could get to flight. I turned up Center Street away from the main drag; I wanted to explore the other side of Provincetown. The wind blew softly and at steady intervals; thick clouds shielded me from the sun's heat. I focused straight ahead, soaking in glimpses of the scenery. I passed by an A&P grocery store, the local bank, and a Cumberland Farms gas station. I crossed the vacant highway, pushing even faster up a long incline. My lungs ached and the sweat drizzled down my temples.

A brown sign that read "Beech Forest" ignited my interest, so I turned onto the small road and ran toward the large oval pond where two swans swam among a web of emerald green lily pads. I followed a dirt path into the thick woods; the scent of pine permeated the air. I was free. On the move, I couldn't feel the rush. Chickadees waking from their slumber chirped a melodious tune above the crickets fading cries almost ready to say goodnight.

A cramp knotted in my side, but I didn't slow my pace. I knew how to push through pain. I ran faster. I checked the time. I was cutting it close, but I wanted to know where this path led. I continued forward, sprinting past my thoughts and eager for the destination, but simultaneously not wanting it to be over.

A half hour later, I remerged at the point where I started, back at the large pond with the swans coasting along the still water and through the lily pads. How had these two swans ever found one another?

Weary and drenched with sweat, I returned to the apartment. I unlaced my sneakers and pulled off my wet socks. I filled a glass of water from the faucet and guzzled it as I looked out the sliding glass door at the white lighthouse across the bay.

Perched on the deck rail, a red cardinal chirped a mating call into the stale air. When I crept onto the back porch to get a closer look, the cardinal cast off the railing and flew to safety in a nearby locust branch. But to my surprise, I found Dylan lying on a lounge chair, wearing only a pair of plaid boxers, and smoking a joint.

"Hey. I crashed here last night," he said, pulling himself upright and to the edge of the chair.

"One too many Buds after hours?"

"You could say that."

We stared mutely at the bay. I looked out at the lighthouse on the sandbar. I heard Dylan suck in another long hit of the joint. He began to beat his foot against the wood balcony. I licked my lips and Dylan cleared his throat, letting out an awkward cough. Finally, I broke the silence and turned to him, asking, "So, what time do you have to be at work?"

"Usually ten-ish or so for the lunch rush. Then, I take a break.

Work the dinner shift," he said.

"Must be nice, to just stroll in whenever it suits you."

"I don't stroll in. I skip in."

I laughed, "You skip? You don't seem to be the skipping type."

"I'm practicing."

"For the Skipping Olympics?"

"Nope. I'm practicing to be gay." He held out the joint.

"No, thanks."

"You don't smoke?" Dylan asked.

"Not really."

"Why not?"

"I don't know. Why should I?" I asked.

"Because pot opens your eyes to the world. And since I answered your question, and you didn't answer mine, why don't you take a toke or two?" He passed me the joint and I carefully placed it between my lips. I inhaled deeply and stifled a cough.

"Besides, nothing matters. What's the point anyhow?" Dylan spoke aloud to himself. Nothing matters? What did he mean?

"Hey, Dylan, I heard a piece of interesting information about you yesterday."

"Really, what's that?"

"Word on the street is that you are quite the lady's man."

"What! That is not true. Who said that?" He was angry and I immediately backed off, realizing that I had punched a bruise.

"What you got to understand about Mona Lisa's is that people thrive on unsubstantiated gossip. If my life were only as interesting as people make it out to be…" He spoke in a monotone voice, gazing at a man pushing a kayak into the water. My insides were queasy, but I believed him. Why would he lie?

"Did you grow up here?"

"No," he said, "ran away from home at seventeen. Thumbed

my way across the country from San Francisco. Landed here and began working at Mona Lisa's."

"Why did you runaway?"

"Bad birthday party."

"What happened? Run out of beer?"

"Something like that. So what's your…"

"What made you become a chef?" I asked.

"Fell into it, I guess," he said, taking another hit from his joint, "you have really beautiful toes."

I glanced down at my feet, wiggled my toes, and laughed. "Yeah, people tell me that all the time."

"Really?"

"Of course. They say you can tell a lot about a person's pinky toe and mine is slightly longer than the one to the left. That means I have an engaging personality."

"What does mine say about me?" Dylan inquired.

"Well, yours is substantially shorter than the one to the left. That means you're an open book."

"Yeah, right," he said, "I can't get enough of talking about myself."

"I can see that. Sharing personal information seems to be your forte," I said.

Dylan grinned and passed me the joint, "Hey, you should come out tonight. We're having a bonfire at Herring Cove beach to kick off the summer season."

Cara burst onto the balcony in a hot pink string bikini decorated with red cherries and struck a pose with her hands cocked on her slender hips. Her eyes darted wearily at me, "Morning sunshine! Did you sleep okay, your first night?"

"Baby." She turned toward Dylan, "Aren't you going to make me your famous egg McDunkin sandwich?" She squeezed suntan lotion into her cupped hand and slowly rubbed the coconut oil into her chest.

"C'mon, Dylan. I deserve a great big yummy breakfast. Here. Do me up." She straddled the chair with her back facing Dylan and tossed the bottle of lotion behind her shoulder.

"Ooooh, that feels sooooo divine," Cara cooed as Dylan rubbed the lotion into her lower back.

"Where's your boyfriend, Cara? I never had a chance to meet him." I asked.

"Uh...he's just somewhere...being an asshole." Cara said and Dylan grinned.

"In Provincetown, 'boyfriend' and 'girlfriend' are very loose terms." Dylan said and I nodded, but really, I had no idea what he meant. There was "dating," which meant an open relationship where both parties were free to explore and then there was "boyfriend" or "girlfriend," which meant the relationship was monogamous.

"Speaking of girlfriends. Ava is going to be a nutcase because you didn't come home last night."

"She's not my girlfriend. She's my ex-girlfriend," Dylan said firmly, glancing quickly at me and returning his eyes on Cara's shoulders.

"Your ex-girlfriend who lives with you so you can still screw her." Cara pouted.

Dylan turned to me and tossed his hands in the air, shrugging, "See. What did I tell you? Unsubstantiated gossip. Ava lives with me because she's looking for a place and I'm not the kind of guy that would kick her out in the street. But we're over."

"Dylan, I saw you in the parking lot with her after the bar, two nights ago." Cara said.

"Yeah, but we were just talking."

"I saw you kiss her."

"I only kissed her once. I was way too drunk and it shouldn't have happened. It was a huge mistake. She's psycho."

"All your girlfriends are psycho. Except for me. I was the only normal babe in the bunch." Cara turned to face Dylan and leaned in slowly with an exaggerated pucker and they kissed long enough for me to turn my head toward the bay in discomfort.

"You two dated?" I asked.

"Yeah, like three summers ago." Dylan said.

"Except it didn't work out because Dylan's a professional rogue," Cara said, raising one eyebrow.

Dylan pondered her statement, as if he were working out a jigsaw puzzle, "Were you the one that told Angel that I was a womanizer?"

"What are you talking about?" Cara said, innocently. Then they began to bicker and I excused myself. It was already half past six. What possessed me to smoke that joint?

༄

After I showered and dressed in my work uniform, a knee-length black skirt and lime green tee shirt with a silk-screened picture of the Mona Lisa, I rushed out the screen door. The restaurant was conveniently less than a quarter mile away from my apartment. Compulsively, I checked my watch. My speed walk transformed into a swift jog.

Commercial Street was still, not yet under the siege of bodies, cars, bicycles, delivery trucks, and the trolley. The tranquility of early morning always amazed me; the masses were bonded together in a deep slumber, hidden from the world's view and nestled in their huts. The sun, sky, and sea owned the moment. Deep down, from Provincetown to Prague, from Afghanistan to

America, were we really all that different?

A firmly toned, shirtless man with six-pack abs sprinted past me. Another unattainable gay Greek God, I imagined, and a reminder that the mind draws conclusions, taps into preconceived notions and stereotypes. Perhaps, it was natural for people to strive to identify with a specific group, like the two swans on the pond at Beech Forest. If that were true, then where was my swan?

An assembly of frantic pigeons fought over a chocolate donut hole on the pavement. They were a precursor of things to come—of strollers, roller blades, bikes, scooters, autos, and feet, scuffling for the right to survive on Commercial Street. At 6:44 AM, I ran through the door of the restaurant with sweat soaked through the armpits of my tee shirt. Lisa greeted me with a stack of plastic containers, a bin of butter, and the order to fill three tin trays because she predicted "complete insanity." It was the Memorial Day weekend. "An introduction to hell," she said.

The following ten hours slipped by without my awareness. I had never imagined that waitressing could be such a challenge. The job pushed my brain and body to the brink of spontaneous combustion.

I sprinted from table to table, scribbling down orders, punching them into the computer, picking up beverages at the bar, delivering the beverages, charging into the kitchen, searching for the white ticket with my number printed on it, grabbing the food, turning off my blinking number on the small computer, stabbing the ticket on a metal spike, picking up another round of beverages at the bar, and delivering them to my tables. Hallelujah. A peaceful moment. I took a quick sip of my pink lemonade.

I down shifted from fifth gear into first. I asked my customers, "How is everything?" The answers meant I shifted back into fifth gear: another Corona, a side of mayo, a decaf coffee, another pitcher of cream, more tartar sauce, a refill of ice tea, balsamic vinegar, Tabasco sauce, honey, mustard, honey-mustard dressing. My explanation, "I'm sorry sir, we don't have honey-mustard dressing," an exasperated response from the customer, "But, you have honey and you have mustard, so you should have honey-mustard dressing."

"Except we don't. We don't have honey-mustard dressing. I can give you honey and I can give you mustard, but I cannot give you honey-mustard dressing, because as I have stated three times now, we do not have it. There is a supermarket four blocks from here, so if you want honey-mustard dressing, you can walk to the A&P and purchase a bottle, and bring it back here and dip your french fries in it. Or you could just settle for good old-fashioned ketchup." He left me two cents on a forty-dollar bill. The cheapskate.

Finally, the Town Hall tower bell struck five rings and my shift ended. I slid into an empty booth at the front of the restaurant, removed my clogs, and rubbed the blister on the ball of my right foot. I pulled a large stack of cash from my apron and began to sort the bills by denomination. Cara entered the front door, singing, "Beast of Burden."

"Hey," I waved to her and she slid into the booth opposite me.

"I'm so wasted," she whispered.

"Why?"

"Oh, well, that would be a long story. You know what I mean? I'm stoned out of my skull. I was just going to have one beer before work. One thing led to another. You know what I mean?"

"I don't know how you could do it. I had a hard enough time fully sober."

"Yeah, well, give it time. I was like you once. It just sucks you in. Did you make any money?"

"Yeah. Actually. Two hundred and eighty bucks."

"Hey. As a little tip. If you get parties bigger than six people, you can add on an eighteen percent gratuity. People end up tipping you double. But, that's their problem. It says it right on the menu."

"Well, thanks. But, it just seems like bad karma to me."

"Gina, no one cares about karma in Provincetown. People love it when you got some drama going on. It gives everyone something to talk about." Cara pulled out a tube of pink gloss and rubbed it across her lips. I wondered if that statement was only true in Provincetown. People certainly gossiped about my father's car accident in Westport.

John Coltrane's saxophone, playing "Dear Lord," floated in from the street. It was him. For some reason, I was glad Mr. Riva had arrived.

"Caesar's here. I better pull it together. I'll talk to you later," Cara said, slipping out of the booth and walking quickly to the bathroom. I returned to counting money.

"So, you're coming tonight, right?" Dylan came up from behind, startling me.

"Coming where?"

"To the beach party."

"Well…"

"Great. I'll meet you there at 11:30 after I get off work tonight. Here. I drew out directions." He handed me detailed instructions, complete with a picture map of ocean waves and a seagull waving his wing. The bottoms of my feet pulsated from sprinting all day and my head was dazed, but I didn't want to disappoint Dylan, especially after his extra efforts to include me in the close network of Mona Lisa's employees.

"Um, I don't know."

"What's there to know? Just say yes. What do you have planned anyway?"

"Oh, you see, the thing about me is that I have this whole system. I wake up early to run. Meditate. Read the *Times*. Drink my coffee. I won't take you through the whole 'Angelina Moreau Rules for Daily Living,' but you catch my drift."

"Rules are for people in prison and concentration camps. C'mon Angel. Live a little. We're in the home of the free and the brave here." Dylan began to hum the National Anthem with his right hand covering his heart.

"Alright, alright. I'll meet you there. It couldn't hurt to join in for one night. Right?"

"Now, you're getting it," Dylan said.

I slid out of the booth to hand my bag of money to the bartender on duty and headed to the computer to clock out for the day. The glass door opened. A warm breeze snuck into the air-conditioned room. Through the door, Caesar swaggered into the restaurant, wearing a black shirt decorated with bright orange carrots.

"Hi, Angelina Moreau," he said, loudly, making a Presidential Address to the entire restaurant.

"Hi, Caesar Riva." I mimicked him, my voice just as boisterous and bold.

Caesar pulled out chapstick from his black pants pocket. He stood beside me on the other computer. "Hey, man, where's the button to order the jerk chicken sandwich?" He asked, squinting.

I moved close to him and pointed to the button, lingering in the deserted island of electricity between us. "It's right there. Looks like you may need glasses. But I bet you're too vain for that. Aren't you?" I said, teasingly, shocking myself with my audacity. He laughed, a bit taken aback. Caesar was accustomed to being the King in his court. Whenever Lisa spotted him driving his Porsche into the parking lot, she'd announce, "Caesar's here!" with an element of fear. That sent the entire wait staff scrambling to clean up the newspapers and magazines sprawled about the front tables. Then she'd order others to set up the front patio and sweep up dirty straws or napkins from the cement ground.

"You're done for the day?" Caesar asked, leaning in closer.

"Yep."

"Wow, Angelina Moreau, we're going to have to do something about this."

"Something about what?"

"We're going to have to put you on the night schedule because that's the only time I work. How am I going to work if you're not here?"

"Where there's a will, there's a way. Where there's a will, there's a way." I picked up my tote bag and headed toward the door, turning back to look at him.

"Honey, that's my motto too. And, I got plenty of will. Trust me." I shook my head and fled through the glass door, smiling. It would have been so cool, if I hadn't looked back.

∽

On my stroll back to my apartment, I dogged the tourists stalled in the street like parking cones. I pulled my cell phone from my canvas bag and turned the ringer back on; I dialed my voice mail. Twelve new messages. All from my mother. I sat down to listen on the bottom step of cement stairs that led to a brick Post Office building. Maybe I should have erased the messages so her words wouldn't hurt or confuse me, but I chose to torture myself.

Her strained voice indicated honest concern. She said, "I need you to be more rational." "This isn't a good idea." She didn't want me to "mess up my life." Mess up my life? My slate was so clean, I wondered if I had been living at all. Were all my choices, up until this point, truly my own? Had I unconsciously lived a program, never knowing what I really wanted? Fear set in. The rush came back again. Watching the tanned legs quickly pass by me, I was alone, sitting on a cold, dirty slab of cement next to a pile of cigarette butts.

I stood up, turned off my cell phone, and continued to walk back to the apartment. I had learned at a young age my mother didn't have all the answers and wouldn't always be there to protect me. My mother went away for a weekend when I was thirteen to visit Grampy M in a nursing home.

She leaves Neely and I alone with my dad. Except Neely is eighteen and she is never home; so really, it is just me and my dad. He heads out of the house around eight o'clock on a summer night. He is going to rent me a movie. He'll be right back. "Right back" turns into five hours. I know he's at the bar, drinking. I go to sleep.

In the middle of the night, I wake up with the weight of his body flopping on top of me, like a nearly dead fish. The whiskey from his breath exhales over my closed lips. He is naked. Only a thin white sheet separates us. His penis presses against my thigh. He kisses my forehead three times, repeating, "You're my Angel."

My body stiffens; I gently plead, "Dad, could you please get off of me?"

He stands up. "Jesus Christ, you're just like your mother. I was just trying to love you." He stumbles out of my room, accidentally kicking the Monopoly game that I am supposed to finish with Molly tomorrow. I hear him bang the bathroom door and turn on the water, shouting sentences I can't understand.

I run down the stairs to the kitchen, grabbing the cordless phone and the note with my mother's hotel room phone number. I pull open the silverware drawer and remove the butcher's knife. I run back to my bedroom, locking the door, grabbing my pillow and creep into the closet.

"Angelina? Why are you calling me so late? Is everything alright?"

From across the hall, I hear him talking rapidly, incoherently. I can make out pieces, "Fucking kill somebody." "I don't deserve this shit."

"Mom. You've got to come home. Dad's not right," I whisper into the phone.

"What's wrong? What happened?"

"He came home from the bar. He's not right. Please, please, please come get me."

"Angelina, I'm five hours away," she said, flatly.

"He was on top of me. Naked. But, he got up. He got up."

"Oh," she said. "Oh." The rush floods my insides. I press the knife into the carpet.

"He'll probably pass out now. Just try to get some sleep. I'll be back tomorrow. I love you, sweetie." She hangs up.

I curl up in a tight ball and I fall asleep clutching the knife. I awake the next morning with a new shell formed over me, hardened to the both of them. I'm a tiny fiddler crab scuttling sideways on the ocean floor.

We never spoke of the incident again. I never told Neely. I don't think my father even remembered. But my mother looked at me differently, her eyes saying sorry in random moments, like when we baked cherry pies for Thanksgiving dinner. We would be laughing and having fun together pounding the dough with our fists. She would look up suddenly, right into me with sorrow and regret. "I should have picked you up," her expression seemed to say. I would smile, letting her know it was okay. I handed her a cherry and we'd begin to roll out the dough.

Back at the apartment in Provincetown, I showered for an hour, harshly scraping my body with a loofah sponge until my skin turned pink. I pulled on a pair of black pants and a black tank-top. I lay on the back deck, reading a biography on Frida Khalo, passing time before the beach party and grateful that I had a place to go.

Chapter Three

Later that night, at Herring Cove Beach, about twenty employees from the restaurant huddled together around a bonfire. Goose bumps covered my forearms. The ocean roared as six-foot waves slashed the shore and gusts of wind spun sand showers into the midnight air. The strong summer wind moved carrot colored flames from the fire to samba to the ocean's sound. My bare toes dug into the frigid sand as I arranged a collection of stones in order by size. Cara lay on her stomach, her knees bent and ankles crossed in the air, snapping a piece of strawberry gum. She spoke to me in a low voice.

"Get this, I heard Lisa's husband is having an affair!"

"Really?" I asked, although I really didn't want to know the details. From years studying Sigmund Freud, Carl Rogers, and Jung, I understood rumors did not reflect the truth about human dynamics. Even if there was some truth in a rumor, a rumor was not the whole truth.

"She doesn't have the balls to divorce him. I would divorce the loser."

Perhaps sniffing out the scandal, Lisa relocated next to Cara. Lisa had innate gossip radar—she always knew the latest scoop and readily passed on the drama of the day. Within Provincetown's small community, gossip was a hobby, much like watching television or reading a novel.

"Lisa! How are you babe? I just love that sweater. It's a fabulous color purple. JCrew, right?" Cara wrapped her arm around Lisa's shoulders and kissed her cheek. Lisa returned the gesture.

I marveled at Cara's conversion. She really was an actress. Ironically, earlier at work, I overheard Lisa acerbically remark to other employees about Cara's promiscuity, "Cara is open for business. Over one million served." The co-workers laughed at Cara's expense while I clenched my lips. I knew I'd be banished if I stuck up for Cara. I wasn't sure which was worse, cast away in solitude with my principles, or embraced by everyone whose principles I opposed. I despised people who judged others, yet I clearly was judging them for their tendency to judge each other. Maybe, I wasn't all that different.

Cara passed me a joint and I took a hit. The white smoke from my exhalation mingled with the thick black smoke from the fire and trailed into the sky, floating toward the Big Dipper. I watched the animated faces encircling the fire; a twenty-eight-year-old gay man with HIV spoke with a forty-five-year-old mother of five about a new antique store opening in town. A middle-aged lesbian couple, raising three adopted children counseled a married woman that was having trouble with her son skipping class and hanging out with the wrong crowd. I loved the fact that the range of lifestyles, ethnicities, and ages between the workers at Mona Lisa's weren't barriers to their friendships. "The white girl from the big city with her miss-smarty-pants-college-education." This was probably how they summed me up. They laughed and teased and drank and hugged and drank and teased and laughed as I watched. I wanted in. I chugged the remainder of my Corona and reached for another.

Cara bragged to the others about my accomplishments, "Angelina just graduated Harvard," and "Angelina was an All-

American soccer player." I blushed and dropped my eyes to the sand, digging my hand underneath. I appreciated Cara's extra effort to include me into conversations, but I didn't want to be set apart. Her fingers, clustered in six clunky silver rings, clawed into my collarbone as she pushed to a standing position, saying, "I feel like playing a little make-out ball." She winked at me and strolled down the beach to meet the boyfriend I hadn't yet met, I assumed.

In the following hours, I drank another three, no, four Coronas, and smoked the remaining pot until the roach singed the tip of my thumb. I was in the moment. I was carefree. I grabbed a hold of a guitar. I had never held an instrument before. As a teenager, I had hidden seven journals filled with my pencil sketches and watercolor paintings under my bed. I'm not sure why, but I eventually stopped painting. My fingers strummed the guitar strings and I sang an improvisational song about the perils of waitressing:

> *"One guy wants a side of tar-tar.*
> *I told him, baby, you better bart-er.*
> *Another wants a cup of chowd-er.*
> *I say, boy, you got to beg a little loud-er.*
> *And, I call that, the Waitressing Blu-ues."*

When I stopped, the group begged for more by chanting, "An-gel-i-na." I saw Caesar from the dark edges of the crackling bonfire, marching toward the group, with a raised chin, holding three cardboard pizza boxes stacked on his head. I wavered for a moment, but didn't stop my little performance on his account; I was enjoying the spotlight too much so I continued. Occasionally Caesar and I locked glances. But I always looked away while he arrogantly continued to gaze at me. What was he looking at, anyway? Now he was standing directly across from me, silhouetted by the moon. The wild whites of his eyes glowed in the dark. I reached for my beer.

Dylan emerged from a sand dune in a blue windbreaker, with a beer bottle in one hand, his black chef clogs in the other, and his linen pants rolled to his knees. He slowly moved my way, supplying me with another Corona. He didn't remain by my side for long, yet every time my Corona emptied, he supplied me with another. He fluttered around like a moth, weaving in between everyone at the party, never settling down in one place for longer than five minutes. When my beach chair cracked and I fell backward, still strumming the guitar, he was there—miraculously materializing like a rabbit from under a magician's hat. Dylan offered his hand and softly brushed the sand from my upper back. Before I had time to thank him, he disappeared.

When saliva quickly pooled in my mouth, I jogged away from the crowd, clenching my abdomen. I had never been sick from drinking too much, not even during senior week in college. The starry sky spun violently. I shut my eyes, but the blackness rotated at an accelerated rate. I prayed to God, "Please, don't make me puke…I promise I won't do this again, but please, please, don't make me puke now." At the water's edge, I vomited pure liquid into the sea. I had to get home to bed. My hands searched for car keys in the front pocket of my black pants. I had lost them somewhere in the half mile circumference of the bonfire.

A sturdy hand rubbed my lower back.

"Are you alright?"

"I don't do this, Caesar. Don't think I do this. This isn't me," I said, turning away.

He intertwined his elbow with mine and I used his body to hold my weight up. My head bobbed from side to side, until it finally rested comfortably on his shoulder. Blood pulsated in my temples as if my heart were beating in my brain.

"C'mon. I'll drive you home," he said.

"Well, I can't drive home until I find my car keys."

"You're not driving home."

"Oh, yes, I am. I'm finding my car keys and then I'm driving home. And, that's what I am doing."

"Okay, Honey. You're driving home. Let's look for your car keys, then."

Caesar ran up to the bonfire. He couldn't find a flashlight, so he twisted two glow sticks together, tied them to the end of a large piece of driftwood, and we combed the sand for my keys. We didn't speak, but a silence throbbed between us. The waves crashed against the shoreline and the wind cried into the night air, sending a shiver up my spine.

"Hey, what are you two doing?" Dylan yelled, jogging up to me. He lifted a damp strand of my hair from my cheek and tucked it behind my ear.

"Looking for my keys," I said, hiccupping. Caesar eyed us, frowning, and turned away. He crouched down, his fingers raking across the sand.

"You've been out here for at least a half hour. You're never going to find them," Dylan said. I had already debated giving up entirely. I wasn't going to stop until I found them. Caesar understood. "Think positive, Honey. We ain't stopping until we find these darn things." He had told me. I squinted along the water's edge, looking for him. I could make out a faint green light from the glow sticks about twenty-yards down.

"I'm glad you showed up, Angel," he said, grinning.

"Really?" I coyly asked.

"Really. I'm really looking forward to hearing more of your scientific theories about personalities and pinky toes."

"Yeah, well, it goes much deeper than that. We still have many other body parts to cover," I said, hiccupping.

"Is that a fact? Like what?"

"There's the earlobe for instance."

"Right, of course, the earlobe. You know, I've read that a connected earlobe means cleverness. Like me. My earlobe is connected. I'm clever," Dylan said, tugging at his ear.

"I don't know. I think that is still up for debate," I said, searching for Caesar. The green light glowed brighter as he returned to me.

"Oh, no. It's as certain as Columbus's discovery that the world is round. I'll show you my research tomorrow."

"Well, I expect concrete evidence."

Dylan laughed. When Caesar approached, Dylan returned to the party. A statuesque young woman held out a beer for him as he met the crowd.

"Who's that girl with Dylan?" I asked.

Caesar squinted toward the bonfire, "That's Ava. A member of Dylan's fan club."

Ava's bronzed skin and black hair gave her an exotic beauty. Dylan and Ava seemed a bizarre pair. She was a ravishing raven and he was a plain robin.

"Hey, man. I found them!" Caesar shouted with his chest plumed out. He had retrieved my keys from a wet section of sand, just before a wave crashed over them. He dangled the keys a foot above my head. When I jumped to reach them, he stretched his hand higher into the air. I placed one hand on my hip and extended the other with a cupped palm, "If you don't give them back to me, I may have to call you Mister."

"Okay. You win," Caesar said, placing the keys into my palm. His hand covered mine and that's when I saw it. A gold wedding band wrapped around his left index finger.

"Oh," I said, frowning.

"Oh, what?"

"Thank you." My head was dizzy. I took a step back, my ankle buckled, and I toppled on the cold ground. Immediately, Caesar reached for both my arms, pulling me upright.

"Do you still think it's a good idea to drive?"

"There's a boulder there. I tripped because there's a boulder there," I said.

Caesar bent over and picked up a white stone the size of a garlic clove, "Sorry, Honey. You're coming with me." He turned and skimmed the rock across the water's surface. It skipped ten times before it sank.

"That was impressive. I mean, as far as skipping rocks goes."

"I know," Caesar said.

Without saying goodbye to the crowd, I followed his footprints up the sand dune and into the parking lot.

My body collapsed into the passenger seat like a rag doll. I hiccupped. Caesar placed a Frank Sinatra CD into the stereo system.

"Are you cold?" he asked.

"A little." He turned on the heat and pushed a button to close the convertible roof. "Can you leave the top down? I want to watch the moon."

Caesar complied, taking a left out of the parking lot. He accelerated the Porsche. I checked the speedometer. He cruised close to fifteen miles over the speed limit along a winding single-lane road. We drifted into the empty land covered only by small scrub trees, lacking lampposts to light the way.

"I think you turned the wrong way," I said, the bitter breeze whipping my hair around.

"I don't take wrong turns, Angelina Moreau," he teased, "I'm giving you a free tour."

I stretched my arms into the air and slowly twirled my wrists, as if I reached the top of a roller coaster. Closing my eyes, I smiled. The wind's resistance pressed against my arms, blowing them back.

"I just love Frank! Don't you?" I asked.

We simultaneously reached over to turn up the volume dial. Our skin brushed. I placed my hand on my lap, tightly crossed my legs, and leaned against the door. I glanced at him from the corner of my eye. He stared straight ahead, his foot bearing down on the pedal, rubbing chapstick across his lips. I looked out the side window at the scrub pines flying past. I felt Caesar, looking at me.

"So, why did you come to Provincetown?" I asked.

"After college, I went backpacking through Europe. I ran out of money and took a flight to Boston. I was looking to hitch a ride to New York. Stay with a friend until I got a job in the city. And this guy at Logan Airport said he was on his way to P-town. I'd never been so I said, 'Why the hell not?' It was in the universe's cards, you know what I mean? What about you? How'd you land here from Harvard?"

We approached a yellow traffic light and Caesar stopped. I told him the story about my plans to work at Morgan Stanley, the angry business woman in Starbucks, and the newspaper ad. He stared into my eyes with large pupils, but I didn't look away. The light changed to green. I lightly tapped him on his forearm, pointed forward, and we crossed the intersection.

"How did you build your restaurant?"

"I started with a hotdog stand on the street. Saved money and bought a small space along the pier. Eventually, sold it. Got into some real-estate ventures. The time was right in the market. I started the restaurant with a business partner and bought him out a couple years ago."

"But how did you know it would be successful?"

"Honey, I just did it. It's like playing golf. You put the ball on the tee and you wail the crap out it. Sometimes you hit a bunker, but you learn as you go. You practice hard enough, and man, one day you'll nail a hole in one." Caesar's words endeared me to him, calling me both "honey" and "man" in the same sentence, spoken at a tone-deafening volume.

"Have you eaten there yet?" he asked and nodded his head at a tiny black shack with a pink neon sign that read "Betty Boop's Burgers", hardly an establishment at which I expected Caesar to dine. However he did dress in faded jeans and a tee-shirt, not a designer fashion ensemble, not to mention his black silk shirt with bright orange carrots. Caesar didn't flaunt his affluence, he flaunted his individuality.

"Man, those burgers are really good. Plus, the counter girl is cute and she has big tits," he said, exploding with a loud and awkward laugh.

Normally, I would have ripped into him with my monologue about respecting womankind. Instead, I laughed, appreciating the fact that Caesar's tongue wasn't on a leash.

"Tell me, Caesar, just how good are the burgers? Are they just okay? Or is it mind-blowing experience?"

"Oh, Honey, trust me. This is gonna blow your mind," he said, deepening the tone of his voice.

"By the way," I said, quickly becoming serious, "my apartment is on Commercial Street. 193."

"193? You live with Cara, then."

"Yeah."

"She moved in with us when she was ten. We adopted her. She was my daughter's best friend…well…I don't want to get into all that," Caesar said, his foot bore down on the gas pedal. "Cara's a babe, but, man, she always dates losers."

"Really. I haven't met him."

"The kid is a creatin'. He's not good for her and I wish she would realize that. I don't get it. Why do women date losers?"

"I'm not sure. Maybe, it can feel good taking care of someone. Gives you a sense of purpose. You don't have time to look inside when you're dealing with someone so messed up," I said, suddenly embarrassed.

We drove the remainder of the ride in silence. As we approached 193 Commercial, I became more disappointed with each passing mile. I didn't want to part.

The Porsche skidded onto the shell-cracked driveway. Caesar stopped the car and pulled up the emergency brake. He inhaled deeply, closing his eyes, saying, "Can you smell that? The lilacs."

I unbuckled my seatbelt. Caesar opened his eyes and I plunged, leaning into him. My lips met his. Our tongues delicately said hello and I cradled his prickly jaw with my palms to draw him closer, moving my hands down his shirtsleeves and bare forearms, until our fingers intertwined. We held on firmly.

I suddenly felt the cold metal encircling his left finger and pushed myself back, "That was a big mistake," I said, opening the car door, fumbling on the floor for my purse.

"Mmm. No it wasn't," Caesar said, shutting his eyes. Underneath his eyelids, I could read him, replaying the kiss in his mind, still savoring the flavor. I rushed to kiss him a second time, deeply and searchingly. Twenty-five years lay between us, I wondered how a kiss so logistically wrong, felt so supremely right. I finally pulled away and slammed the car door without looking back.

Cara was hanging out the second floor window, smoking a cigarette and flicking her ashes toward the street as I passed. Our eyes met. She knew. I stumbled into the apartment. Without removing my sandy sneakers, I flopped onto my bed fully clothed and quickly fell to sleep.

Chapter Four

The next morning at 8:32 AM, Lisa phoned annoyed and impatient. I was an hour and a half late for work. "That's unacceptable," she said, "and you may want to lay off the two-in-the-morning drives." With a dry mouth that tasted like vomit, I pulled on work clothes from the day before—my tee shirt was drizzled with balsamic vinegar dressing and splattered ketchup. I ran to Mona Lisa's, pushing through the pain that was like a drill slicing into my skull, tripped on my untied shoelace and skidded against the pavement, scrapping my knee. I fought the mist in my eyes and sprinted faster, trying to recall last night's events. "Lay off the two-in-the-morning drives." What in the world was she talking about? I felt anxious I had committed an inexcusable act, and horrified I could not remember what exactly I had done.

I entered the restaurant as if a land mine would detonate at any minute. I searched into the eyes of my co-workers for evidence of condemnation, but demanding customers consumed their attention. They didn't notice my arrival. I tied on my black apron, clocked into the computer, and checked the table-station chart on the host-stand. Lisa stuck me on the back outdoor patio with the six tables farthest from the door. I spent most of the day running from the tables into the kitchen and back, occasionally taking breaks on the outdoor station tucked on the side of the restaurant, sipping water and gazing at the lighthouse across the bay. The day passed quickly and without a comment about the previous night. I swiftly counted my money outside and walked to the front of the restaurant with my eyes fixed on the dark gray carpet to clock out of the computer.

"Hey, Angel. One too many Coronas last night. Huh?" Dylan approached me with a knowing smile.

"Not really. I just set my alarm clock for PM instead of AM," I said, punching the first number of my code into the computer.

"Making out with the boss cuts into a quality night of sleep, I guess."

I stopped, forgetting the next number of my code and remembering Caesar's tongue looping around mine. "I kissed him. So, what?" I spoke softly, my arms crossing over my chest and my eyes surveying the room for people close by.

"You know, I'm worried about you. You really have to be careful with drinking too much," Dylan said.

"Don't worry. After last night, I'm going into detox for awhile."

"I'm not saying stop drinking. Just don't let booze turn you into something you're not."

The topic of "alcohol" was a grotesque harelip I had surgically corrected long ago. I wasn't an alcoholic. It was my dad. Not me.

"Who told you about that, anyway?" I asked.

"Lisa."

"Lisa?"

"Cara told Lisa," Dylan said.

"Does everyone know?"

"Not yet. But, it's safe to say that if Lisa knows, news will have completely spread in the next twenty-four hours."

Strong cologne flooded the air—sage, nutmeg, and a hint of lime. Caesar appeared with an extra macho snap in his step.

"Great. Here comes trouble," I said, biting the bottom of my lip.

"No trouble, Honey, no trouble," Caesar said, clocking into the computer screen next to mine.

Caesar's indifference unnerved me. "Oh, you're definitely trouble. Trust me," I said.

"Really? Why is that Angelina Moreau? Why am I trouble?" He had obviously been here before with a woman other than his wife; a kiss was not a shock to his spirit. Who knew how many mistresses he had stored away?

"Hm," I scowled at him.

"So are you gonna share with me and Dylan here why I am trouble? I would really love to hear you present your case."

"Fine, I'll tell you. You really want to know?"

"Yeah, man. But, hurry up. I don't got all day," Caesar said, playfully. He rubbed his shaved chin and leaned against the wall. He crossed one black boot over the other. All the while, he had a cocky smile plastered on his face. Dylan was like a fly on a bowl of fruit, buzzing about, positioning his body between ours.

"Oh, forget it. You're impossible," I said.

Caesar kissed the tip of his fingers and tossed it out to me. I swung my bag over my shoulder and stomped away, but in my hurry to exit I dropped my bag and the contents fell on the floor—my wallet, lipstick, house keys, and change. Caesar bent down to help me gather my belongings while Dylan walked away. A penny rolled along the rug before settling flat. I reached over, saying, "It's heads up. For good luck. Here." I dropped the penny in Caesar's hand.

"Thanks. I'll put it in a special place." Caesar tucked the penny in the top pocket of his striped shirt, tapping his hand over his heart two times.

Cara passed by and I shouted, "Hey, Cara! Wait up!" My clogs shuffled against the carpet as I ran to catch up to her before she entered the handicapped bathroom.

"Can I talk with you for a second?" I asked.

"Sure, c'mon in." She held the door for me.

"Listen, I know that you know," I said with my arms tightly crossed against my chest.

"Know what?" She innocently asked as she scrunched up her short black skirt to squat over the toilet.

"About the kiss," I said.

"Oh, that. So, what."

"Well, I really wished that you hadn't told everyone."

"I didn't tell everyone. I just told Lisa."

"Well, I wished you didn't tell her." She flushed the toilet and moved to the sink, staring into the mirror and pouting her lips.

"Do you think I'm pretty?"

"Cara, you're gorgeous."

"Really?" she asked, wide eyed, waiting for my response.

"Really, really, gorgeous. You're movie star gorgeous." How could she not see that? Right in front of the mirror. The truth. How could she not see?

"You're not just saying that?"

"Hey, I'd trade my skinny bum for your tight, heart-shaped rear any day."

She turned around and stood on her tippy toes to examine her bottom. "Really?"

"You're perfect, Cara," I said.

She turned back to the mirror, unzipped her cosmetic bag, and began to apply black eyeliner above her lids. "Anyway, you don't have to stress out about kissing Caesar."

"Well, I'm not exactly proud of it."

Cara rolled her eyes, saying, "Gina, you're so damn innocent."

"No, I'm not."

"We're one big, incestuous family here. It's called Mona Lisa's Seduction for a reason. We have one of those Don't Ask, Don't Tell policies. Sex is for sale. Believe me. I mean, it's just sex."

"Is it really that simple? All the time?"

Cara scrunched her eyebrows, pondering the question. I waited for her reply, but she turned back to the mirror to apply blush along her cheeks.

"Well…whatever, I'm not here to mess around with the staff," I said.

"What is someone like you doing here, anyway?" Cara asked with curiosity that led me to believe she had already been contemplating this ever since I arrived.

"I guess, sometimes in life, you just have no where else to be."

"So 'freedom's another word for nothing left to lose' Huh?"

"Or perhaps I'm searching to be bound to something. Something worth holding on to."

"Yeah. Me too. That's why I'm saving my money and moving to LA in the fall. I don't care. I'm just going." She rummaged through her polka dotted purse, saying, "He'll see." She pulled out a large bag of white powder.

"Cara? What are you doing?"

"It's just sugar. Relax."

"Oh. Okay."

"Just kidding. It's coke. See, I told you. You're soooooo innocent. Are you like the Virgin Mary in disguise or what?" She tossed the bag of cocaine at me and it fell through my hands like a scalding hot platter.

"What are you doing with all that?"

"I'm CEO of my own private company. CCC. Cara's Coke Corporation. That's how I'm going to get out of here." She picked up the bag of cocaine from the yellow tile floor and hugged it to her chest.

"If the police don't bust you first," I said.

"In Provincetown? Have you checked out these summer cops? They can't handle two cars at a four stop intersection." She unlocked the plastic bag, licked her finger, and dabbed it into the bag of cocaine. She ran the powder over her top gum.

"Hm. Just like candy. Want some?"

"No."

"Why not?"

"Because, I don't."

"Why don't you? Aren't you kinda curious?" Perspiration began to bead on my lower back. I didn't like the situation one bit, trapped in a room with a bag full of cocaine. A knock on the door made me gasp.

"Just a sec," Cara said, applying a layer of pale pink gloss on her lips. Meanwhile, I paced the bathroom like a bull in a pen seconds before the rodeo.

"Listen. I need you tonight." Cara said.

"For what?" I asked.

"You'll see. Just trust me. Meet me at The Claw at 10:30. It's just past Town Hall." She unlocked the bathroom door. "Put the coke in my bag," she mouthed the words to me, adding, "act cool."

Caesar stood outside the door. Of course. "Why were you girls taking so long? Making out together in there or what?"

Cara laughed and lightly punched Caesar on the arm. She opened a second door to the dining room and cruised at racetrack speed to the front of the restaurant, leaving me alone with him.

"Yeah…two women making out…Ha…in your dreams,

Caesar Riva," I said.

"No. Just you," he whispered, barely audible.

"What?"

He was silent and boyishly nervous.

"What did you say?"

"In my dreams. Just you and your siren song." He looked directly at me, shining with a tender sensitivity.

A foreign feeling rose inside of me. I gnawed a cuticle on the edge of my pinky nail, inhaling the scent of his nutmeg cologne. "What are you wearing anyway?"

Caesar dropped his eyes, seemingly embarrassed that I noticed he had applied cologne. "Uh…it's called. 'Contradiction.' Kinda corny name, right?" He laughed, forcibly.

The door opened from the outside, pushing my body into his. Attempting to dodge him, I ducked my head under the bridge he formed by his arm on the top edge of the bathroom door.

"Oh, sorry. Are you in line?" A man asked. Caesar's fingertips skimmed my lower back.

"No…no…I was…uh…just leaving," I said.

Caesar entered the bathroom and I walked into the dining room. The thick wood door clicked shut; I stood with my back against the wall, thinking, "Contradiction. No, Caesar. It's not all that corny."

Chapter Five

I arrived at The Claw at 10:30 sharp. Cara never came home after work, so I didn't have a chance to tell her that I wasn't going. That was why I showed up at The Claw. To tell her I wasn't going. The bar was small, but big enough to pack in forty bodies. The popular fisherman's hangout constructed from ship wood, rank of alcohol sweated out the day after a hangover. Bruce Springsteen belted out "Glory Days" from the 1960's jukebox in the back corner. I sensed the year-rounders' resentment for the college students, leaning over their shoulders and flapping twenty dollar bills in front of their noses. The middle-aged regulars at The Claw understood the value of a dollar; the crows' feet wrinkles around their eyes spoke of the endless hours under the sun—pounding nails, painting houses, pulling weeds from gardens, or hoping for the big one, the big tuna or lobster catch of the day. They drank another Bud with paint splattered and calloused hands to ease the disdain for the kids on summer break from college, celebrating the fact that they had their whole lives ahead of them. Another shot. Another round. The party was just getting started. I didn't want to be there.

The Claw reminded me of the local bar my dad hid away in, during one of his binges, between the months he struggled to stay sober. When I got my driver's license, Neely and I argued over who was going to be "the one" to pick him up. She said it was my turn automatically because she had suffered for the couple of years before I had my license. I refused to allow her to bully me. It wasn't my fault I was born last. Rock, paper, scissors. That was how we managed to negotiate the clash. It was imperative that one of us arrive at the bar before eleven, or else Dad may have gotten too drunk. He could arrive home wasted, dangerously drunk, and who knew what would set him off into a tirade? Who knew what would cause him to beat my mother, his fist whacking against her flesh? However, we couldn't appear before eleven because he wasn't drunk enough to allow us to drive him home. Neely and I had mastered the skills of "the pick up" with world-class precision.

One. Two. Three. Shoot. I always threw out the rock. Neely always threw out the paper. I usually let her win, unless I had a final exam or an essay to crunch out. This time I threw out the scissors. I knew I had tougher skin than Neely. She knew too. She confronted my parents more than I did, saying things like "you guys need some serious professional help like pronto" or "please tell me I was adopted into this insanity." Then she would slam a few doors or blast heavy metal music from her bedroom. But all her rage was a shield from her flimsy, paper-doll spirit. That was why I was the rock and she was the paper.

Every episode is the same. I walk into the bar and say "Hi" to Ted, the bartender. My dad's drinking buddies joke that the old maid came to whip him into shape. For a year, I laugh with them to mask my discomfort. Until, one night, I snap. I tell them, "Do me a favor and just shut up for one night, because someone you love is having their heart break because of your passion for booze. Do you think this is fun? Yeah. Look. I'm having a blast." I do a little tap dance, then I freeze with my right leg extended and my arms outstretched in an L, "Ta-daaaaa!" They shut up. In fact, they stop joking about me all together and their eyes would only meet mine in sharp darting glances.

After Ted helps me drag my father into my Toyota, we drive home in silence until he begins to speak about the time at UConn when he and his fraternity brothers ripped off a scarlet red door to some rich guy's brand new corvette and placed it on my dad's beat up Pinto because his door got busted when he side-swiped a bush. He put the clutch into drive, instead of reverse, and ended up inches from slamming into my mothers' parents' home, adding , "Me and your mother just started dating…a month later…we got a kid on the way." I want to remind him, "The kid's name is Neely, Dad." Instead, I tighten my grip around the steering wheel.

He only tells college stories on our drives home and they always end with the same period mark: "college was the best years of my life." He continues, babbling, "It wasn't easy being a father so young. Too young. Plus, I was born with only one kidney." At the kidney story, I draw the line. I pop in my Beatles CD, fast-forwarding to Lennon's "Imagine." My father sings loudly off key and I sing with him.

My father never asks me about school or my boyfriend or my college search but he always asks me about soccer practice. When "Imagine" ends, he turns to me. "How many goals did you score today?"

"Two."

"Good job, kiddo. You know, I talked with a college scout at your last game?" My father said, smiling. He had never missed a game.

"Really? What did she say?"

"I told her that you're tough. And, you're ranked third in your class."

"What college was she from?"

"Then, I told her you're the highest scorer on your team. But that's not the whole story. You have more assists than goals. You're a real team player," he said, patting my head. I jerk, knocking my head against the driver's seat window.

"What did she say?"

"I didn't know your SAT scores. What are your SATs?"

"1440."

"Is that good?"

"I guess, Dad. It's out of 1600."

"Well, wherever you want to go, Angel, I'll pay for it. Princeton…Yale…Harvard. You should go to Harvard."

"Thanks, Dad."

"I love you Angel."

I clear my throat, "I love you too, Dad."

Without soccer as a source of conversation, my father just talks at me, over me, through me, and beyond me. Still, I savor our time together in the car because I harbor a snowflake of faith. He will change. One oppressively hot summer night, a week before I plan to leave for Harvard, my car pulls up the long driveway between the perfectly manicured green lawns and lit up by tall black lampposts. "Stop," my dad mumbles, "Look at it." He points to our white, three-story Colonial home, refined and symmetrical, rectangular windows with jet black shutters, ivy twisting up its tall Corinthian pillars—in honor of his childhood home in Savannah, Georgia. A light fog hovers over the tree tops, and covers the brick chimney on the roof. My dad turns to me, saying, "You know, when my father died of a heart attack when I was nine, we lost everything. I watched them seize our house. Pull out the furniture. Everything. Ma did the best she could. She did the best she could. Then she married that louse. I know why she did it. She wanted to make sure your aunt and I had things…she wanted to give us a future. I told her not to worry. One day, I'd make sure that I had the perfect home.

Nothing bad would ever happen again. The perfect home." He chuckles and I turn to him, watching his eyes gloss over. "And, I did it. We have five-thousand square feet of perfection. Two point two acres of perfect land. Great kids. Great wife. God, Nancy, why do you stay with me?" he said, grabbing his head and pulling his hair, "All those hours working…weekends…deal after deal…for this perfection. Who ever thought I would be the stain?" He looks at me, tears falling from his eyes. I take him in my arms while his body shakes. "I'm a bum, Angel," he said, "I'm nothing but a bum."

"Shhhh. It's okay. I love you, Daddy. We can help you. You can get better."

"My Angel," he said, pulling away and wiping his eyes. He smiles wearily, lightly tapping his hand on my cheek, and I smile back.

I drive the Camry into our four-car garage, right in between my father's Bentley and my mother's SUV. He quickly exits, leaving me alone in the car. He went inside, calling, "Nancy, honey, I'm back!"

Seven days later, Neely and I play another round of rock, paper, scissors. I pick him up at the bar. On the way home, I sing "Imagine" alone.

I found an instant comfort in The Claw; the same comfort I found in catechism classes my mother forced me to attend as a little girl. I couldn't understand what brought everyone together, and I wasn't sure if I really wanted to be there in the first place, but once I got used to it, I relied on the routine. It was just…normal.

"Angel, what's going on?" Dylan asked. He scooted onto the splintered bench beside me.

"Hey, Dylan! I'm just waiting for Cara," I said, checking my watch, adding, "Actually, she was supposed to meet me a half hour ago."

"What? She told me to meet her at the bar across the street.

That's why I came to The Claw. To see if she came here instead."

"That's bizarre," I said.

"No. It's just Cara being Cara."

"What does that mean?"

"Yeah. I don't know, I just thought it sounded good," He said and we laughed—Dylan muffled a few hee-hee-hee's as if he were stifling a sneeze and I clapped my hands together, releasing the sound exuberantly and entirely.

"Let me buy you a drink." Dylan said.

"Okay."

He wormed through the crowded bar, which was two rows deep in customers pleading for drinks. Some people waited quietly with hands in their pockets, others pulled rank by calling the bartender's name. It took Dylan twenty minutes to buy the beers, not because of the busy bartender, but because he paused to chat with a dozen people. All women. Young women, too young to legally be in the bar. Curvy women. Beautiful women, I was surprised gave him the time of day. Women with husbands or boyfriends nearby, that warned him with their intense stares to tone down the flirtation. Dylan played all of them like a checker champion, jumping from one end of the board to the other, until he got his fill, until his eyes said, "King me." When he was ready, he raised his right hand and yelled, "Theresa! Can I get two Coronas!"

"Here you go." Dylan handed me the Corona with the lime propped on the edge of the rim.

"Aren't you going to fix it up for me?" I asked and he grinned, exposing his dimples. He slowly pushed the lime into the bottle with his thumb and turned the bottle upside down until the lime bumped against the bottom.

"Is that to your likin' Ms. Angel?"

"Well, let me give it a taste test. I'll let you know." I took a long, savory sip. "Hm, hm. I think you've found a new calling. Perfect dispersion of lime and liquid."

Dylan scooted back into the booth. We matched one another beer for beer, until I suggested we step it up a notch, and kick back a shot of tequila.

"I thought you were in detox," he said.

"This is detox. From twenty fours years of living by the rules."

"Yeah, I've been detoxing myself for about nineteen years. Since, I left San Fran." Dylan was much older than I had assumed. He ran away from home when he was seventeen, so that made him…thirty-six! No way. He had the anxious energy of a teenager with attention deficit disorder, not my image of a thirty-six-year-old man.

"Dylan, you're like a man." I blurted out and immediately wished I hadn't drunk the tequila shot.

"Thanks a lot," he said.

"No. Please. Don't take it the wrong way."

"What did you think I was? A drag queen? 'Like a man!'" He mimicked me, forming quotation marks into the air with his forefingers. "At least you use original material, Angel."

"No. Really. It's a compliment." I laid my hand on his forearm. I leaned my forehead near his cheek, my eyelashes almost brushing his pasty skin.

"What are you doing?"

"I'm investigating."

"Great. Now you think I have some skin disease. Or, maybe, I'm 'like an alien.'"

"No. I know you're not an alien."

"Why's that?"

"Because, I'm an alien," I said, "and I don't recognize you from my planet." He shook his head, smiling. "I'm searching for wrinkles. You don't have any wrinkles. No frown lines. No crow's feet. Nothing."

The screen door swung open, Dylan turned his head, and slid his body away from me.

"Stop for a sec," he muttered. I glanced at the door.

It was Ava, wearing tall black high heel boots, a jean mini skirt, and an oversized Polo shirt tied in a knot at her waist. She looked like a dancer in an eighties punk rock video, but she was so striking, it didn't matter. Ava glared first at Dylan and then at me.

"Hey, Dylan. Can I talk to you?" Ava asked.

"Not here," he said, picking up a lime and squeezing it into his beer.

"When then?"

Dylan looked at me and then back to her. "Tomorrow. After work."

"Okay."

"Hey, is that my Polo?"

"Yeah. Sorry."

"That's my favorite shirt. You can't just take that without asking, Ava."

I picked up a straw off the wood table and began tying a knot.

"Well, you left it at my apartment." Ava tilted her chin, maintaining an air of indifference, but she cleared her throat and immediately fled the bar. The screen door slammed loudly and a few heads turned to look at the exit. I had just broken up with John. I got it, the uncertainty of a dying relationship, the pull to return to the familiar. Dylan and I enjoyed a slight flirtation, but Ava had nothing to worry about. We looked at one another and simultaneously said, "Let's get out of here."

Dylan and I shared this character trait: avoidance. We easily engaged in conversation with people—asking questions, flirting, and making them smile. But if the discussion dug beneath that surface layer, producing an uneasy feeling, we suddenly had somewhere else to be—Dylan had work and I had to run.

I employed the tactic with John. Instead of confronting him about a rumor I'd heard that he had cheated on me with his ex-girlfriend, I swallowed my discomfort. But two sentences played over and over in my mind: "He cheated on me," and "I'm not good enough." The idea of his unfaithfulness slowly corroded my heart. It wasn't the idea of him with another woman that bothered me; it was the fact that he had hidden it from me. A-void-dance. That was what happened when I kept my mouth shut, and that was probably the real reason I broke up with John. Perhaps the break up had little to do with his color-coordinated sock drawer and everything to do with my unwillingness to tackle the messiness of intimacy. Had John really cheated on me? Would he have lessened his drinking if I had asked him? I would never know.

"You know, Dylan, you can tell me if you're still dating Ava. I mean…if you left your shirt at her apartment…well…"

He looked at me with a sideways glance. We speedily walked through the crowd. "I mean, I know how hard break-ups are. And it just seems like you guys have a lot of unfinished business. You know? It's safe to tell me."

"I already told you. Ava's psycho."

"Maybe everyone's psycho. If you take the time to get to know them." I walked faster, a few steps ahead of Dylan. Maybe people had to learn to be psycho together? Maybe that was the point? We don't have to be psycho alone.

"I wonder what the heck happened to Cara tonight?" Dylan changed the subject.

"Yeah, does she make a habit of blowing people off?"

"Cara is a diva. That's why it didn't work out between us. She's too high maintenance. I need to date carefree women," he said, adding, "Not my mother."

"Carefree?"

Dylan slowed his pace. "Why did you say it like that?"

"Like what?"

"'Carefree.' With a sarcastic attitude."

"I wasn't being sarcastic."

"Yeah. You were clearly sarcastic."

"No."

"Yes, you were. Admit it."

"Dylan, I'm not admitting something that's untrue. In all sincerity, I wasn't being sarcastic. Unless you need someone to say things that are false so you can feel better." How had we become trapped in a verbal tug-of-war? I wanted to get home. As we approached my apartment, I realized that I had left my car in the parking lot at Mona Lisa's, because the neighbors had asked me if they could use the driveway for company coming to stay the night.

"It's not for the sake of feeling better. I feel fine," Dylan said.

"Good."

"Fine," he snapped.

"Hey, do you think it's okay to leave my car in the restaurant lot for the night?"

"Nah. You better move it. Delivery trucks have to come in the morning."

We turned the bend in Commercial Street, passing two men holding hands and laughing. Dylan walked on the brick sidewalk and I strolled on the opposite side of the street, closest to the bay. The water was silent. I glanced between two homes. The tide was low and under the moonlight small pools of water were glistening between the vast sandbars that appeared to stretch for miles.

We arrived at the restaurant parking lot. Dylan had to lock up and phone in food orders for the following day. Walking toward my car, I turned to ask, "Do you think that's really possible? I mean, carefree seems like an unattainable quality to demand in someone."

"Well, I'm carefree," he jogged to catch up to me.

"Really? Are you really?"

"Yeah. That's why I don't have any wrinkles."

I laughed as I unlocked the car door. Dylan pressed his hand against the driver's seat window.

"What are you doing?"

"Nothing."

"You're standing in front of my car door."

"So."

"So, I'm trying to get into my car door. See?" I dangled the keys in front of his nose; he snatched them from my hand and ran.

"You're too drunk to drive." He shouted and I chased him across the street to the restaurant.

"Dylan! Give it back."

"What are you going to do?"

"Call the cops on you. For stealing something that doesn't belong to you."

"Yet," he said, grabbing hold of my shirt and pulling me close. "Come here," he leaned down to kiss me, but then drew back.

His pause suddenly sparked my curiosity, "Why not?"

"Not here," he said.

"Why?" I scanned the vacant restaurant. Only a black cat could see us, but even he was busy, licking his paw and rubbing it over his pointy ear.

"Because, next thing you know. Everyone knows."

"Everyone, who?" I pried.

"Lisa. Then, she'll broadcast it to all the workers at Mona Lisa's.

After that, the whole town will know. Trust me. I understand how this place operates."

"Well, then, you must be lying to me, Dylan."

"I'm not lying to you."

"You still must be involved with Ava. And that's fine. But, why are you so hesitant to honestly share that information?"

· "You're too young to be so jaded," he said.

"I'm not jaded. I'm realistic. Darwin said it himself…"

"Survival of the Fittest," he finished my sentence.

"Exactly."

Dylan walked across the street back to the parking lot and I followed him to my car, "Get in. I'll drive you home."

Dylan clicked on the CD player. He leaned back into the driver's seat with his eyes barely above the dashboard, while gripping the steering wheel. I turned up the volume on the music.

"No. Angel, please. It can't be…"

"What?"

"Frank Sinatra. Please tell me a stranger broke into your car and put this ridiculous CD into your stereo system. No. Strike that. Pathetic. Pathetic CD." He turned it off.

"Nope. I love Frank. Actually, this…what's that you called it?…oh, right, 'pathetic,' Yeah, this pathetic 1960s box set compilation is my most prized musical possession."

"You've got to be kidding!" He drove fast up Bradford Street and I clutched the handle above the passenger's window.

"Do you see me laughing?"

"Well, I guess, I'm just going to have to overlook that."

"Don't," I said.

"Don't what?" He stopped short, slamming on the brakes and squealing around the corner onto Commercial.

"Don't overlook that. Look right into it. Frank Sinatra understood life. In a way that you probably don't." Alcohol had short-wired my better judgment, I didn't consider the consequences of my words.

"What's that supposed to mean?" He asked.

"I mean he lived the full spectrum of the emotional experience. Without restraint. Frank knew what it means to be human." Through the side window I saw the late night crowd stumble down Commercial Street. Couples strolled arm and arm in opposite directions- avoiding collisions by scuttling sideways before stepping forward. Some people wandered wide-eyed, still in search of something more, in the hopes of hearing the scoop on the after-hours party. In front of Town Hall, Ella swayed with her microphone in hand, singing "Is That All There Is?" I read her sign again: "Living the Dream." Where was Caesar among this chaos?

The ride lasted an eternity; my focus remained outside the window. The quaint shops with bright orange "closed" signs hung crookedly from the glass doors. Lace drapes blew against the window screens of second floor apartment buildings; an elderly woman rocked in a chair, watching the kaleidoscope of strangers meandering on the pavement below. A stranger stubbed his toe on the curb, "Damn it." A stranger wept, sitting on the green bench—and another stranger was consoling him with his arm draped over his shoulder. A stranger bent down with a plastic bag to pick up his Chihuahua's poop from the brick sidewalk. A stranger yelled, "Come back. You sexy thing!" A cluster of women strangers pounded through the crowd like a marching band, drinking from cans covered by koozies. Two strangers kissed, leaning against the pole of a flickering street lamp light. A stranger puffed on a cigar, watching smoke rings fade into the starry sky.

"You act like Frank is God or something."

"He is God. To me."

Dylan's knuckles whitened as he grasped the wheel tighter, his back stiffened, and with his right elbow he began nudging my arm off the armrest between us. "Christ! Frank is God? Now, I think, I'm gonna puke."

"Well, just roll down the window and make sure to stick your head way out….so you don't vomit across the side of my Camry. And, be sure to take the wind resistance into account. I really don't want to have to clean your dried throw-up tomorrow."

"Damn, Angel. The least you can do is have a bit of respect for me. I'm being a good friend. Driving you home when you're wasted!"

"Hey, I'm just being a good friend, too. Warning you about the wind resistance when you puke, because you've made it abundantly clear that my love for Frank Sinatra makes you that sick."

"I didn't have to drive you home," Dylan said.

"No, you didn't. In fact, I tried to get my keys back from you in the parking lot. Remember? I'm a survivor. I'll make it home just fine. I don't need any handouts."

"This isn't a handout. It's someone actually caring about you."

"Really, this is what this is? You. Caring. For me?" I asked.

"What's your problem?" he asked.

I could have asked him the same question. Instead, I turned the CD player back on with the volume loud enough that strangers on the street began looking inside the vehicle.

"Why are you acting so tough, when you're really not?" Dylan asked.

"Dylan Duncan, I am not acting anything. I am who I am. And, I am a whole lot of things…but, I'm not carefree. I'm stressed out about the war…and why innocent people have to die…and I'm annoyed that I think about this with pearls pierced in my earlobes…and…I'm worried my mother will disown me because I'm here—instead of there…and I feel awful because I haven't spoken with my father in years...even though I've heard he finally got help," I said, licking my lips, adding, "and...I'm afraid I've been drinking too much...that I may end up like them...and I'm just burning inside...to...," I sighed heavily. I was burning inside to get naked, not physically naked, but stripped bare—soul to soul. I wanted someone to rip off my armor, someone who could smile when I was "psycho," someone that could speak and live the truth with me—the raw-soul-truth-of-it-all. I turned to Dylan, saying, "So...you see...I'm on the 'not carefree' side of the coin here. And I'm curious, are you truly looking for that? Or do you pick girls like Ava and Cara because you can boss them around?"

With a clenched jaw, he snapped off the music. "You think too much. Frank Sinatra is just a loser. That's all. I'm done talking about it."

I turned the radio back on and "I've Got You Under My Skin" blared out, the bass vibrated through the speakers, pulsing in my chest.

Dylan turned off the music, puffing out his reddened cheeks. "His songs are lame."

I turned the dial on. "Can't hear you. Weren't you done talking, anyways?"

Him. Off. "You're really something else, Angel."

Me. On. "At least, I'm not a liar."

Off. "I'm not a liar."

On. "Oh, Please! Now, you're lying about the fact that you're a liar."

Off. "You don't know anything."

On. *"...a part of me"*

Off.

On. *"...warning voice"*

Off.

On. *"...step up, wake up to reality"*
Off.

The Camry pulled into the driveway and Dylan shut the engine off. We rotated our shoulders and crashed into an angry embrace. His fingers clawed inside my indigo blue tank top, my hands clenched his chest, not sure whether to push or pull him, when the top button to his Polo shirt popped off. Our tongues dove into the darkness between us and with my eyes shut, I straddled him, needing more, and needing more.

"C'mon. We should go inside. Before someone sees us out here," Dylan said, breaking from our frenzy. He opened the car door. His head darted left, then right, and like a militiaman in combat, he sprinted toward the stairs to my apartment. "C'mon," he said, waving me over with his hand.

I casually walked—making a point not to hurry—and unlocked the door.

"Check to see if Cara's home," Dylan said.

"Nope. Her light's not on," I said, suddenly, no longer wanting him to enter my apartment.

Dylan relaxed. He followed me up the stairs and into my bedroom like a stray cat in search of a late night treat. My eyes scanned his body, lying there on my feather comforter, and I wanted to tell him this wasn't right, but Dylan pushed his thin tongue into my mouth. I let him kiss me, hard.

"Um. What would you like?" he asked, nervously.

It was as if I'd pulled up to a Burger King window to place my order. I was starving, but I didn't want to eat here, not this way. We undressed and my mind wandered. Why was I doing something I didn't even want to do?

"Want me to go down on you?" His voice sounded anxious and far away.

"Yeah, sure," I said, detached. What was he trying to get from me? What was I trying to get from him? Couldn't he tell this wasn't right? The questions raced through my mind as he knelt down at the base of my thighs, my eyes staring at the "Road to Nowhere" poster on the wall across from my bed. The man and woman were dressed in trench coats, her arm intertwined with his, walking side by side across a sandbar. I held my breath. A parasite. Thriving. On my host. Nasty. Get away. Get away from me. Get off me. You parasite. I faked it, then. My orgasm. I didn't return the favor. I needed a shower. I needed to disappear. I was single, but felt I had cheated on someone. Myself, maybe.

I turned onto my side, away from him, sobs thickened inside my throat, but I didn't make a sound. I pushed them down to the pit of my starving stomach.

"Hey. I got to go back to the restaurant. I forgot something," Dylan said.

"No problem," I turned toward him.

"I'll be back," he said.

"That's okay," I whispered.

He mumbled a faint, "Oh." He pulled up his pants. Buttoned up his Polo. Bit his lip in a half-smile. "I guess, I'll see you later. Maybe we can play tennis tomorrow. I'll call you," he said.

"Alright," I said, as he walked out the door.

When he was gone, I took a shower.

Chapter Six

Dylan phoned the next morning. I spotted his number on the caller ID, but he didn't leave a message and I was grateful. I grabbed my beach towel. It was a perfect beach day. The tide was high, the breeze slight and steady, the sun hot, but not sweltering. My head ached, so I skipped my run. It was just one day, I told myself. I searched for my tote bag while the Great Danes chased me around the apartment.

"What do you want?" Big Fred jumped up, his front legs hitting my hips, and knocking me onto the couch. Thankfully, the door opened, someone had arrived to save me from suffocation. I struggled to peek around Big Fred's heaving belly and slobbering tongue. It was Dylan, holding two bottles of Gatorade.

"Hey! Perfect timing. Could you help me out of this one?" Big Fred was licking my face with his long tongue.

When Dylan snapped his fingers Big Fred backed off me, and moped, with his head hung down, he settled in the corner of the living room.

"How'd you do that?" I asked.

"Fred and I speak the same language," Dylan replied.

"Hey, thanks for driving me home last night," I remembered our argument and wished I hadn't been so belligerent.

Dylan sat down beside me. "I don't get you, Angel. You're

always speaking in secret code."

"Well, luckily, I get me. About 89 percent of the time, anyways."

"What about the extra 11 percent?"

"That's the part I'm still trying to figure out."

"Last night was pretty crazy, huh?"

"Yeah, I'm breaking a lot of my rules, Dylan."

He chuckled. "Listen," he said, "I just wanted to say…"

"I know. I know. We should keep this a secret."

Dylan blinked, surprised. "Yeah, okay. Right. Whatever you say," he sputtered, looking down at his feet. He held out a Gatorade and leaned forward to kiss my cheek, but I stood, moving to Big Fred. I leaned down to pat his belly, saying, "Good Boy." I needed to keep my motives clear with Dylan. The line had blurred under the influence of alcohol; from now on I would remain sober in his company.

Dylan walked to me. "Here, I bought you a Gatorade."

"Thank you. That was thoughtful," I said, unscrewing the cap.

"Make sure to come to the restaurant tonight. There's going to be a pretty decent band playing."

"Pretty decent?"

"Well, it's Caesar. He always schedules some obscure jazz band. But he arranged a benefit for the AIDS Support Group."

"Wow. I'll definitely come then. Plus, I love Jazz. It nourishes the soul. Ya' know?"

"Yeah. I guess, Jazz is alright," Dylan said. "So, I'll see you around eleven?"

"Great."

Dylan left the apartment. When the door swung shut, Big Fred charged at me, pushing me onto the couch. I wriggled under him, trying to get away, but clearly it was a no-win battle, so I surrendered to Big Fred and allowed him to lick my cheek. Finally he settled down, losing interest. I went out to the deck in search of my sunglasses.

Below, in the backyard covered in knee-high beach grass, Dylan crouched beside Cara, who sprawled topless on a lounge chair with her hands behind her head. I crept closer, straining to hear.

"I told you to be nice to her, not to screw her," Cara said, scowling.

"I didn't screw her, Cara. I like her."

Cara pushed her sunglasses to the bridge of her nose, exposing, I imagined, a frosty look in her blue eyes. "Dylan, you like anything that doesn't like you. That's your thing."

"Jesus, Cara."

"I'm sure that's whose name she was moaning last night."

"Nothing happened. Why did you tell her to meet you at ten thirty last night, when you told me the same thing?"

"Sweetie, I'm tired. I need my beauty rest." She shielded her eyes with her white sunglasses and, turning over onto her stomach, she lowered the plastic lounge chair into a flat position and reached for a *Cosmo* magazine on the ground. She began flipping through the pages.

"You're up to something, Cara. What are you up too?"

"Nothing, really. Be a dear and step out of my sun. You're going to give me an uneven tan."

Dylan stood and shook his head. "This is why we can't be together," he said.

Cara closed the magazine and looked up at him.

"Just leave me out of it Cara. And, leave Angel out of it too."

"What are you? Her knight in shining armor, now?" Cara snapped.

"I'm going to work," Dylan said, walking away.

I gasped, startled by Big Fred, who'd bounded onto the deck.

Cara looked up.

"Uh….hey…I'm just getting my sunglasses," I said.

"Right."

"What happened to you last night?"

"Oh, I'm super, super sorry about that Angel. I just got side tracked. I'll make it up to you somehow. You don't mind me, calling you Angel? Seems like that's what everyone's calling you these days."

"No one calls me Angel."

"Dylan does."

"Really? I haven't noticed," I said.

"You know, I was only trying to look after you that day, when I told you Dylan is nothing but a womanizer. I guess, now, you're just going to have to learn the hard way."

"Cara, I'm just here to make some money. Figure things out. I'm not getting involved in anything," I said, sighing.

"Angel, babe, you're already involved. Like it or not. Welcome to the great big dysfunctional family."

I grabbed my sunglasses off the deck railing and left the apartment with my bag weighing heavily on my shoulder. The sun beat against my back as I walked down Commercial Street toward the end of town and to Herring Cove. I had at least a mile and a half walk ahead of me. I considered the perfect comeback that I could have said to Cara, wishing I had been wittier on the spot, "I already have a dysfunctional family. One is enough, thanks." What did she know about me, anyway?

꘎

A gust of wind blew against the back of my bare neck, sending a chill down my spine. From behind, I heard "Somethin' Else" chugging toward me like a steam train, drowning out the sparrows twittering their steady series of cheeps. Mile Davis's trumpet spoke in short, simple phrases, with Cannonball Adderly's alto saxophone answering in long complex sentences. The brass flirtatiously sauced up the flavor of a fever deep down. The two instruments chased one another, never interrupting, but never allowing the other to catch up.

Beep. Beep. A car horn sounded behind me.

"Hello. Angelina Moreau." Caesar pulled up beside me, slowing down.

I stepped into the road, in front of his convertible, forcing him to apply the brakes.

"You better be careful. You're going to go deaf listening to your music that loud," I yelled over the saxophone, slowing walking backwards, his Porsche creeping up to me.

"Honey, I'm already deaf. It don't matter," Caesar said, over the trumpet.

"Well, then, you're going to make the rest of the human population deaf and you're going to have one heck of a law suit on your hands. "

He revved his engine to indicate I take my place back on the sidewalk. I stopped walking all together. "What are you going to do? I double dare you." I outstretched my arms and tilted my head back.

Caesar laughed. "Do you want a ride?"

"What?"

"Want a ride?" He asked again.

I hesitated for a moment, glancing down Commercial Street. It was still a hike to the beach. But, a ride with Caesar? I wasn't so sure.

"C'mon. Get in. I'm going to the beach anyway. I got to pick up my kids," he said, leaning across the car to open the passenger's door.

With the mention of the word "kids," I felt secure. He was

going to pick up his *kids* at the beach and I was going there too. "How did you know I was going to the beach? Are you James Bond?" I asked, sitting down on the leather seat.

"The bag, the towel, the flip flops. Those bathing suit strings hanging out of your skin tight tank top."

I shook my head at him and sighed. "You're playing your theme song right now. You do know that, don't you?"

"No, honey, you're the one that's something else." Caesar drove slowly, saying, "I was just thinking on my drive up here about what we got to do to change the world."

"Make me president," I said.

"Of course. The world needs more women leaders."

"You've got to be kidding!"

"What?" He asked, innocently.

"How can I put this…diplomatically…"

"Honey, why are you biting your tongue? Are you shy all of a sudden? Could I be making you shy, Angelina Moreau?"

I was enraged by Caesar's bold and cocky prodding, more so by his accuracy- he was making me shy. "Well, for your information. I was trying to be polite. Because, not everyone just says what's on their mind. All the time."

"Why not?"

I wished I'd never gotten in the car with him. I could have tranquilly strolled among the tourists, a sea of strangers who wouldn't reduce me to a cocktail of unrecognizable feelings. "Because, nobody does," I said, "You need to use a censor sometimes."

"I don't think you want to use a censor. Ever. I can see that. So, why resist? You should never resist what you want to do."

I nibbled on the inside of my cheek. A Fed Ex truck was parked in the middle of the street, blocking the cars and piling a line of traffic.

"Are you not speaking to me now?" Caesar asked.

"I'm thinking."

"You're thinking about what you're going to say to shut me up," he said.

The truck drove forward, allowing the cars to flow.

"Actually, I was thinking about remaining polite and not saying what I wanted to say in the first place, which was that I can't believe that you, you of all people, would make a comment that the world needs more women leaders and sincerely mean it, because I've seen you in action. You are a dirty, chauvinistic, 'men are the dominate species of the Earth,' kind of man. That's what you are."

Caesar burst into exuberant laughter, slapping his knee. I thought about opening the car door and jumping out.

"What's so funny?" I asked with my arms crossed over my chest.

"Nothing, Honey."

We passed Mona Lisa's and Caesar honked the horn, waving at Lisa who stood on the outdoor patio with a stack of menus in her arms. I placed my elbow on the compartment between Caesar and me, covering the side of my face with my hand.

When we had fully passed the restaurant, I dropped my hand and turned to him, "Apparently, something was humorous. I'm not sure what was so funny, but I would sure like to know."

"I was just thinking that's why the world needs more women like you," he said.

I smiled and he pulled the Porsche up to the curb into a no parking zone.

"What are you doing?" I asked.

"I just need to stop in this gallery to pick something up. Are you coming in?" he asked, leaning in, the cuff of his turquoise shirtsleeve brushing against my bare arm.

"All right. But, is it such a good idea to leave your car here?"

"Why?" I pointed to the "no parking" sign. "Yeah. So what? Regulations. They don't concern me, man."

I walked closely behind him. Somehow Caesar's stride created a space for me in which I could glide more smoothly; like a Canadian goose at the head of migratory "V." His muscular forearm was crisply defined as he held the door open for me. He caught me looking at him. I shifted my gaze into the gallery.

Caesar greeted the woman on duty, giving her a scan down the body like an ex-ray machine at airport security. How could his wife possibly deal with all this? What was he searching for? I barely knew him. Yet I realized then, I trusted him. I trusted him because Caesar Riva was fully there—in his words and his actions—absolutely unconcealed. As I stood beside his right shoulder, watching his forehead wrinkle and his lips turn upward, listening to the woman talk about how her husband had wrecked his new Harley in less than a week, it became clear to me that Caesar Riva was someone I wanted to know. I was fascinated by his turquoise shirt and khaki cargo shorts hanging down past his knees, and the way his squeaky, faintly lisping voice rose to an obnoxiously loud, "Man," then fell back to a deeper tenor.

I wandered into the back of the gallery, mesmerized by the work of a local artist who painted Provincetown scenes with strokes of crimson and chartreuse, splashes of lemon yellow and lime green. She captured the essence of Commercial Street—the seclusion among the pandemonium. I stopped in front of a painting in which a young woman, wearing a long gray raincoat sat on a curb, lost in a stream of legs walking past. Her hands were cupped under her chin and her eyes set on the mango sky. My body jerked when Caesar rested his hand on my lower back. I had forgotten he was there or that I was there, for that matter.

"I'm ready. Let's go," he said.

"Look at this Caesar. I mean, really look at this."

"You like it?"

There are a certain number of things that one is drawn to over a lifetime, sometimes places or sometimes people, objects of desire that emit a certain energy that cannot be denied or defeated. Objects that a human soul cannot resist because they are the crucial pieces of cracked ceramic sent from the universe to complete an individual's mosaic. That painting, that painting knew me. The me, that I had hidden so well over the years, until it sat there on the baby blue wall, hung before me, sucking me into my internal reality. The void that my flesh and bones protected, like a fortress up in the air, but my estrangement from others, my protection from those legs passing me by, were really a testimony to the cavity I didn't know how to fill inside of myself and the fear of not knowing how to stand up, away from the curb.

"Yeah. I like it."

"How much is it?" Caesar asked. I glanced at the white card below the golden frame.

"Two thousand dollars! I guess, it's not meant to be."

"By the end of the summer, you'll be able to buy it."

"Maybe," I took my last look of the painting and followed Caesar back to the car.

We drove along the road that wound through the salt marsh toward Herring Cove. Tall strands of sharp sea grass were reflected in the tidal pools flowing in between them and into the crevices, creating an intricate maze. I felt secure with Caesar beside me, listening to Miles and Adderly bee-bop, something was happening to me, there, at the edge of the world.

We turned around a sharp bend and entered the parking lot of the beach.

"I wanted to be an artist once," I said.

"Oh yeah. Why aren't you?"

"My mother wouldn't have approved."

"What about your father?"

"I don't have one," I said.

"Oh."

"So, when are you going to start painting?" Caesar asked.

"Me?"

"Yeah. You got to begin. Tell me one good reason you shouldn't."

I wanted to say I hadn't painted since I was seventeen, but that wasn't a legitimate reason. I wanted to say I wasn't any good, but I could be. If I practiced, I could learn again. I could paint. Why couldn't I paint?

"Tomorrow. I'm going to the Ace hardware store tomorrow to buy supplies. And, I'm going to paint when I get off work."

"See, Angelina Moreau. With that initiative, you could run the world." Caesar down shifted to first gear and I rested my hand on top of his.

"Thank you," I said.

"For what?"

"I don't know…um…I just feel grateful for what you said…I guess."

He scrunched his eyebrows and stared straight ahead. "You're…uh….welcome," Caesar sputtered loudly.

His two daughters waved from the hotdog stand at the edge of a dune that dipped steeply down to the shore. They had wiry bodies and confident smiles and wore matching purple bathing suits with white polka-dots. A plump woman, perhaps ten years older than Caesar, stood beside the girls, collecting change and handing them orange beach towels.

"Who's that woman?" I asked.

"The nanny. She takes care of the kids when Carol's gone. Which is like most of the time nowadays," he said, pulling up his Yankees cap to wipe sweat from his forehead.

"What does…um…Carol do?" I asked.

"Who knows."

"What do you mean? You've been married for over twenty years. Right?"

"Well, she's a psychiatrist for criminal cases. If that's what you mean. So she's away a lot on business to different cities. DC. New York. That sort of thing."

"You don't speak much?"

"We speak plenty. About the kids," he said, rubbing his nose.

"How many children do you have?"

"Three. Total. The twins. They're ten." He nodded toward the girls. "Then, there's Marcus. My son. He'll be five next month." I smiled, imagining a miniature version of Caesar.

"Well, if he's really mine. I mean."

"What?" I asked.

"Who knows. Let's just say…over the last ten years, Carol and I haven't really been…"

"Physically connected."

"Connected. Period." Caesar laughed awkwardly, "But, I have really great kids," he said, beaming.

"Your children are beautiful," I watched them brush the sand off their small tanned feet.

"Yeah, man. They take after their mother. I guess."

"Oh, come on. You're pretty sexy yourself," I blurted, "I mean…back in your day, I bet you were a heart throb."

"Of course I was. And, now, you're giving me my second wind, honey."

"I should probably leave now," I said.

"Okay."

We both turned toward the backseat and reached for my tote bag, grabbing the handle. Our eyes connected.

"I'm leaving," I said.

"Yeah…sure. That's what you said a century ago," Caesar said.

"What?"

"That's what you said a second ago."

Caesar beeped the horn to signal to his girls and nanny to hurry up. I left the car and walked toward the ocean. When I looked back at his daughters, one of the girls was staring at me and I overheard the other ask, "Who's that lady?" I stepped onto the warm sand, realizing then I'd forgotten my sunglasses in the car, but it was too late. I yelled, "Caesar!" into the salty air, flavored by grease from the grill, but "Somethin' Else" blasted from his Porsche. He was facing forward with two hands on the wheel, unaware of me wildly waving my arms.

༶

I made the most of the beach day, carefully laying out my towel, *Time*, and Poland Springs water bottle. I removed my flip-flops and let the hot sand squish between my peach painted toenails. I lay down on the soft bed of sand, that took the form of my body, sighing deeply, and released my stress into the horizon. When I was a child I couldn't wait until I was big enough to swim to the end, where the baby blue sky touched the inky water, where it all came together in a perfect straight line. In the third grade I had told Ms. Ketchum my secret dream and she had smiled warmly, saying, "Dear, the world is round."

Near the water's edge, a father with a farmer's tan and white belly hanging over his swim shorts, carved out a mote around his son's sand castle.

"Not like that Daddy. With this." His son handed him a yellow plastic shovel.

"Okay. Champ. Thanks for the help."

Champ?! It sounded so *Brady Bunch*. During my adolescence, I was a fanatical *Brady Bunch* fan. I would settle in at five minutes before five to catch the opening song and at five thirty, I switched to channel 38 to catch a second episode. In my favorite episode Mike had helped Marcia with her homework and missed his business meeting, so she decided to enter her step-father in the "Father of the Year" contest. One night, Mike caught her sneaking out her bedroom window to mail the letter; Marcia refused to explain why she was hanging out the window in her nightgown, so Mike grounded her from the upcoming family ski-trip. Marcia mailed the letter anyway and Mike won the "Father of the Year" award. Twenty-five minutes later, he apologized, Marcia became a hero, and she hadn't missed the family ski-trip. All the laundry came spotlessly clean in the confines of a half an hour. My best friend, Molly, told me that every family had at least one person who passed on a screwed up definition of love to the next generation. She said the point wasn't to waste your time day dreaming of existing in a normal family, the point was to define love for yourself.

"Darling, you need me to rub some sun screen on your shoulders? You're getting pink." The father shouted up to his pregnant wife who sat on a beach chair reading *Oprah Magazine*, under the shade of a floppy straw hat. He walked up to her with a shy grin, like a teenage boy making his way over to his crush who was waiting by the hallway lockers. He massaged lotion onto her shoulders, kissing the back of her tilted neck.

"Daddy, come in the water!" The red haired boy with freckles yelled. The man picked up a yellow rubber tube and jogged toward his son.

What were they hiding? Perhaps he was really a heroin addict or a child pornographer, or the wife was having an affair and the baby wasn't his. There had to be something underneath the surface. It couldn't really run so smoothly. Could it?

My father took me to the beach every week in the summer. When I was eight-years-old, after a fight between my parents, my father planned a family day. He purchased a water cooler and filled it with every junk food item that my mother refused to buy Neely and I, sour cream Pringles and strawberry Fruit Roll-Ups. He also bought me a pink dolphin inflatable raft.

I straddle it and hold the two black handles, while he leads me around in circles across the water. When a wave approaches, he places his hand on my back, making certain I don't fall.

Neely lies on her stomach reading *Teen Magazine* all day, repeatedly asking my mother when we would be "done with the bullshit." That provokes an argument with my mom, because profanity is "a classless way to prove a point." If my father is drunk, however, then this rule, all rules, don't apply. Neely began to figure out that my mother isn't as in control as she pretends to be. So, at the beach, Neely escalates the fight by calling her a "real uptight bitch." My mother's mouth drops open and she scans the area for judgmental eyes cast upon her; an elderly couple walking nearby stares back. She furiously mouths to Neely to lower her tone.

I see them arguing on the shore. I am safe with my father, winding along the water on my pink dolphin. A girl from my class at school doggy-paddles to us, saying, "Hi, Gina." My dad smiles and looks at me, "Maybe, it would be nice to let your friend up too?" I nod and he lifts Kimmy onto the raft behind me. When my dad begins to shiver he asks, "Baby, do you want to take a break?" I shake my head and we stay in.

Finally, the argument between my mother and Neely grows so explosive that my mother waves us back to shore. We have to leave the beach. Kimmy runs back to her parents, her mother stands with a white towel spread open, covering it around Kimmy's body. I wipe my runny nose with the back of my hand and sit down on the sand in my wet bathing-suit. My mother hands me flip-flops and begins shaking the sand out of the towels. My dad pulls my hair back in a pony-tail and kisses the top of my head. Neely is always messing it up.

When Neely entered high school she pierced her nose and when the resulting parental fire subsided, she pierced her nipple. She actually raised her "Clash" tee-shirt to show the metal ring to my mother. She was grounded for a month, but Neely snuck out her bedroom window every night. Skipped school. Smoked dope. Slammed doors. My mother began to administer daily Breathalyzer tests during which Neely laughed—she knew pot would never show up. Neely fought with my parents over a misplaced toothbrush and this ignited a larger argument, leading to a scene in which my sister screamed at my father for being a drunken loser. This sent him out to the bar a couple hours earlier, and then my mom sent Neely to her room.

During these hurricanes, I went into my room and studied with headphones on, I played blasting music to drown out the storm. When it blew over, they hugged and embraced. There was nothing to discuss, I just moved on, I just kept moving on.

The afternoon of the accident I was home from Harvard on spring break. Ted, the bartender from Billboards, phones me because my father shattered a bottle of Gordon's vodka against the back wall and now he's swinging the Grey Goose over his head like a lasso. When I arrive at the bar, my father hovers over a woman about four years older than me; his hand strokes the top of her thigh. I tap his shoulder.

"Hey, Neely! Here's my girl! Everybody it's my girl!" he shouted.

"Dad, come on. Let's go." I wrap my arms around his waist and he nudges me with the back of his elbow.

"I'm not going anywhere. I have to go to work."

"Dad, it's Sunday. Come on." He stumbles off his barstool and pulls his car keys from his khaki pants. "No! I'm driving. You're coming with me," I tug at the back of his green dress shirt, but he swats at me, as if I am a distracting housefly and strides toward the exit. I jog to keep up.

"Dad. C'mon. Please. My car's right there. Don't be stupid."

"Christ. You're just like your mother. Who would've thought?" He collapses inside his Bentley and starts the ignition. I jump into the passenger's seat, the car slowly moving forward although my father was looking in the rearview mirror, intending to back the car out of the parking space.

"Jesus, the gears are all messed up," he said, maneuvering onto the street and cutting off a car that let loose a long honk.

"Dad…"

"Just calm down. Just calm the fuck down, for Christ's sakes!" he shouted.

I put on my seatbelt, my heart races as he weaves from side to side in the lane, the left tires trimming the double lines, but not crossing completely over. My father takes one hand off the wheel to search inside his pants pocket.

"Christ. I think I left my wallet back there," he said, his right arm reaching into the back seat. He turns his head.

"Dad!" I screamed. An SUV faces us. The brakes squeal. We swerve to the right, tearing over a lawn. We drive through rose bushes and smash into a mailbox. My neck snaps forward and slams back against the headboard. My father rolls from side to side in the front seat, saying "Jesus Christ" over and over. Blood pours from his nose.

I unbuckle my seatbelt. "Dad, don't move. I'm going to call the ambulance."

"No...No...No..." he said, cupping his hand under his chin, the blood pooling up.

I glance in the rearview mirror. The SUV is stopped on the side of the road fifty-yards down. The driver's door opens and I squint, recognizing the thick, silver hair. "Dad, Mister O'Donnell is running this way."

My father starts the engine; the car scrapes against the rose bushes as he pulls onto the road. He presses down on the gas pedal.

"Dad, you can't just leave."

"Do you think Jerry saw us?" he asked, pulling his shirt up to his bloody nose.

"Yes. He saw us," I said, turning to him, "and when I get home, I'm calling the police."

At Herring Cove, the father swam underwater toward his son with his hand raised like a shark fin. The boy giggled. The wife glanced up from her magazine from time to time and waved at them.

As the sun began to set, the sky was splashed in tangerine streaks, boldly peaking through the peach, fluffy clouds. Beach goers began to shake out their towels and close their umbrellas. When I pressed the skin on my breastbone, it left a white impression that quickly became bright pink. I had been in the sun too long. It was clearly time to leave. I dusted the sand off my feet, put on my flip-flops, and slowly began my mile and a half journey back to Commercial Street.

When I arrived home, the sunset enticed me to walk down to the bay. I sat down on the sand, tucking my knees under my chin. Through the wispy clouds, the sun radiated a cherry glow and the light scattered across the surface of the sea like rubies.

My fingers raked through the coarse sand, searching for treasures. I picked up a smooth black stone and stood. Walking toward the sea, I cocked my elbow back and snapped the flat stone across the water's surface. It bounced like a mini jet ski, hitting the water ten times. Ten times, just like Caesar's white stone at Herring Cove. I smiled, thinking of his crooked lips.

A wave lapped at my toes, offering me an open oyster shell, the two halves were connected by one hinge, but faced opposite directions. Inside each half were two identical purple stains. I shook the water from the shell and carried my treasure back to my apartment.

I placed the shell on the nightstand near my bed and flopped down restlessly on my comforter. Had my mother been right about my decision to become a waitress? After all, they hadn't spent thirty-five thousand dollars a year on my Harvard education so that I could work in a restaurant.

I wandered into the living room and slumped onto the couch. Cara's bong, packed with pot, sat in the middle of the glass coffee table. I picked up the remote control and clicked through a hundred stations on the television set. I reached for a florescent orange lighter, my thumb flicked over the ridge, sparking the flame a couple of times. I watched the fire burn to the sound of the newscaster's deep voice, reporting live from Afghanistan. I knew that I should have a little perspective, considering the insignificance of my so-called problems, and that aggravated me, because I didn't. I felt hopelessly aware of myself and the world at large, but I didn't have the slightest clue what to do about it all. Bent over Cara's bong I inhaled three large hits of pot.

I thought about Caesar's comment in the car on our way to the beach. "The world needed more women leaders." He was right. Mostly men ruled countries and frankly the over saturation created an imbalance of energy. What if history had reversed and women had led nations? What would the world look like today if that had been the case? Perhaps just as chaotic, but it could not be any more chaotic than today. Someone needed to point these things out. There should be a hotline for times like these, a 1-800 number to the President for pot-thought emergencies. I'd tell him, "Hello, Mister President, I was just thinking about the way energy works. You know…the high and low tide of life. It's the same with power and the same with love. High and low tide. You see, Mister President. The very same reason an empire rises and falls. No nation beats history, Mister President, because history is just a large repeating decimal and we keep choosing the same course of action every time. Just for fun why don't we create anew? Try something a little different this time around."

Big Fred pranced to me and nudged his head into my lap. I raised it with both hands and looked him in the eyes, asking aloud, "Right Fred?" I was lonely then. I entered the kitchen, searching for something to drink. I turned on the faucet to pour a glass of water, but a brown sludge sputtered out. I poured a glass of Merlot instead. Just one glass. I wandered into my bedroom and opened the closet door; I ran my fingers across my hanging clothes—white shirts, gray and black pants, peach, cream, pale yellow. I found it, my crimson strapless dress. I would dash down to Mona Lisa's Seduction for the AIDS benefit to listen to some jazz. Just for an hour. I would return home early and get a good night sleep.

After taking a shower, I plugged in the hair-straightener and blow-dried my hair. The curls fell loosely past my shoulders. I picked up the flat iron, pulling a section of hair to the side and looking into the mirror, I decided against it. I would leave my hair curly. I sat back down on the black leather couch in my crimson strapless dress and sipped my glass of Merlot, passing the time, waiting to leave, waiting to escape to Mona Lisa's Seduction, waiting to see Caesar.

Chapter Seven
༄

I arrived at the restaurant around ten-thirty. Every seat near the five piece jazz band was occupied, so I leaned against the wooden host stand, off to the side. My limbs seemed to dangle off my body as I stifled nervous giggles. I tugged on the corners of my strapless dress. Cara lightly pinched the side of my waist, saying "Hey, babe," as she hurried to a table, carrying a bowl of mussels over linguini in a garlic cream sauce.

I smiled at Cara and closed my eyes to fully consume the music. My hips slowly swayed and my shoulders rolled from side to side, dipping to the deep plucking of bass strings. The melody crept closer. With my eyes shut, I felt it swarming around me like a pack of lions and I lingered there. Dancing with even less inhibition, dancing as if I were alone, my body merged with the drummer's solo—his brush lightly tapping the cymbal and his foot firmly pressing a pedal that drove the mallet to repeatedly knock against the bass drum on the floor. The saxophone boldly entered. The audience applauded and whistled. I opened my eyes. Across the room, sitting alone in a corner booth, he clapped, fixing me with an expression of admiration and longing.

If only I looked away, but instead, I gave him permission, tilting my head and sending a coquettish smile. The commotion of the restaurant, the cheers and applause, and the crowd of faces through which waitresses wove in and out, swirled around me like a tornado with Caesar and I centered in the eye.

"Hey, Angel," Dylan stood in front of me. "Here. It's on the house." He passed me a large glass of foamy beer.

"Thanks." I took a large gulp. "Are you almost done with work?"

"Yep. Another day…"

"Another dollar."

"Right." After a long pause, he said, "That's a fabulous dress."

"Hey, baby cakes," Cara emerged from the kitchen and kissed Dylan slowly on the lips.

I took another long guzzle from my beer and watched how Dylan willingly accepted Cara's lips. He didn't lean into the kiss, but he didn't exactly pull away either.

"Hi, guys." Caesar strutted toward us, his eyes set on me. "Angelina Moreau, what's the occasion? You look beautiful this evening."

"Me," I said, feeling airy as a balloon drifting through the clouds, "That's the occasion. I'm celebrating me."

"Man, I wish I could get a ticket to that party."

"Sorry, Caesar Riva. It's all sold out," I said. He chuckled. Cara cupped her hands around Dylan's ear. Caesar leaned back, placing his elbows on the host-stand beside me, as he swayed to the music, his long metal chain knocked lightly against the side of my thigh. He stopped swaying and his chain stopped knocking. We stared at the band. I slithered sideways with a small step. With my hip pressed against his, I glanced around the room to see if anyone noticed us standing close together.

"Angel, I forgot," Dylan said and I stepped away from Caesar. "I brought a present for you." Cara glared at me as if I were hatching a secret plot against her.

"Why didn't you bring me something special?" Cara pinched

the stretchy fabric of Dylan's black and white checkered chef pants. She suddenly placed her hand on the buzzer clipped to her apron, "I think that's your dinner, Dylan." Cara reached for Dylan's hand and dragged him reluctantly to the kitchen to pick up the order through the swinging door.

    I glanced up at Caesar. I couldn't help but feel uneasy, thinking he knew the secret I kept about him underneath my dress.

    "I didn't know you had so many suitors, Angelina Moreau. Although, I'm not surprised. So, what's the deal?"

    "What deal?"

    "What are my chances?" Caesar asked.

    "Your chances? I'd say, about one in a trillion." We tapped our feet to the saxophone, the suggestive howls did the talking, until I couldn't stand it any longer. "Well, I'm going to get another beer. Your chances will move up to two in a trillion in about five minutes."

    "Wow. That's great. I didn't know my chances were that high."

    I walked toward the bar, sliding my fingers along the oak wall for support; my legs wobbled and a thick fog was cast over my mind. In the bar room, people stood, packed closely to those seated with their drinks in hand, laughing and speaking over one another. Two women got up from their stools and I quickly scooted into a seat. Across the bar, Cara was whispering again into Dylan's ear, and I wondered why they consistently congregated in their conspiring underworld. Dylan caught me staring at them. I swiftly shifted my gaze to the television set and sipped on my Sam Adams. Dylan snuck up beside me.

    "Is this saved for someone?" he asked.

    "Depends."

    "On what?"

    "If you're planning to sit there," I said.

"What if I were?"

"Then, I'd say: depends."

"On what?"

"If you're planning to tell me why Cara is always whispering sneaky things in your ear?"

"Hm," Dylan rubbed his chin.

"What?"

"I can't figure you out."

"Trust me. I'm not that mysterious."

"But you are hard to figure out."

"People aren't cocktails, Dylan. You can't just measure out the formula of this and that and get a drink. People are complex."

"I can figure people out."

"Really? What's your secret?"

"You just formulate a conclusion and stubbornly stick with it." Dylan said.

"You know, Dylan, you seem like more of a riddle than me. With all that sarcasm."

"It's not sarcasm. It's irony."

"Same thing."

"No. Sarcasm contains a bitter undertone. Irony just points out…points out…the…"

"The what?" I asked.

"The irony."

"Sarcasm and irony are adjectives," I declared.

"No they aren't. Looks like I might have actually stumped the Harvard girl," Dylan said.

"Do you have proof?"

"Yeah. In the back office. I have a dictionary."

"Fine. Let's see it."

"Okay. Meet me at the side door outside," Dylan said, glancing at Cara across the bar. Her eyebrows scrunched in anger, and then her face muscles relaxed into a pained look.

Dylan left the bar and headed to the back office through the kitchen door. I chugged the remainder of my beer and immediately asked the bartender for another. Caesar slid into Dylan's unoccupied seat, holding his dinner plate—veal covered in a plum glaze with mashed potatoes. The potent garlic whipped into the potatoes dissipated into the air. I focused on the Red Sox game on the television above my head. I pretended he wasn't beside me, but every time he lifted his fork, his knuckles rubbed against my upper arm. I didn't push my arm toward him or pull it away. It remained and I impatiently waited for the next tingle along my skin.

I stared at the television, thinking how the choices you make determine what people enter your life. Yet you cannot control the course of Mother Nature's plan. She seduces you with her glorious temptations. She creates an abnormally warm day in April, just warm enough to wear a short sleeve shirt for the first time after a bitter New England winter; and with canary yellow tulips in full bloom and the samba sound of bumble bees back in business the world feels tipped upside down with the sea painted in the sky and the clouds like pillows under your feet, a day when gravity pulls you upward. On days like those, we forget about the reversal, that percentage chance a thunderstorm could set in any minute, and any minute trapped outside without an umbrella with the weight of the rain pushing your shoulders downward and your soles of your sneakers glued to the cement. You even disillusion yourself into thinking that you can control the perils of nature and if you just chose to step out of her way, you would outsmart her, but you don't. Instead, you fall prey to the seduction of her balmy spring day, you cling to her splendor to avoid the possibility of her destructive force, and that is why Mother Nature controls you everyday, until you accept her process. Until you learn that behind every rainbow lay a rainstorm merging with the sun.

I wasn't sure what sort of day Caesar Riva was, but something told me that I better keep my umbrella close at hand.

"What are you thinking about, Honey?" Caesar asked, not looking up from his plate.

"Um…excuse me?"

"You do that a lot you know. Your wheels turn and turn. One minute you're here. Then, all of a sudden…Snap…you get lost away into your own world," Caesar said, cutting his knife into the veal. I swiveled the chair slightly away from him. The crowd around the bar booed loudly and Caesar snapped to look at the television, shouting, "Yeah, man…go…go…go. Oooh…Oooh…Yeah, Yeah, Yeah, man!"

Derek Jeter hit a grand slam. Caesar tore into the veal, eating like a child in the Great Depression, protecting his plate with his two elbows. But Caesar was hardly poor. He was a millionaire. Yet he lacked the pretentiousness that I'd been accustomed to in Westport. He sporadically used "ain't" and said things like "you got lost." His contradictions magnetized me to him and made me feel I still had so much to learn about people.

"You're a real caveman, Caesar. You know that? First of all. You're rooting for the Yankees. That's a war crime in the state of Massachusetts. Second of all. You sound like you're watching a porn film. This is baseball. And, lastly, you have plum sauce on your chin." I grabbed his white napkin from his lap, wiped the sauce from his chin, and put the cloth back on his knee. His eyes glowed with affection.

"Would you like a taste?" He stabbed a slice of meat with his fork and held it up to my mouth.

"Not sure. Is it worth it?"

"You tell me," he said, feeding me the veal. Being with Caesar was like bumping into a childhood friend after twenty years, through the years you had ripened, yet somehow you still knew each other at the core.

"That's phenomenal," I said, suddenly feeling too close for his examination. Caesar returned to the food on his plate. I rose from the barstool, adding, "You know, it's really nice that you donated tonight's revenue to the AIDS charity."

"Naw. It's nothing. It's what we're supposed to do," he said without looking up, "I only wish I could do more." I patted his shoulder and slid through a couple standing behind my chair.

"Where you going?" Caesar asked, grabbing my hand.

"I'll be right back."

"Ain't no sunshine when she's gone," he said, chewing the meat with his mouth open.

ೞ

I was pressing my palms against the front glass door when Cara yelled at me from behind, "What are you doing?" She carried a bucket of ice and champagne on her hip.

"Nothing."

"Angelina. Be careful," she placed her hand on my shoulder.

"Cara, I'm fine. I'm not involved in anything. Really."

"He's a womanizer, Gina."

I knew that she was referring to Dylan, but I was tired of her assumption and I wanted to put her at ease. "I'm really not interested in Dylan. Not the way you're thinking."

"Really?" she asked and the tension around her eyes relaxed. "Good. Because, I've been on the checkerboard. I have watched Dylan jump from one woman to another to another. I just don't want to see you get hurt like I was," Cara said.

I appreciated her concern, however I questioned her sincerity. I was uncomfortable with contradictions, the gray area in human relationships; I learned that gray areas only led to disappointment. I struggled to maintain neutral.

"Thank you for your concern Cara, but I'm fine. I'm great. So, please. Stop worrying," I said. She placed the champagne bucket down on the host-stand and opened her arms, offering me a hug. Regardless of my suspicions, I welcomed it.

I swung the glass door open to breathe in the summer air, sultry and thick, beads of perspiration swelled on my collarbone. I quickly dodged through the tables in the front patio and the side-station where Nadia sliced bread and another server sat on a white plastic chair smoking a cigarette. I rapped lightly against the door. The beige shades were drawn shut without even a slight crack to peek inside the room. I ran my hands over my sides to smooth the wrinkle on the waist of my dress, and then the door opened.

"Hello, I'm looking for Mr. Sarcastic," I said.

"Hm. I don't know anyone by that name. I do know a Mr. Ironic."

"Well, cough up the evidence or I'm leaving. I'm not waiting around for you forever."

"You're not?" I playfully punched him in the stomach and walked inside the office. Photographs of Dylan and (what I concluded were) a Hall of Fame of former girlfriends decorated the lime green walls: Cara rode piggy-back on Dylan in front of The Claw, her arms clinging tightly around his neck, Ava stood behind Dylan with her chin resting on his shoulder in front of a clear blue Caribbean sea, another girl sat behind Dylan on a motorcycle, peering out from the side. One photograph stood out among the rest. Lisa stood next to Dylan with glowing eyes and a toothy smile, Dylan was looking at her tenderly. I moved a pile of cookbooks and a pair of khakis onto a stack of clothes piled on the floor in the corner, and relaxed onto the blue loveseat.

"Well, this office says a lot about you, that's for sure," I said.

"Uh-oh."

"Why do you always assume that I mean something hurtful?" I asked.

"I don't always assume that," Dylan said.

I pointed to the photograph of Lisa and Dylan, asking, "Did you two date?"

"Naw," Dylan said, laughing. "But, I tried my hardest. I used to follow her like a puppy when I moved here. Before she married. I had the biggest crush on her."

"Have or had?"

"Well, it's unrequited love. It's like…perfect," he said. I opened my mouth, but quickly shut it. Dylan moved to the desk, opened the top drawer and pulled out a CD.

"A peace offering," he said, handing it to me. "Frank Sinatra. The Early Years." I laughed.

"Thanks Dylan. You know…I'm…."

"Me too," he said, pulling the dictionary off the bookshelf.

"Aha! Here it is." He sat on the loveseat, handing me the book and pointing to the entry under 'sarcastic.'

"Sarcastic," I read aloud, "caustic, acerbic, bitter, cutting, and contemptuously derisive." Dylan gazed sheepishly at me. "Well, it's official. You proved me wrong, Dylan."

"I looked up irony. It means 'use of words to convey the opposite of their literal meaning.' See…chef's can be smart," he said, flipping the pages of the dictionary.

"Of course they are. Intelligence has little to do with having a formal education. In fact, the longer I'm here the more I realize that I'm completely ignorant when it comes to certain things."

"Like what?" Dylan asked, placing his hand on top of mine.

"Well…I could spit out facts. I could tell you about every detail of the Geneva Convention in 1864. I could have gone to work at Morgan Stanley and played the corporate game brilliantly. But…um…I don't know…what about that hidden layer inside all of us. What about people? How do you ever know their intentions? What's trust? What's love?" I leaned back against the sofa and the dictionary dropped from my lap. "And, since I've been here, I've noticed how happy and beautiful so many of the workers from Jamaica are. And, I bet they didn't grow up with a quarter of the money my family has. Why is it that my family had so much money, but we couldn't do the simple things?"

Dylan lunged toward me, slithering his hand underneath my dress, swiftly moving up my thigh. His lips pressed against mine. An image of Caesar's large pupils with flecks of orange in the iris of his eyes flashed like a camera bulb in my mind. I turned my head. Dylan's fingers circled over my underwear and he lightly bit my ear.

"You think too much," he said. I hovered above our bodies as if observing emergency doctors operating on a patient. I gazed at the photograph of Dylan and Lisa, inhaling deeply I smelled the beer on Dylan's breath. I pressed my hand against Dylan's pulsing heart, pushing him away.

"This isn't the answer," I said faintly, shaking my head.

Dylan rolled off my body and clasped his hands behind his head, staring at the ceiling fan, the blades lapping around in circles. I saw pain in his eyes. I wanted to say something comforting. "It's not you, it's me," or "I think it's better if we remain friends." But I knew those rehearsed statements were not comforting at all.

"Can't we just have fun?" He asked.

"We could. But…"

"But, what?" Dylan asked.

I glanced up at the photographs. I wanted to tell him it wouldn't be long before we'd become a picture hung on the wall and he wouldn't look at me the way he looked at Lisa. Instead I placed my hand over his, saying, "It's not you, it's me."

"Wow. I've heard that a hundred times," Dylan stood, "But, I'm the one that says it." He shut off the ceiling fan, the blades whipped slowly to a halt. "Well, we better get out there, before people start wondering," he said, walking to the front door of the office. I reached for the doorknob in the back.

"Angel…."

"Yeah?"

Dylan fidgeted with a button in his shirt, looking at the pictures on the wall. Maybe he would prove me wrong a second time. Maybe he could see in those pictures, his addiction to the chase and his love for unavailability.

"Forget it," he said, walking through the door and into the kitchen.

෴

The wind blew against my bare shoulders, forcefully slamming the door shut behind me. The back patio had cleared, except for a couple lingering with a bottle of champagne, their bodies leaning toward one another as they were speaking. I squeezed through two tables, but they didn't disconnect their gaze. I peered into the large glass window. Pressed in between a tall blonde and a tan brunette, both vying for his attention, Dylan sat motionless in a booth, both hands clutching his draft beer, his eyes on the rim of the mug. The blonde woman pinched his cheek and Dylan feigned a smile, but his eyes were stark. I saw his face like a blank canvas—how could I make it vibrant? If I was drawn to Dylan, it was because of this look. I wanted him to tell me why it was there and I wanted to fix it.

My high heels were scraping against my tendons, ripping into the blisters. I had pushed through the sting for three hours, but I couldn't ignore the evidence— blood was dripping down my ankles. I slipped my shoes off, my soles welcoming the pebbled pavement, and tiptoed toward the pier that extended into the choppy sea. The moonlight hit the gazebo like a spotlight. A gust of wind canopied my skirt and a crashing wave sprayed my legs with cold seawater; I jogged to seek refuge inside the gazebo.

Hung against the back wall was a glass-encased replica of the Mona Lisa. For centuries, historians and artisans debated the infamous painting, searching for a definitive answer about her mystery; an answer that perhaps you could only truly determine for yourself, after all, the knowledge of her identity would not resolve the elusive question "what hid behind her smile?" What emotion really lay behind those slightly upturned lips? What secrets did she conceal? Was her smile a legitimate expression of contentment? Or was she cleverly masking the pain of a broken heart, broken dreams, and a broken spirit—disillusioned by life's harsh realities. Unrequited love, for example. Or requited love fated to end tragically by a lover's premature death. She portrayed the wisdom that one only earns through having lived a full life, for having exposed her vulnerability, for having risked greatly, for having lost miserably, for having explored the uncharted territory, the darkness of what it means to be human. Yet her wisdom was not jaded by bitterness or regret. To look at the Mona Lisa was to feel a dying person's final inhalation and exhalation. She was eternal peace encapsulated in that moment. Maybe her smile was not a veil to mask her secrets. Maybe it was just the opposite.

The Mona Lisa was truth. And her smile was a reminder that we were the ones hiding.

I watched her watching me. I swayed to the left and to the right of her silver plated frame. Her espresso eyes followed. She wouldn't allow me to get away from myself, so I stepped in closer to stare her down. Millimeters away from the tip of her nose, we locked eyes.

"For Christ sakes, Gina. What the hell are you doing? Planning on slipping her the tongue?" Cara's voice snapped me back from my stare down.

"How long has this been here?" I asked.

"Never noticed it before."

"Well, who put it here?"

"Caesar, I assume. He's weird like that. Who knows."

"What do you see when you look at her?"

Cara rubbed her chin like a mathematician analyzing an algebraic equation. "I see cosmic energy swirling around her head like a halo. There's like a big white light right above her forehead." Cara sat down on the bench that circled the inside of the gazebo. She curled her legs Indian style and I sat down beside her.

"What?"

"Earth to Gina. I'm joking. It's a god-damn painting, Gina. And, that broad's a real dog, if you ask me. I don't get what the big deal is. What makes her so famous, anyway? Would you really want to hang an ugly chick on your wall?"

"There's a rumor that she isn't a 'she' at all. That Leonardo da Vinci painted himself in drag. Which could explain the mystery behind the smile. But, I think…"

"You think way too much and if you keep it up, you're gonna think yourself right into the nuthouse. You have to learn to just go with the flow." Cara pulled an aquamarine pouch with gold sequins out of the pocket of her waitress apron.

"That's beautiful."

"It was a present. From Dylan." She tugged on the zipper, continuing, "But, now, allow me to introduce you to something really beautiful." Cara removed a small plastic bag of coke from the pouch, lay a checkbook down on the wooden bench, and tapped a quarter of the cocaine onto the surface. The wind had subsided and the sea was eerily quiet. Cara inserted a rolled-up twenty dollar bill into her nostril and inhaled a trail of the powder.

"Ahhhh," she pinched her nostrils together and wiped the remaining powder on her top gum. "Are you ready?"

"No, I'm going to stay out here for awhile."

"I mean, are you ready for a bump?"

"I already told you Cara. I'm not into it."

"That's not true. You've never done it. How can you sit there on your high moral horse and tell me that you're not into something that you have never done? I mean, like really, that's like high-po-critical." Cara spoke so fast I could barely process her words.

"Hypocritical," I said, cringing at my correction. It was just like my mother. She was always there to point out to everyone else exactly where he or she had gone wrong.

"I just love this place. Don't you?" Cara said, without waiting for an answer. "I mean, things aren't so bad here. They could be worse. I could be in a wheel chair or I could be blind, or could be a schizophrenic and hear crazy people talking to me all the time, imagine that? or I could be one of those android people, you know, like have a vagina *and* a penis, and not know if I'm male or female, that would really, really, suck."

"I don't know…just because it could be worse, doesn't mean you should stop creating something better," I said.

"Or I could have three nipples. I saw that on *Ripley's Believe it or*

Not. Or I could be one of those bearded ladies. Although, I just found a hair on my chin yesterday. Maybe I'm becoming one of them. A freak of nature. But, it's probably nothing. If I end up sporting a bushy beard in a month, do me a favor and put me out of my misery."

"I guess, you're right Cara. You could look a hell of a lot worse than you do now."

"Here. It's just a small one," Cara smoothed out a thin line of cocaine on the checkbook and nudged it toward me on the bench, but I shook my head.

"Ava's in there." Cara nodded her chin at restaurant.

"Really?"

"Yep. And it looks like she and Dylan might be getting back together."

"What makes you say that?" I asked.

"Their hands are all over each other. Well, more like, Dylan's all over her, but who wouldn't be. She's gorgeous. What more could she ask for? Except…"

"Except what?"

"She's a wild girl. Ava parties a bit harder than Dylan would like to for an 'official' girlfriend."

"Well, Dylan isn't exactly a public service announcement for sobriety."

"Yeah. No kidding," Cara laughed.

"So, then, why would he care if his girlfriend drinks?"

"Ava doesn't drink. She's a drunk. There's a big difference."

"Well, then, why is he getting back together with her?"

"It's comfortable."

"What's so comfortable about taking care of an alcoholic girlfriend?" I asked.

"Dylan's got a past. Just like the rest of us, Gina. It's a hell of a lot easier to stick with what you know, no matter how miserable. After awhile you're so used to the misery that you just accept it and you believe that's all there is. It's just normal. It's like this…you've been driving a beat up old Camry for years, right?"

"Yeah…" I nodded, wondering where she was going with the analogy.

"And, it's fine if you get into accidents because it's busted. You hit curbs, scrape the paint against a pole in the Stop and Shop parking lot. No problem. Everything's cool. You don't really care all that much. And no matter what happens that beat up Camry stays with you. You're in control."

"Uh-huh. Except what does that have to do with Dylan again?"

"Yo'. I'm not finished. I'm being deep here," Cara mocked herself, "But, then imagine this: what if someone gave you the keys to a new convertible Ferrari? What if you could drive it around Provincetown for the day? Imagine the pressure. Sure, the car runs better. And, it's shiny and new. You feel fucking fabulous in the Ferrari. But, it's so freakin' stressful. So many gadgets you don't understand. So, many elements you can't control. And, there's so much potential…to drive fast, but that only adds to the pressure. You love sitting in that Ferrari, or maybe, you like the idea of driving it better, because deep down you don't want to get too attached. Because it's only on loan for the day. That's super scary. Losing something like that. So, you stick to the beat up Camry because you understand how it works. No matter how dysfunctional or busted. That Camry is a loyal piece of fucking machinery."

"But wouldn't you want to learn to drive the Ferrari? I mean, isn't it better to experience the ecstasy? Love something in the face of fear? Even if you may lose it? Because if you just stick to the beat up Camry, you miss out. You'll never grow."

"It's safer not to know what you're missing, Gina. Convince

yourself that's all you want anyhow. That's most people. That's Dylan, anyway. Like I said before. We all got a past. And, as much as we snub personal history, we keep driving the same route in the same car." Cara looked across the bay toward the lighthouse's blinking green light.

"Cara?"

"What's up?"

"Thank you."

She rolled her eyes. "For what?"

"I don't know. I guess, I just appreciate that you shared that with me."

Cara covered her hands over her frosted pink lips and giggled. "I have thoughts. Plenty of thoughts. I just keep 'em inside. Don't take it all that seriously. We're all here for a short time anyhow. I want to play as much as I can before it's over." She pointed at the line of cocaine still stationed by my side.

"What does it really do to you anyhow?" I asked.

"It's just a pick me up. Like a couple of glasses of wine. Not a big deal, really. It's just fun."

A small breeze blew against my back, drying beads of sweat on my neck. I yawned and checked my watch. It was time to leave. I had already broken my self-imposed curfew. It was two hours past my bedtime. "Cara…"

"Shhh! Check that out." She pointed to the office door at the back of the restaurant and queasiness mounted in the pit of my stomach. Ava crouched on the step, cradling a large martini glass with both hands, and sobbing uncontrollably. The couple had left the patio, leaving their half-full champagne glasses on the table.

"Cara. We should leave," I said feeling guilty.

"What! And miss this drama? No way. It's better than a reality TV show. C'mon. This is our very own special episode."

Ava fetched a mirror out of her purse. She wiped off the smudged mascara under her eyes and rose to her feet. Her black mini-skirt barely covered her behind, her lean legs traveling for miles. She bent over and flipped her head back, shaking the thick mane of black hair until it settled onto her large chest. What was it like to be that beautiful? To walk into a room and turn the heads of men and women? Dylan opened the door before she had a chance to knock.

"We can't, Ava. I can't do this anymore," he yelled.

"You! You can't do this. What? Now, you're just going to toss me out. Just like that. For what? That new girl? What's her name?" She screamed. Their voices carried across the black sea water.

"Who?" Dylan asked.

"Annabel? Anastasia? Angelina? That's it. Angelina. Cara told me all about her. Don't deny it."

I glared at Cara with raised eyebrows. She shrugged her shoulders.

"Ava…" Dylan reached for her hand and she let him caress it.

"What did you say about me?" I whispered to Cara.

"Shhh. This scene isn't over yet. Trust me. It's gonna heat up." I felt irritated that Cara was enjoying the scene. I could have walked away, but something kept me glued to the bench.

"Don't touch me. Ever again. You see this." Ava raised her martini glass. "This is a woman's heart…." She turned her back on Dylan. "And, this is a woman's heart after meeting Dylan Duncan." Ava rocketed the martini glass at the cement. The glass shattered and she kicked a plastic chair.

"What did I tell you? Movie producers would salivate for footage like this," Cara said.

"What the hell Ava? What's the point? You're just going to have to pay for another vodka martini. What's that anyway? Your fourth glass?" Dylan shouted.

"You, don't tell me what to do. Ever again. Go ahead. Screw that new girl. I don't know how you can lower your standards. She's got a crooked tooth and a bump in the middle of her nose. Not to mention, could she be any flatter? Dylan, she's like a little boy. You're just one step away from coming out of the closet."

"That bitch," Cara said, "I'm gonna knock her prissy nose in." Cara stood and began to march down the wharf, but I grabbed hold of the back of her tee shirt just in time.

"Let it go," I whispered.

"But, she's talking…"

"About me. I know. It's fine. Look. Do you see any cleavage here?" I asked, squeezing my breasts together with the palms of my hands.

"You're too good, Gina," Cara said.

Ava collapsed onto the ground, her sobs growing louder. Dylan watched her, standing with his arms crossed. "I hate you," she screamed. Dylan's face went blank and he wrapped his body around her like a walnut shell.

"C'mon. Ava. Come inside," Dylan pulled Ava up from the pavement and held her close as they entered the office.

"What an asshole," Cara said. I'm not sure why, but in that moment, I desperately needed…something.

"Here." Cara set the checkbook with a line of coke into my lap and handed me the rolled twenty.

I inserted the bill into my right nostril, bent down, and sucked the slate clean. My head snapped up, alert and rejuvenated, born again. My heart was beating so fast and loud I could hear the bongo drum of it, banging to bust out, holding in numbness. "Hey. I need another one of those."

Cara grinned, set me up with another line of coke, and I

inhaled it, making certain to suck in all the loose powder. We walked away from the gazebo. I was in the lead.

"Hey. Joan of Arc. Wait up!" Cara called from behind. I didn't slow down. My jaw was clenched like a screw wound too tightly and my teeth were grinding in a circular motion. When my toes touched the cold pavement, I slipped my tan shoes back on my feet; the raw skin of my heels no longer throbbed. I was beyond physical pain.

We cut through the back patio toward the side station. When Cara passed by Dylan's bicycle locked against a chain-link fence, she hacked up a ball of phlegm and spat on the leather seat.

"Now, was that necessary?" I asked.

"Necessary. No. Reasonable. Yes. It's not my fault that Dylan's bicycle just so happened to be in the path of my spit's trajectory."

"Poor guy," I said, softly. I sensed Dylan's desire to break free from his patterns, but just like me, he relied on them, afraid and not knowing how to act otherwise.

"Poor guy? Damn, Gina. You're not wearing rose colored glasses. You're just blind. Don't feel sorry for him. It's his own fault that he's such an asshole."

"Cara, let's lay off the topic."

"But…"

"But, nothing. I'm done caring…"

"But…."

"But, this." I pulled up the back of my dress, exposing my cherry satin underwear, and flashed Cara. She laughed, but looked at me skeptically.

"Uh. Like what's going on? You're scaring me Gina."

"Boo!" I sprung at Cara with open palms. "Just kidding. I'm ready to have a good time. That's all. I hope you can handle it."

"I still have to cash out and get out of this grubby uniform.

But, trust me, I wouldn't miss this for the world. What are you scheming up?"

"I don't have an agenda. No secrets. Just looking for a little innocent fun."

"They don't go together."

"What's that?"

"Innocent and fun."

༄

We approached the front patio to Mona Lisa's Seduction. Customers sat outside under the moonlight, talking and drinking cocktails. Cara jogged past me and entered the front door of the restaurant. Caesar stood alone, holding the door open with his back resting on the metal edge of the door, swaying side to side to the jazz music with his hands tucked behind him. His chest puffed out as if he was posing for a portrait and his upturned chin completed the impression he was an aristocrat from King Louis's court.

As I approached, Caesar swayed toward the right, shut the door, and blocked my entrance. "What's the password?"

I leaned toward him with my lips close to his ear and whispered, "Come dance with me." Caesar smiled innocently. He fumbled in his pocket, pulling out a tube of chapstick.

Caesar had full lips that didn't match: the top lip rested a tiny bit farther to the right of his lower lip, making them appear slightly crooked. Caesar removed the cap from the chapstick, rubbing one coat slowly across his top lip and then across the bottom. He had performed this ritual countless times over the summer.

"You ever get wild and crazy and use two strokes on each lip instead of one?" I asked.

"What?"

"I think you have a serious addiction to chapstick. You apply it every hour on the hour, and always just one stroke."

"That's all I need. I take only what I need. No more. No less."

"You're addicted to that stuff. You might want to think about rehab."

"The way I see it, a human being is programmed for addiction. Nowadays, I make sure I'm addicted to positive things."

"Chapstick? How is that positive?"

"Honey, this ain't any chapstick. It's special."

"Oh, yeah. What's so special about it?" He turned the tube around and held it up so I could read the label: "Kiss So Soft."

"It's the best around. Look how smooth my lips are." He puckered his lips. "Plus, it's SPF 15. You gotta protect yourself. Global warming is on the rise."

"C'mon, what's the real reason you apply chapstick…wait …no…sorry…I mean, your special 'Kiss So Soft' every hour?"

"Nerves. It calms me down."

"Am I making you nervous?"

"You always make me nervous."

I couldn't tell if he was playful or sincere, I could never really tell with Caesar. "What about the first day you met me? Were you nervous then?" I asked.

"Yep."

"You seemed a lot of things but nervous wasn't a word that came to mind."

"Well, I guess…you read me wrong," he said, "By the way. I know I said it before, but it's worth saying again. You really look beautiful this evening." I tilted my face up to him and puckered my lips. Cupping the bottom of my chin with his hand, he carefully glided the lip balm over my lips. I smudged them together.

"Now you're going to be addicted, Honey."

"Would you do me a favor?" I asked.

"Anything for you, Honey."

"Stop calling me 'Honey.' I'm not your Honey. Save it for the rest of the female species."

"Okay. No problem, Sugar."

My nostrils flared. "Don't patronize me, Caesar Riva. I'm not like the rest of them."

"I know that. That's why you're my Sugar. It's the real deal. Pure sweetness."

"You know, I'll bet it's been decades since you've let your guard down."

"Yeah," he said, becoming serious, "You're probably right."

A lamppost across the road flickered and then the bulb blew out, shedding darkness across a section of Commercial Street. The last of the customers had left the front patio. A busboy winded through the tables with a broom, sweeping crumbs, pieces of lobster shells, and empty sugar packets into neat piles. I wanted to rewind the night, but it was too late. I spied Dylan inside the restaurant window, with his arms crossed, watching me. What was taking Cara so long? Caesar bent down to untie his shoelace, retying it again in a double knot.

Tapping Caesar's shoulder to break the tension, I said, "Did I get the password right or not? Are you going to let me through, your Majesty?"

"Not right exactly. But, it'll do for now," he said, standing and opening the door. "After you, my dear. Is it legal for me to call you that? Or are you going to send me into exile?"

"Don't worry. After this night, I'm ready to go into exile myself."

"Wow. Our own little private island in exile. What do you think would happen to us there?"

"Caesar," I said, widening my eyes and giving him a sharp look. "Uh-oh. I'm in trouble again."

"Just come dance with me. And, be a gentleman."

Caesar scratched his temple with his finger, saying, "Hey, Kid. I'm not sure if that's possible."

"Everything is possible," I said, leading the way into the restaurant.

Caesar followed closely behind me, with one hand delicately holding the small of my back. "They're playing our song," he said behind my shoulder, his breath tortuously tickling my neck.

"Our song? Is that right? Well, that's news to me. I wasn't aware that we had a song, Caesar," I said, stepping forward.

"Shhh. Listen." Caesar took a hold of my hand, lightly kissing the back. We settled arm and arm onto the small dance floor, joining four other couples turning together to Nat King Cole's "Unforgettable." My feet resisted his direction but Caesar pulled me closer and I surrendered. Caesar took the lead. He twirled me around with one hand gently supporting my lower back, he dipped me, his face close to mine.

"How's this? Is it up to par, Ms. Moreau? Perhaps you are all wrong about me."

"Maybe. Or, maybe underneath it all you're a dirty dog."

"Maybe. But, I'm trainable. I'm like one of Pavlov's dogs and you're my bell ringer."

"You're…..you're…just…"

"Shhh. I told you already. Listen to the words of our song."

A buxom red-head in a jade sequined gown crooned into the microphone, and Caesar lip-synched along with the lyrics. Caesar dipped me back, my curly black hair nearly touching the floor, as the band's music trailed off. Nearly losing my balance, I clung to Caesar's waist. He gracefully lifted me up and I found myself pressed against him in a snug embrace.

"You didn't warn me that you're a real danger on the dance floor. Does the department of national security know about you?" Caesar said. "Sugar, you're blushing."

"I am not." I shook my head, unable to look him in the eye.

"It's about time you let your hair down. It's beautiful that way. It suits you." He added.

"Really? My mother used to spend hours straightening it. I kept doing it…out of habit…I guess."

Caesar lifted a strand of curls veiling my right eye and tucked them behind my ear. "Thank you. I can't even think of the last time I've danced like that," he said, softening his voice, "It was a real pleasure, Angelina."

"You're welcome," I said, squeezing his hand. It was time to go. I scanned the restaurant, looking for Cara. I spotted her in a lilac booth at the back. "Bye, Caesar," I wiggled my fingers in a half wave. He held his "Kiss So Soft" in the air like a champagne glass and toasted me.

The customers had all left the back dining area and the kitchen was closed for the evening. Cara sat with one knee pulled under her chin and was sorting her money. She had changed into a white tank top tied at the waist, exposing her tan, flat stomach, and a navy blue Red Sox's cap.

I slid in the booth across from her. "Hey, what took you so long?"

"I had to make a few phone calls." She placed a wad of fifty dollar bills in her pocket.

"Wow. You cleaned up tonight. How did you make so much money?"

"Uh…yeah…I was super busy," she picked up a glass and gulped her margarita, licking the salt from the rim with her tongue. "He really likes you, you know."

"Who? Dylan?" Maybe, she had drilled him about the evening and elicited some information.

"Ha. That's funny," Cara said. I picked up a cocktail napkin and began shredding it into strips. "Uh. Sorry. Was I being harsh? It's just. Dylan doesn't know what he likes. He's like that person at the Ben and Jerry's counter, when there's a long-ass line out the door, who takes twenty minutes deciding which flavor of ice cream he wants. Like so totally unaware. And then, once he finally decides he complains that he should have ordered something else."

I nodded my head, but I didn't really understand what that had to do with me. I reached over the table for Cara's margarita glass. "Do you mind?" I asked.

"Not a bit. What's mine is yours, babe."

"Thanks." I took a sip from the straw.

"I'm talking about Caesar. He likes you," Cara said, suddenly steering the conversation off the road entirely.

"That impossible creature?"

"It's Attraction 101, Gina. It's like totally obvious."

"He's like fifty."

"Forty-nine," she said.

Forty-nine, a twenty-five year span between our ages.

"He's married." I said.

"And?"

"Caesar was just flirting. The way he flirts with any other woman or drag queens for that matter. He even flirts with men. It's just his nature."

"Yeah. He radiates a certain sexual energy. But, clearly not with me. I was best friends with Isabella since kindergarten. His daughter. When my mom got remarried to Satan, they decided to move to Michigan. I was only ten, but I wasn't going anywhere. Not after what that bastard did to me," she took another long swig of her drink.

"What did he do?"

"It started out…tickling on the couch…he moved his fingers over my boobs…rubbing his hard-on against my leg…"

"Oh my God, Cara. Did you tell your mom?"

"Oh yeah. I told her. And you know what she said? 'I shouldn't make up stories.'" Cara pulled down the visor of her hat. "I told Isabella. Next thing you know Caesar and Carol invited me to live with them. They're really great people. But I'm not so sure they are great together."

"What do you mean?"

"Well…it's strange…I always thought Isabella had the perfect life. Her parents were together and they lived in an enormous house. But once I moved in, I started to notice things. Carol and Caesar barely spoke. Except for questions like 'what's for dinner?' or 'have you seen my cell phone?' And maybe that's just normal marriage, but they never touched. In the eight years that I was there I never saw a hug, not even a peck on the cheek. Carol went away on business trips more and more. Caesar involved himself in a billion community activities. Charities. Real Estate projects. The Art Center."

"What about Isabella?"

"Oh, they both loved her so much. No doubt about it. But when she got to high school she fell in love for the first time. That's when she told me, she knew it would be better if her parents just got divorced. I mean, she never would have said anything to them. But, it's bizarre. You could tell Carol and Caesar stayed together for her. Maybe all their love for her made her grow up to love them even more. I mean, every kid wants their parents together but she loved them enough to think they should let it go. I guess after awhile people get so used to their program, they kind of numb out. It's scary when they don't even realize it."

I clawed the pile of shredded napkin, picking it up and releasing it. The pieces sprinkled over the tablecloth like snowflakes.

"Hey. Don't look so sad," she said, sliding the drink toward me.

I collected the napkin shreds into a tight ball, "What makes you think he likes me, anyway?"

"Caesar doesn't dance," Cara said.

"That's your big reason? Maybe, no one asked him before."

"You asked him?" Cara placed her elbows on the table, resting her chin in her hands, "Interesting."

"What's so interesting?" Dylan nudged me with his hip as he slid into the booth.

"Gina asked Caesar to dance," she said.

"Cara….please…drop it," I said.

"That is interesting," Dylan said.

"What's so interesting about it? I love jazz. I love to dance….Caesar stood blocking my way…."

"And, now, was that song by Frank Sinatra? Your Holy Savior."

"Dylan. Don't start," I said. Dylan laughed and rested his head on my shoulder.

Cara snapped her fingers in front of our faces, "Why? What's up with Frank Sinatra?"

"Long story," Dylan and I answered simultaneously. Dylan pinched my waist and I scooted further to the window to put more space between our bodies. Grabbing a white napkin and waving it in front of my nose, Dylan said, "I surrender, I surrender."

I swatted it away, smiling.

"And, by the way your hair really looks great like that," he said.

"Yeah. Caesar thinks so too," Cara said. I didn't know how Cara overheard my conversation with Caesar, but I didn't appreciate whatever it was she was attempting to get at.

"What's your point, Cara?" Dylan asked.

"When's the last time you've seen Caesar dance?"

"Never. But, I'm not keeping tabs on the guy," Dylan looked at me, "I think we need a change of scenery. Where are we going, Angel?"

"Where's Ava, Dylan? Shuffled her to the bottom of the deck? So, soon?" Cara asked.

"What's your problem, Cara?"

"Maybe, I should go." I nudged Dylan with my shoulder, hoping I could escape whatever volcano was about to erupt.

He rested his hand on top of mine, saying, "I agree. We should go." Dylan stood and pulled me from the booth.

With a cunning grin, Cara said, "Yeah, sure. Go ahead. But, both of you will come back to me. It's only a matter of time."

Dylan linked his arm through mine and we walked through the dining room. But before we got out the door, he released his grip. "I forgot about the office door. I'm just gonna lock up before we leave. Put in some food orders."

I moved outside. People had made their way back onto Commercial Street, joining the web of activity, in search of another enticing place to spend the witching hour. At a plastic table in the middle of the patio, Caesar sat alone with a bottle of Cabernet Sauvignon. He gulped down the remaining glass of wine and immediately reached for the bottle to refill it. Caesar slumped in his chair and stared straight ahead at the remaining cars in the dark parking lot, the strangers on the street criss-crossed in front of his line of vision. When a middle-aged couple passed, holding hands, the man yelled, "Hey Riva, you did it again. Best gig in town." Caesar nodded his head to acknowledge them, opening his mouth to speak but before he had a chance the man grabbed the woman and spun her around. She let out a playful shrill and Caesar looked down at his glass of wine, pinching the stem with his fingers.

"Hey. Are you alright?" I put my hand on his shoulder, startling him.

"Who? Me?"

"Yeah, you."

"I'm fine. Perfectly fine."

"You had a lonely kind of look in your eyes. That's all."

"I ain't sad. I don't get sad." He said, pulling himself upright and taking another sip of wine. I sat on the white plastic chair across from him, pulling his wine glass and the bottle of Cabernet Sauvignon toward me.

"What are you doing?" Caesar asked.

"I'm being your mirror. What do you see when you look at me?"

"I see a beautiful woman with the most gorgeous wild hair that I have ever laid eyes on."

"Oh…Caesar…you're…so…"

"Sugar, help me finish this. I've had too much," he said, reaching across the table and filling the glass with the last of the wine.

"Me too."

"Well, then, we'll have too much together. Let's celebrate."

"Celebrate, what?"

"You need a reason?"

"Yeah. I need a reason."

"Alright then. Let's celebrate the Summer Triangle."

"What?"

"Come here."

I dragged my chair around the table, setting it beside him. Sitting down, Caesar placed his hand on my arm and pointed to the sky. "See that bright bluish star?"

"Uh-huh."

"That's Vega. The harp. And, that one is Altair, the eagle." My eyes followed his finger. "The one over there is Deneb, the swan. It's almost a perfect right triangle," he said, "in Chinese mythology Vega and Altair were two lovers separated by a great river…the Milky Way. And once a year, a huge flock of magpies formed a bridge over Deneb to allow the lovers to spend a night together."

Wind swept the air and the leaves of a locust tree began to murmur.

"Oh, well," Caesar said, his eyes tracing the triangle of stars.

Looking at his profile, my eyes fell upon the small, flat mole on his cheekbone and I wanted to place my lips there.

"If you never feel sad then, well, how can you ever feel happy?" I asked.

"I'm always happy."

"Is that right?

"What about it?" Caesar asked.

"So, you just live in denial, then."

"Denial is not such a bad thing. Everyone needs a good dose of denial to get through. Especially, someone in my situation," he said, "Hey, have you started painting yet?"

I leaned toward the table, propping my chin on top of my closed fist. "Not yet. Someday," I said.

"Tomorrow."

"Sure. Tomorrow."

"Oh, before I forget." Caesar reached into his pocket and pulled out a folded postcard, handing it to me.

I spread out the paper. It was an invitation to an art opening at the Bangs Street Gallery. "Thank you." I creased the card and tucked it inside my purse, noticing the screen on my cellphone: 1 missed call. It was John's number. I zipped my bag.

"What's wrong?" Caesar asked.

"I'm just thinking about something you said. About denial and life."

"Don't, kid. It ain't worth it." Caesar guzzled down the last of the wine in three long swigs, adding, "It's just the way it is." He placed the wine glass down definitively, like a period mark.

I reached for his hand underneath the table. It was resting on his thigh, and as I held it, he stroked my palm with his thumb in the pattern of a figure eight. Caesar began to hum and I shut my eyes, feeling my heart beat out of synch.

"There you are. I've been searching all over for you," Dylan said. I let go of Caesar's hand as Dylan pulled a plastic chair up to the table.

"Are you ready?" Dylan asked.

"Ready for what? You ain't just gonna steal her away from me that easily, man. Not without a fight," Caesar said, playfully.

"Give it up old man," Dylan said, "She's out of your league."

"Old! Who's old?" Caesar picked up the bottom of his silk shirt, exposed his lean stomach, and patted it with his hand. "Let's see your abs, Dylan. You already got a beer belly going on, man."

"No, I don't!" Dylan lifted up his blue tee shirt.

I rose from my chair, announcing, "Gentleman, as intriguing as this moment is, I think, I'll leave you to your caveman antics."

"Hey, where you going?" Dylan shouted.

"To sleep," I shouted back without turning around.

"Bye, Angelina Moreau. I'll miss you!" Caesar called out after me.

꙰

I crawled into my bed, pulled the sheet tightly under my chin, and dialed into my voicemail to hear John's message: "Hey, Gina…I'm just calling…to see how things are going? Your mom called me today. I guess you're not in New York. I don't know…it just doesn't sound like you, Gina…Gina…Gina…Bo-Bina…I love you…um, right…I'll see you tomorrow…this is John."

He was drunk. I deleted the message and placed my phone on the nightstand. Through the skylight, I looked up at the sparkling stars, searching for Vega and Altair. The harp and the eagle. I couldn't find them, so I closed my eyes, and slid my hand inside my satin underwear.

PART TWO

⁕

"Life is a process of becoming,
a combination of states we have to go through.
Where people fail
is that they wish to elect a state and remain in it.
This is a kind of death."

—Anaïs Nin

Chapter Eight

A month had past and it had become impossible to differentiate a Saturday from a Wednesday—the days melted together in a combination of work and partying. One evening, a week after the AIDS benefit, Lisa had called me to come to the restaurant. A server had quit in the middle of a crazy rush and she needed to put me on the floor. I handled it flawlessly, so I began working four nights a week—on top of my five day shifts. I noticed that my nightly section of tables rotated, depending on whether Caesar hosted inside or outside—I was positioned in the stations closest to him. I always lingered at the restaurant after work, usually eating my dinner by Caesar. He would talk to me about politics and the history of religion. Sometimes, we would silently sit in a booth and listen to a jazz band. Cara always pulled me away from him to head downtown to The Claw. She informed me that workers had begun to gossip about our relationship. People thought we were having an affair. I told her that was ridiculous, but I sensed she didn't believe me. After that, I avoided Caesar. He eventually asked me what was wrong and I explained what Cara had told me. Caesar just laughed and said, "Angelina, are you going to spend your whole life worrying about what people think?" So I returned to sitting by his side.

Planning to catch up on sleep, I was already in my bed when

Cara had opened my bedroom door. She tossed me a nude color halter-top dress, saying, "Get ready for the night of your life." I told her I wasn't in the mood, but she said, "You can sleep when you're dead." She also mentioned that it was Caesar's birthday. I didn't say anything in response, but I got in the shower. After tying the string of fabric around my neck, I turned to look in the full length mirror on the back of Cara's bedroom door, the dress cut dramatically to reveal my whole back. I told her people were going to think I was a hooker. She said it was impossible because everyone in P-town knew I was "some sort of genius."

We wove through the bodies on Commercial Street, Cara's red high heels tap-danced against the pavement and I took in the scent of blueberry taffy emerging from The Penny Patch candy store. I grabbed Cara's hand, pulling her inside, "We have to make a pit stop."

The taffy was stored in large bins in a rainbow of colors. I knew what I was looking for, Atomic Fire Balls. I found them in a plastic container next to the Boston Baked Beans and purchased two for twenty-five cents. As kids, Neely and I would hold contests to see who could last the longest without pulling the candy from our mouths. I usually won, allowing my eyes to tear-up and taste-buds to numb. When Neely turned fourteen, she stopped playing the "Fire Ball Challenge."

As we approached Town Hall, Cara and I popped the candy in our mouths. When we passed the benches a man whistled and another yelled, "Ladies, where are you going?"

"See, I told you. They think I'm a prostitute," I said.

"Alright. That does it." Cara grabbed my hand and pulled me toward three tall drag-queens, all wearing fluorescent green, spaghetti-strapped dresses, orange platform shoes, and blonde wigs teased at the crown. Their faces were thickly caked with foundation, false eyelashes, blue eye-shadow, and red lips. A family of five stood in front of them, smiling widely as if they were posing with Mickey Mouse, and an elderly man took a photograph.

Cara pulled a disposable camera from her bag. When the father thanked the drag-queens, Cara nudged me with her elbow, "Go on."

As I walked toward them, the tallest flipped her wrist, exclaiming, "Oh, Honey, I need to get in touch with your stylist. You look delicious."

"That's what I've been trying to tell her," Cara shouted, putting the camera in front of her face.

"Say: it's not easy being queen-y," they said in unison, and I giggled along with them as the camera bulb flashed.

We continued down the street and Cara linked her arm through mine. "This place is unbelievable," I said.

"Years ago...like back to Pilgrim times...there used to be a town near Herring Cove. It was named Helltown. It was basically a mob of smugglers, outlaws, pirates. They didn't have a church or any laws. A bunch of hoodlums on a large sandbar. I guess, P-town carries a little bit of that left-over feeling. You know, like the outcasts come to live here. But now all the 'normal' people come visit. And look at them," Cara said, outstretching her arms, "They're having the time of their lives."

I crunched down on the center of the fire ball in my mouth, noticing that my eyes hadn't even watered. "Hey, are you done with the candy?" I asked.

"Are you kiddin' me? I finished that thing ages ago." Cara said, yanking my arm, "C'mon. I'm taking you to the A-House."

We walked down a small dark alleyway.

"What's the A-House?" I asked, moving past a long line of

men, waiting to enter a white two-story inn with a wrap-around porch. Deep bass beats of electronic House music pumped from the rickety building. Cara forced her way to the front.

"Another little history lesson. This place used to entertain some of the best jazz around. Billie Holiday. Ella...what's her name?"

"Fitzgerald!" I said.

"Yeah."

"That's amazing."

"Yeah, but just wait to see what's inside now. Hi, Bobby." Cara kissed the cheek of a tall man wearing a white tank top that showcased his toned biceps.

"Darling. So, nice to see you. You coming in to play?"

"Always," Cara said, sweetly.

"Be good." He said.

"Never," she responded, giggling. He didn't check our ID's and allowed us to slide into the club without paying. We entered the dark room; the ceiling was held up by wooden posts, the cracked floor shook with the movement of fifty or so men, dancing closely together to the throb of the music. A black light made the white tank tops on a dozen of men glow with a purple hue.

"This is unreal!" I yelled above the music. Cara made her way pulling me with her, through the small spaces between bodies. Occasionally someone's arm, drenched with sweat, rubbed against mine. The heat was unbearable. Within five minutes, it was as if I had been sitting in a sauna for two hours. I wiped perspiration off my forehead with the back of my hand.

"This is my religion," Cara said and I laughed.

"Why is that?"

"Fifty beautiful and smiling gay men. And they love women, but without any other motive. It's so safe. Know what I mean?" She started to move her hips to the beat, closing her eyes. I had never been in a gay bar before, but I soon realized she was right. I was safe. One man grabbed my hand, "Hey beautiful." He spun me around and I shut my eyes, moving to the music and throwing my arms in the air when the song changed into a techno version of Madonna's "Like a Prayer." Cara stepped onto a black dance platform and the men whistled. She bent over, reaching for my hand, but I shook my head.

"Oh, c'mon Mary Magdalene," she said, lifting me up to the platform to join her. From my new view of the A-House, I saw a lot of men dancing bare-chested with their rolled t-shirts hanging from the belt loop of their tight designer jeans. Cara quickly followed the trend, ripping off her tank top, and displaying her lace bra. I glanced around the room, but no one paid attention. I danced to the pulsing music, losing myself under the purple luminosity. Glow sticks swirled in the air, creating trails of pink and green light like shooting stars.

"We better go." Cara shouted above the deafening thump of the bass.

"Where?"

"The Pixie."

"Oh, let's just stay," I said.

"Don't worry, dancing queen. You can dance your heart out at Caesar's party," she said, pulling her tank top over her head and jumping off the platform. I quickly hopped down to the floor to meet her. Cara's lips rushed at me, she pushed her tongue into my mouth and pulled away. Startled by her move, I looked at Cara curiously.

"Oh, don't get your panties all in a bunch. I was just seeing if there was any chance I could bat for the other team."

"And?"

"Unfortunately, I'm condemned to a life of heterosexuality," she said, becoming serious, "How is it possible to love a guy, but he doesn't really love you back in the same way?"

"Cara, if I had that answer, we could bottle it, sell it, and become billionaires. Gay or straight and everyone in between."

༺

We entered the Pixie. The brightly lit room was filled with a dozen young tourists and twenty or so recognizable faces—restaurant and shop workers that stayed through the summer season and I had seen in the Claw and at Mona Lisa's. In the corner of the room, a man shot a dart at a dartboard and his teammate slapped his back when he just missed the bulls-eye. A group of people surrounded a pool table, impatiently waiting for a chance to get in the game. Behind two black doors across the room, a disco song was playing loudly. Cara stopped to talk with a girl I didn't know and I searched around the room, noticing Dylan at the bar ordering drinks. I snuck up beside him.

"Add a couple Coronas to that order," I said.

"Hey. You're finally here," he said, widening his eyes. He pulled a wooden stool back, saying, "Here…I mean if you want to sit down…here…or whatever."

I sat down and Dylan passed me a Corona.

"Hey, guys. I'm going to tear it up in there." Cara said. I noticed that she didn't shoot her usual suspicious glance at Dylan and me. I handed her a Corona, and she walked through the black doors into the back room, tossing her arms in the air.

"I don't like you hanging around her," Dylan said, nodding at the closed doors.

"Well. I appreciate your opinion, but…"

"You should keep away from her."

"As I was saying, thanks for your opinion, but I'm fully capable..." I paused.

"Yeah?" Dylan urged me to continue, sitting down on the stool beside me.

"That's all. Thanks for the advice. I'll keep it in mind."

"That's it? I don't believe it. You're thinking something else. I know you," he said.

"I have been meaning to ask you something, but it's sort of personal, I guess," I said. Dylan squirmed on the stool, tightening his grip around the bottle. "I'm just wondering...about that day...at my apartment...when you told me that you ran away from home. Why did you do that?"

Dylan stared at his Corona and talked about the night of his seventeenth birthday party. His mother had arranged a big affair to compensate for the last week she had stayed in bed, crying and chain smoking Merits. "She was really starting to get on my nerves...saying things like 'a martini a day keeps the doctor away'...all the lies I had to tell to cover up for the fact she was an alcoholic." Dylan went onto the terrace to smoke a joint and he saw a homeless man below, sitting on the curb and fumbling for a lighter. Dylan dropped his down. "That's when I asked him, 'is it scary being homeless?' He told me, 'I got a home. Look around you kid. If you want to see scary just visit my parents in Boise, Idaho.'" When he returned inside, people had gathered and his mother was half in the bag, mingling around with her phony Botox lips. He sat on a leather recliner, looking at the crystal Tiffany's clock hanging above the fireplace, the fireplace they didn't even use except on holidays when his mother ignited fake logs to create the illusion of a Norman Rockwell Christmas. He watched how all his extended family would circle around his grandmother. "She had Alzheimer's Disease. And you want to know why they were talking to her? Because she was sitting on forty million dollars. It was disgusting. All of it," Dylan said, pulling his Corona to his lips, "Then, my dad shows up out of the blue. He divorced my mother when I was eight. It took about fifteen minutes before they started up. Screaming about me. My grades. My future. So I walked to my bedroom, stuffed some crap in a backpack, stole five thousand bucks from my mother's nightstand. Slipped out the door. They didn't even notice. I wanted to go back to the beginning, start over with a fresh new start. So, I made my way straight across country from San Francisco to here. As far away as possible."

"Did you ever see your parents again?" I asked.

"I called my mother when I turned eighteen. She was going to AA. Step 9 or something. The past is the past, Angel. Don't dig into it. It's done."

"You're right, Dylan. It's already written. Time to create a new chapter. Cheers." We clicked our bottles together and the night continued on, a shot of Cuervo Gold, a couple more Coronas. Dylan looked uncomfortable, his eyebrows furrowed, and I could tell he was mulling something over.

"It's okay. Dylan. Whatever it is. It's safe to tell me."

"About what happened….a month ago…in the office…."

"Yeah?" I squeezed his hand, encouraging him to continue.

"You're so smart and beautiful and I bet a billion guys would love to be with you…" He played with a plastic straw, twisting it into knots.

"It's okay," I started to say, to spare him the discomfort. But, he was drunk. He needed to talk. He turned his head away from me, looking at a man cuing up his pool stick. "When Mister Right comes along, then what am I left with? You and I are different, Angel. I'm just…a…."

"Don't say it Dylan. It's not true."

"I'm a bum," he said, his face wincing, exposing the tiny wrinkles around his eyes. "It's just so complicated. I don't know. When did it get so complicated?"

"No. It's not. All you have to do is un-complicate it. Whatever it is. You can change it," I said.

"I'm trying. But, I got too many people involved. I lost myself in this insanity and I took too many people with me. I don't want to get you involved too. I've got to find a way out." He said. I wasn't sure exactly what Dylan meant, but I didn't pry. What had he done?

His cellphone rang and he checked the caller ID. "I have to take this. I'll be right back." He placed the cellphone to his ear and headed outside. In search of the restroom, I walked up a staircase where I saw Cara at the head of a line of women waiting to enter.

"Gina! C'mon," she waved me up to the front.

"Ow!"

"Oh. Excuse me. I'm sorry," I said. I had accidentally stepped on a woman's sandal, scratching one of her mocha painted toenails.

"Yeah. I'm sure you're real sorry," Ava said, flipping her hair over her shoulder

"Ava. I didn't see you there! You've been going through quite a nightmare this summer, huh?" Cara said.

"What are you talking about?" Ava asked. I knocked loudly on the bathroom door, hoping the woman inside would hurry up.

"Oh. My mistake," Cara said, "I was just out back the restaurant, when I saw you like totally break down about Dylan. It's harsh you guys are breaking up, but hey I told you this was going to happen when I found out you two were cheating on me. Remember? When I was Dylan's girlfriend and you were my best friend. And you two thought you were pulling a fast one on me. I told you it would come back to haunt you."

"Get over it, Cara," Ava said.

"I am over it. But don't act surprised that you're hurting over Dylan. Do you even know what I've been through?" The door opened, a woman emerged shooting me a nasty look, and I grabbed Cara by the knot in her shirt, yanking her inside, and locking the door.

"I'd really love to smack her!" Cara was yelling.

"I didn't realize she did that to you! And, she was your best friend?"

"Whatever. They both did it. And, I was too stupid to realize. Who knows. Dylan told me that he's trying to change now. But, it's hard to believe." Cara pulled her package of cocaine out and laid down two trails on the bathroom sink. She blew the lines up her nose.

"Well, I think Dylan is trying to change, to be a better friend. Why don't you give him the benefit of the doubt?" I asked, realizing this wasn't the best time for a heart to heart. A month earlier, I never would have imagined I'd be in a bar bathroom with a pile of cocaine.

"Dylan will never change."

"We were just talking and I can tell that he's trying. He said…" I began, but Cara interrupted.

"Look, I won't deny it. Dylan is drawn to you. But, that doesn't mean that he can be with you. You're a Ferrari, Gina."

"I am not a Ferrari." I said, placing my hands on my hips.

"Gina. You graduated from like Harvard Ivy League University. Okay. You're an All-American athlete. You're sexy and strong. You ain't here for long. You're just getting started. It's only a matter of time until you burn rubber out of here and leave skid marks on Dylan's back."

I looked over Cara's shoulder into the cracked mirror, pulling the elastic band from my wrist, and tucking my hair back into a tight ponytail. What had all those accomplishments been worth, really?

"Why can't you see what's so freaking obvious, Gina? It's almost insulting."

"Well, you're going to get out of here too. After this summer, you're moving to LA and you'll be on your way to becoming a big movie star," I said.

"Yeah. Sure." Cara snickered.

"But, you are, Cara. You could do or be anything."

"You're sweet, Gina. But, you know, deep down I'm not going anywhere." She dabbed cocaine onto the counter top and handed me a rolled twenty. "Here. I'm going to head out." Cara said, sneaking out the door. I locked it behind her, moved to the sink, and bent over the cocaine. I met my reflection in the mirror.

"Hey. What's your deal?" A voice yelled from the other side of the door.

"Just a minute," I shouted, sweeping the cocaine into my cupped hand and moving to the toilet. I clapped my hands over the toilet bowl and flushed it all down.

When I returned downstairs, I couldn't find Cara or Dylan, so I walked to the back of the room and opened the door. A disco ball spun circles of light around the dark room, tightly packed with people. Swaying a bit from side to side, I pushed my way through the strangers who were flailing around the dance floor to "Need You Tonight" by Inxs. Like a ping-pong ball, I bounced off their heated bodies until I emerged through to the other side, where another crowd of people stood idle in front of the deejay, not drunk enough to dance. Cara rested her back against the wall talking to Caesar.

"And, I was like so, upset, but, like, who wouldn't be…" Cara babbled on and I steered myself toward the bar, grabbing a hold of the brass ledge to watch from the sidelines. He nodded every now and then, but his hazel eyes weren't focused on her. Caesar stretched out his neck like an ostrich, jerking his head from side to side, I waited patiently, as if I were four-years-old again and Neely was coming to get me. I wanted to be found, but terrified of the consequence. Finally he saw me, already looking at him. He relaxed then and offered me a tender smile.

With his eyes upon me, Caesar moved through the crowd, most people stepping out of his way when they saw him coming. I ducked my head, playing hide-and-go-seek. His expression went blank when I was out of view, until he caught a glimpse of me and his eager eyes returned. I sat on the barstool, waiting for him to approach me. "I won," he said, pressing his thighs against my kneecaps. "You shouldn't let those lovely legs go to waste. It's your turn to come dance with me." He reached for my hand.

"Did you go to school to learn that womanizing lingo? What is it all about? I hope you know I'm not seduced by that sort of thing. I'll tell you that right off the bat."

"You're not? Well, I better punch that into my womanizing database. File it under your name. 'Not seduced by womanizing lingo.' So, what are you seduced by then?"

"Something that a person from your generation probably wouldn't understand."

"Ouch. Now, you're making age jokes. And, on my birthday! That ain't nice, kid. Aren't you supposed to be politically correct with that Harvard education and all? What are you seduced by?"

"You really want to know?"

"Of course," he nodded. I placed my two palms flat against his chest and opened them like a book, saying, "Everything inside there."

"I believe that too," he said, with unwavering eyes.

"I don't know. I just don't understand you." I remained skeptical, waiting for Caesar's eyes to shift, but they didn't blink. They only opened wider.

"Angelina Moreau, you understand me. I'm an open book and you're an excellent reader."

And with that, Caesar led me to the dance floor.

Chapter Nine

The next morning, I awoke to Cara's Great Danes plunging through my bedroom door, chasing a red cardinal that fluttered in circles around the ceiling's perimeter. The bird continued to fly around the room, desperately searching for a way out, unable to see the only way out was the way in, through the open skylight above my bed.

My head ached with a sensation like a thousand fire ants stinging my brain cells. I kicked the covers off my body, quickly noticing that I was wearing the backless nude dress from the night before. I grabbed the dogs by their spiked leather collars, each in one hand, and yanked them into the living room, closing the door behind them. From the other side, their nails scraped against the wood, but, they settled and their barks dwindled to whimpers.

The cardinal was still fluttering around helplessly and sporadically screeching at a pitch that aggravated my headache. I grabbed a plastic hanger from my closet, stood on my bed, and tried to lure the creature toward a new direction of flight. Finally, after a half an hour, the cardinal escaped out the skylight into the open air; his scarlet wings cut through the gray sky. I collapsed onto the bed, my hands folded behind my throbbing head, and glanced around my room.

Something wasn't right.

A full glass of water rested on my nightstand near a bottle of

Tylenol. I unscrewed the cap and swallowed three pills, washing the warm water down my parched throat, trying to dispel the lingering taste of stale beer. A blue windbreaker was draped across a cream-colored chair in the corner and it haunted me from afar. I had seen that blue windbreaker before. It belonged to Dylan.

Above the bureau, a pink note was tacked against the mirror covered in bubbly cursive. It read: "Forgot to tell you. Your father called yesterday. He's coming to visit." I reread the message. "He's coming to visit."

I had only seen my father once since his trial. We hadn't spoken more than three words. How he tracked me down, I wasn't completely certain. But I was sure my mother had something to do with it. What could he possibly have to say after all these years? With the exception of a weekend excursion to Vegas back in '86, my father never left the state of Connecticut. To cross the border into another state was considered international travel. I knew his trip must be critical. I felt guilty. Had he been diagnosed with cancer?

I carefully pasted the note back to the mirror. Like a detective at a crime scene, I was eager to unravel the mystery, but overwhelmed by information. I replaced the evidence, not yet ready to make sense of the clues.

Still clutching the plastic hanger, I scooted over the bed and, holding my knees to my chest, wrapped my hands around my ankles. The skin on my heels had been rubbed raw from all the extra hours at the restaurant; two large band aides were stuck to the backs. Someone had cleaned the cuts. On the other side of my bed, the pillow held the shape of someone's head. I picked up the pillow in the hope I could miraculously figure out who had been there. I lifted the pillow and underneath was a single rose.

The questions stacked up like a deck of cards. Three names sprung to mind: Cara, Dylan, Caesar. But, the question of all questions was: Which one could I trust to tell me the truth?

I stood up from my bed. The rose. The windbreaker. The note. When I shakily wobbled to the closet to replace the plastic hanger, I tripped over a yellow high-heel and landed in the back of the closet. I bent down on one knee, crouched beneath my hanging clothes and rested my right hand on the back wall. A wood panel suddenly swung open and I collapsed onto a pile of shoes. I crawled through the small opening into a room five feet in all directions and filled by thirty black Hefty garbage bags. I carefully untied the plastic handles—immediately wishing I hadn't been so curious. Stacks of hundred dollar bills filled the bag. I opened another bag. Forty smaller clear plastic bags of cocaine were stored inside.

I heard a knock on my bedroom door.

"Gina?" Cara shouted. I rapidly retied the bags. Hearing the sound of my bedroom door being opened, I scrambled back through the opening, closing the panel door. I jumped up to standing and pushed my clothes to the center of the rod to cover the secret stash.

"Just a minute, Cara," I called out.

"What's going on in there?" Cara asked as I emerged from the closet. I flashed her a toothy grin.

"Nothing. Really. Oh. Nothing at all." I said, running my fingers along the seam of a pair of black pants, "I'm just looking at my clothes. I own way too much black."

❦

I sat on the edge of my bed, haunted by what I had discovered inside that secret storage room. I needed to talk to someone. When I heard Cara showering, I snuck into her bedroom, immediately finding what I was looking for in her address book: Caesar's phone number. I wrote the number down with a pen on the palm of my hand and tiptoed out of her bedroom. I waited for her to dress and blow-dry her hair. She invited me to go grocery shopping, but I declined. Finally, she left.

Perhaps, I should have confronted her, but I was afraid of her reaction. I transferred Caesar's number to a slip of paper and decided to shower, hoping it would cleanse my thoughts. A hour later, still confused, I sat on the couch with the phone clutched in my hand, studying Caesar's number, sometimes pressing a few digits and then hanging up.

Finally I pressed all the digits. He answered on the third ring, but I hung up as soon as I heard his velvety voice. My body had become electrified by his mere "hello." Forget it. It was safer to pretend my discovery never happened. The phone rang and I jolted.

"Hello," I answered, tentatively.

"Who is this?"

It was Caesar. Embarrassed for having hung up earlier, I asked, "Who is this?"

"You first," he said.

"No. You first." I said.

"Well, considering you just phoned me, and hung up when I answered, it's your responsibility to answer me first. That's how it works." He must have dialed star 69. That was the problem with technology in the twenty-first century. I couldn't even get away with an innocent hang up.

"It's Angelina," I said.

"I know."

"How?"

"Sugar, I'd recognize your succulent voice from Pluto. Are you kidding me? I'm soooo excited you called."

"Trust me. It's not all that exciting, so you can calm down." My stomach flickered with nervous energy.

"No, I can't calm down. This is the most exciting thing that's happened to me in months. Well, it doesn't beat dancing with you, though."

"What are you doing?" I asked.

"That's it. You just called to ask me what I'm doing?"

"You're not going to make this easy. Are you?"

"I just went shopping at the health food store."

"Where are you driving?"

"I'm going to the restaurant. I'm just passing your apartment actually."

"Stop the car. Can you come in? I need to talk to you about something."

"You want me to come in?"

"I want to talk to you about something. I can't do it at the restaurant." I looked out the living room window. He was sitting in his red Porsche, parked in my driveway, holding his cell phone to his ear.

"You need my help?" he asked, provocatively.

"Yeah. Okay. If you want me to put it that way. I need your help." With the phone still held to my ear, I ran down the stairs, and opened the front door. Wrapping my white cardigan around my sun burnt shoulders, a breeze blew against my lavender and white polka dotted sundress. I leaned against a beam on the porch with my arm hugging my waist.

"Wow. Angelina Moreau. Don't move."

"Why?" I asked. Caesar looked up at me through the windshield of his car, taking off his sunglasses. "I'm taking a mental photograph."

My cheeks flushed. "Are you done yet?"

"Don't rush me. I want to savor the moment. This...this is a magnificent moment."

"Come here," I said, slowly waving him in.

"I'm coming," he opened the car door with his cell phone glued to his ear.

"Is that so? Then, you better slow down."

"You don't want me to come then?" He said, freezing mid-step.

"I didn't say that exactly," I said.

"Well, then, I'm coming."

"You can hang up now," I said.

"You hang up first," he said.

"Are we starting this again?"

"I didn't know we had started something," he said, walking toward me, his sandals crunching on the cracked shell driveway.

"We haven't started. A thing."

"Nothing? Huh?" he asked, only inches away from me. I shook my head, feeling the warmth of his breath. We clicked off our cell phones.

He followed me through the door and up the creaky wooden stairs. As I reached for the doorknob Caesar placed his hand on my waist, running his fingers along the seam of my sundress. We entered my apartment and I locked the door behind him. With his back pressed against the door I leaned toward him, but stopped short to study his crooked lips. Caesar tilted toward me, but I pulled back. We rocked back and forth, our lips close but not touching. It was a game to see who would cross over first. "Wait. Stop. I got to warn you. This isn't a smart idea." Caesar stood straight, knocking his head lightly against the door.

"Why not?" I knew the answer. I wanted to hear it from him.

"I'm married. I'm almost three times your age. You really don't want to do this," he said, "because, we aren't going anywhere, Angelina."

I looked at him, examining his face, the fine lines around his eyes, the speckles of gray glistening in his unshaven chin. I circled my finger around the dark mole on his cheekbone.

"I should go," he said.

"Yeah. You should go," I said, but Caesar didn't move.

"I'm going then."

"Okay. You're going." Our lips came closer to the line of scrimmage. I don't know who crossed it first. We kissed deeply.

Caesar pulled me to him, clasping his arms around my back. With our chests pressing tightly together, his mouth moved down my neck, blowing against the trail of kisses before meeting my lips again. The tip of my tongue lightly stroked the edge of his bottom lip and Caesar waited with an open mouth for me to reenter. Without ever shifting our hands, we kissed for what felt like hours.

"God...I could kiss you forever," he said, nibbling my ear. I remembered Cara had left awhile ago.

"Cara could be back any minute."

"Well, in that case," he said, flipping me around. My back pressed against the door. Caesar cupped my breast over my dress; his mouth moving over the other and lightly biting my nipple. The flash of pain only heightened the pleasure. He collapsed to his knees, coasting his hands down my hips. Starting at my calves, he kissed one and then the other. My palms spread against the door and I began to squirm when his head slid underneath my skirt, moving his way slowly up my thighs. His tongue skimmed against the elastic of my underwear, and I squeezed my legs together fighting the desire until my strength let go, begging him to come to me. Except he didn't rush, he caressed my stomach and hips; he finally made his way inside. My knees began to waver, my back sliding against the door and dropping to the floor when he had finished.

    He took a hold of my waist and stood. I clutched his head, kissing him urgently and pushing him toward the couch. I unbuttoned his shirt as he pulled off his pants. He removed one sock, but before he had a chance to get to the other, I lifted my dress, draped my legs around his waist, and I fell upon him. "Oh, my!"

    A dog barked loudly and I bit the skin on my shoulder to keep me from screaming again. I could hear them panting nearby as we locked eyes, smiling, then wincing. "Oh, No," I whispered, shaking my head. We circled our hips slowly, speeding up, slowing down, stopping, holding in and holding on this way.

    When it was over, the current of energy still shook through me. I closed my eyes and my body couldn't stop trembling. My head dropped onto his shoulder and Caesar hugged me tightly. I pulled back to look at him, his eyes were soft and slightly wounded, "See, I warned you, Angelina."

    We showered together and then he left. When I dropped onto my bed, my eyes fell on the closet door and I remembered the piles of cocaine and hundred dollar bills. Now I harbored two disastrous secrets. How could I conceal them both?

Chapter Ten

Seven hours later, I was working my shift at the restaurant, nervously expecting Caesar's arrival. Every fifteen minutes, I checked my watch. He pulled up in his red Porsche with Louis Armstrong's throaty voice crooning "Kiss of Fire." Cara stood by my side with her arms crossed. Caesar marched right up to me with his silver chain dangling against his thigh and his shoulders arched back. His wide hazel eyes sparkling amicably like an ally, he said, "Hi, Angelina Moreau."

"Hi, Caesar Riva," I said casually, but I longed to hug him. I wanted to kiss those lips. I buried my hands in my apron pockets. Caesar kissed my cheek and entered the restaurant.

"What was that all about?" Cara said.

"I'm not sure," I said and it was true. I didn't know what Caesar and I were all about. I saw Dylan through the large glass windowpane, looking at me as if he were a houseplant I had not watered in a week.

I collected the black bill holder stuffed with money off a table on the patio. I couldn't wait for the elderly couple who were sitting there to leave. It was my last table of the day and I had to get out of there. I sped through my cash out, hiding out on the side station, the coffee carafes, water pitchers, and an empty plastic table. I walked into the restaurant filled with anxiety. Caesar was speaking with

Dylan at the bar, discussing the restaurant's lunch profits. He didn't stop talking when he saw me, but he glanced in my direction long enough for Dylan to turn around and see what Caesar was looking at. I handed my blue bag filled with my daily earnings to the bartender, who deposited it into the safe underneath the cash register. I left the restaurant without saying a word.

I strolled home along Commercial Street, stopping to get my usual vanilla skim latte at the Coffee Corner. My clogs shuffled against the pavement and I dragged my tote bag behind me. Caesar Riva branded inside my brain.

༄

After taking a shower, I sat out on the deck in the padded lounge chair, with my hooded Harvard sweatshirt pulled up over my head, and a glass of ice tea by my side. I finished the biography of Frida Khalo and closely examined the pictures of her artwork. I admired the vulnerability she expressed in her paintings. I didn't think I could ever have the courage to paint that way.

I went back inside, eyeing the books on my bookcase. I picked up *The Magdalene Legacy*. During my freshman year, my roommate at Harvard had given it to me after we spent endless hours discussing religion. I had been conflicted about religion, considering my parents were Catholic, even my father. If anything, it provoked more questions. How could we have gone to church on Sunday while my dad beat my mother? I opened the book, reading the inside flap. Mary Magdalene was one of the most painted and sculpted figures in history, yet she had been denigrated by the religious institution. Why? Perhaps, the words would lead to something more conclusive, something non contradictory.

I returned to the deck. The book hypothesized about the role of Mary and Jesus as mortal humans, lovers even. As my eyes sailed over the treacherous pages of the book, a snake of guilt slithered inside me. I had committed adultery and I had to put an end to Caesar Riva. I read the story of Jesus and Mary until the strawberry sky faded into twilight. While my eyes tore through the sentences, not even stopping for dinner, a seagull cawed out in the distance. On his drive home from work, Caesar phoned me. Just like I prayed he would. A new story was being written. Right or wrong, depending on how you looked at it. And, maybe, it was both: right and wrong. All at once.

∽

For another full month, Caesar and I fueled the affair. Our clandestine world grew more unmanageable at Mona Lisa's Seduction. He called me. I called him. Sometimes three times a day. Sometimes, to come over and talk. Sometimes, to check in. Sometimes, to touch. We kept looping around one another until we were so tangled together that neither one of us knew how to unravel the fraying knot.

PART THREE

۶

"Life shrinks or expands
in proportion to one's
courage."

—Anaïs Nin

Chapter Eleven

I wished that I could have blamed it on the full moon. Earlier in the day, I dropped in Snippy Snaps to have my hair dyed. It wasn't something I had planned. Just my luck, Danny had a slot open. He handed me sample hair colors, suggesting some streaks of lighter brown, but when I flipped the page to a variety of rich red shades, I pointed to a bright burgundy. "That's going to be a drastic change. Are you sure?" He asked. I told him I wasn't sure, but to do it anyway. Three hours later, I exited the hair salon as a red head. It was drastic and I loved it.

That night I was alone in the apartment and Cara was at work. I was free to turn up the volume on John Coltrane's, "Dear Lord." Cara said she didn't get how on earth I could listen to the crap, it was a chaotic mess of random sounds and to show me, she pulled out a pot and slammed a wooden spoon against it and stomped around the living room.

Listening to the mystical music I thought of him, so I phoned, but he didn't pick up. I left a message and hopped in the tub. I closed my eyes, allowing the spout to spray over my scalp like a cleansing rain shower. When I opened my eyes, I saw the dye had painted the water deep red and burgundy droplets had drizzled down my arms and across the dip of my stomach. My hip bones were visible enough to make me realize, for the first time, I had probably lost twenty pounds in the past two and a half months since I had arrived in Provincetown. I shut off the water and stepped out of the tub. A cool breeze came through the window, blowing the pastel pink curtains and making goose bumps rise up on my skin. I wrapped a towel around my body and picked up my cell phone. One new message.

"Hi. It's me. Um. I'm…just calling you back…uh…I don't know…I guess…call me back…I mean, if you want…to call me back…you know…okay…um…" There was a long pause, in which I heard him breathing into the receiver, "I love you," he said faintly and with a quiver in his voice. The words echoed in my ear.

I dialed his number. He said he would be at the apartment in ten minutes. I dressed and towel-dried my hair, staining the white towel with splotches like burgundy clouds. I sat down and waited, unable to think about anything, anticipating his light knock against the door, two soft taps. I wasted time waiting, waiting for that moment when I opened the door. Tick. Tock. The sound of waiting was like hands moving on an old-fashioned grandfather clock. Tick. Tock.

I opened the door.

"Hey, beautiful," he said, planting a kiss on the spot between my eyebrows as he always did when he entered. Carrying a large rectangle panel wrapped in the *New York Times* and a plastic bag, Caesar walked toward the couch, clumsily knocking his knee against the coffee table.

"What's all this?" I asked, sitting down beside him.

"Happy Birthday, kid." Caesar placed the large panel across my lap.

"It's not my birthday."

"Well, you're going to have one eventually, right?"

I had already lost track of how many times he had come to me in the past month, the tally marks had added up too quickly, so I stopped counting. I didn't necessarily feel wrong about him coming to me, yet I didn't exactly feel right about it. That's what made it elusive, as if it wasn't really happening, as if the consequences didn't matter, because in dreams, no one really got hurt.

I carefully tore a piece of tape open, moving slowly to the next bit.

"I'm going to be dead by the time you finish."

I raised my eyebrows, saying, "Hey, don't rush me. I'm savoring it, mister." I worked my way down the paper, pulling the Metro section to my face, I began to read: "Traveling Reverends Sell Faith to N.Y.ers." Peeking over the top edge of the paper, I said, "Fascinating."

Caesar placed his hands over his heart, "I think I'm having a heart attack."

"Alright, alright," I said, tossing the rest of the paper to floor. He stood, helping me turn the frame over. It was the painting from the art gallery, the woman on the curb.

"Do you like it?" Caesar's voice cracked and he searched my face for a reaction.

"No one…no one has ever…done that," I said, searching for the right words, "I can't believe that you…could have…"

"Go on. Look in the bag," Caesar said, pulling the painting from my lap and leaning it against the wall. I peeked inside the plastic bag. There were canvases, paintbrushes, an acrylic paint set, a palette, and a beginner's book to painting.

"Wow. I'm speechless."

"Don't say anything. Just paint me something."

"Okay," I said, walking to him. I threw my arms around his neck, looking into his eyes. He broke our embrace, and moved toward the kitchen. "Do you want any wine?" He asked.

"Please," I said, sitting on the couch sideways.

He handed me the glass, pulling my legs up. He sat down and replaced them across his thighs. Caesar stroked my legs as we talked for the following three hours. We debated the artwork of Frida Kahlo and Diego Rivera; he thought she was a much better artist, although he never explained why. I read him Pablo Neruda's *Ode to Opposites* from beginning to end, first in English, the second time around in Neruda's native tongue. After hearing me speak Spanish, he asked me to read it again. He said he like the way my lips moved when I said *fuego*. He spoke to me about the history of the Knights Templar, and about new theories on religion. We exchanged ideas and opinions on politics, on foreign and domestic policy, on why no peace would ever come from war.

"I could talk to you forever," Caesar said, slumping on the couch and hugging a pillow.

"Are you okay?" I rubbed my hand over his hair.

"Sure. I'm a little confused. I guess."

"Confused about what?"

"I don't know. I don't know. I rather not talk about it." He rested his head against my breast.

"You have small hands," I said, holding his hand up to mine, palm to palm. The tips of my fingers were a few centimeters short of his.

"Yeah. So do you," he said. "Except they aren't that small for a woman, but still, I bet you can't palm a basketball."

"Nope. I can't. But, it looks like our hands match perfectly. My hands are like the female version of yours."

"That's because you are the female version of me."

"Hey. Did you ever think that you're the male version of me?" I said, playfully.

"Well, I was born first. So, that means you got to take after me.

Logistically, speaking."

"Man, you're a real piece of work. You know that?" I tickled under his arm.

"Yeah. I know. And, so are you."

He kissed the back of my hand, pecking his lips in between each of my knuckles. I straddled him, my knees on either side of his lap. We kissed with a tender passion. I ran my fingers through his fine hair and rubbed the sides of his smooth jaw. I inhaled the fresh scent of his skin, like lush ferns. I wanted to bottle his smell, because I knew we were on borrowed time, like Cara's secret storage room in the back of my closet, eventually someone would find out.

He lifted me up in his arms and carried me to the bedroom, my head bumping against the corner of the door.

"Ouch. Careful, Rhett Butler," I said and we laughed. He kissed my temple and I kicked off my flip-flops, lying back onto my bed and tucking my hands behind my head. He sat on the edge and leaned over to pull back the Velcro straps of his Teva sandals. Sometimes I helped him undress, but, sometimes, I liked to watch him shed each piece of clothing and wait for him to come to me and slowly strip away all my layers.

"Why on earth do you always wear socks with your sandals in the middle of the summer?" I asked.

"I don't like things in between my toes. That's why."

"Well, I bet that's not completely true," I said.

"Nope. It's true. I even wear socks to the beach, because I can't stand sand in there. Drives me nuts."

"I bet you'd love me in between your toes," I said and he smiled.

"You. I love anywhere. And, I don't know why. I mean why, I'm so pulled to you. It's like..." He didn't go further. He stood, walked to my stereo, and turned on the radio. The Buena Vista Social Club's,

"Candela", played on WOMR. I pushed myself onto my knees, starting to dance to the Cuban music, shaking my hips and snapping my fingers above my head. Caesar pulled his blue t-shirt with a quarter-size hole in the stomach over his head, dropped his boxer shorts, and lay down naked on the bed. Looking up at me, he said, "Dance for me."

I moved onto the floor, pulling the elastic from my ponytail. With my back to Caesar, I looked at him through the reflection in the mirror above my bureau. I hadn't even begun to dance, yet I could already see his desire for me. I rolled my hips as my fingers skimmed up my sides into the air. I spun around sharply, pulling my tank top off and playing with the straps of my black lace bra. Dancing on the balls of my feet, one leg stepped in front of the other and I flicked my hip to the sound of the bongo drum. Caesar was watching my face as I wiggled out of my jeans. I stepped onto the bed, placing a leg on either side of his body. He held on to my ankles and I unclasped my bra. "*Fuego*," I said, teasingly. I snapped the bra at him and it landed across his face. I covered my mouth, laughing, and Caesar reached for my hips, saying, "That does it." He pulled me down and I screamed playfully. He covered first my stomach with ravenous kisses, then my belly button, and lightening his touch as he moved down. I closed my eyes. I let myself sink into the quicksand, my thighs tingling from the heat of his mouth. I gently rolled him onto his back, languidly skating across his body with my tongue, holding his wrists firmly against the bed. Caesar flipped me over, raised my arms over my head, he held them with one hand, the other squeezed my breast, and he kissed me deeply. I wriggled free, turning him again, my fingers working him like clay, and my teeth marking his shoulder.

We eventually settled on our sides, facing one another, locked together with the tips of our noses touching. His lips opened, sucking in air from the cracks between his teeth. His body went limp and mine began to tremble like it always did after he came. The current pulsed through me, causing me to shiver a few times.

"Oh. My," I said and kissed his chest, above his right nipple. He turned on his back, his arm bent over his forehead, breathing heavily with his eyes closed. "God," he said.

"They write books about this, you know," he said, his fingers sifting through my hair.

"Yeah. But, those books have happy endings," I said, staring at the stars through the skylight.

"What made you decide to dye your hair?"

"It's my scarlet letter. Since, now I'm your mistress."

"You're not my mistress," he said, shaking his head, apparently hurt.

"What exactly am I to you?" I asked.

"Um. You're like my really really good friend," Caesar said.

I pulled away from him and sat Indian style on the bed. The sweat ran down my neck, the honey between my legs still leaking.

"Okay. 'Really good friend?' How do you explain that intensity then? Or do you just so happen to share that with all your really good friends?" I said, perplexed, "You're killing me. One cell at a time." He sat up, brushed his hand against my cheek, and pulled me back with him to the bed.

"Please say something," I said.

"I don't know what to say."

"Say whatever you feel. There's no right or wrong answer," I said, staring at his closed lips. "Look. If this is just about getting laid…" I said, but didn't go on when I saw pain in his eyes. He blinked and turned away, picking up the oyster shell on my nightstand, and pressing his finger on a purple stain.

"Is that your family?" He pointed to a photograph by the lamp.

"Yeah."

He picked up the photo to get a better look. "You were so cute. Look at you with those chubby cheeks." He brought the photograph closer to his eyes and squinted.

I must have been around three. I sat on top of an orange counter at the Dairy Queen, wearing my pink two-piece bathing suit, my pudgy belly hanging out and tiny tongue licking a vanilla ice cream cone. My father hovered over me with a proud smile, wiping chocolate sprinkles from my chin with a white napkin. My mother stood on the other side with my sister piggyback behind her, Neely's wiry arms clinging to her neck.

"It looks like you have a really great family," he said, pinching my cheek. I grabbed the photo and placed it face down on the nightstand.

"Looks like it," I said.

"Is that your Dad? I thought you said you didn't have one?" Caesar asked.

"I do. Except we don't talk anymore."

"You don't see eye to eye?"

"Eye to eye? We're on different planes of reality."

"Yeah. I can relate to that," he said. "So, why do you keep that photo there, then?"

"I don't know. It's a reminder. To have hope. In that second in time, we were all…on the same side. Sometimes, I can't help but think that I'm conning myself."

Caesar let out a long sigh and got up from the bed, leaving me alone with the wrinkled and stained sheets, the potent smell of us.

"Why do you act like that?" I followed him into the bathroom.

"Act like what?"

"Like the Tin Man. You put up this armor," I said, "I mean, if it's just about sex, then tell me."

Caesar cupped my face in his hands like a chalice. "This is not just about sex," he said, his eyes fixing me with overwhelming adoration. In his gleaming eyes, I heard the words he didn't say. Caesar loved me. It struck me then, how much I loved him and I was horrified. What would become of a love like this?

"C'mon. Get in here." He took hold of my wrist and pulled me in the shower. I shivered and he moved me in front of him, under the hot water.

"What about what's-her-name?" I asked.

"What about her?" Caesar asked.

"Wouldn't she be hurt by this?"

"She don't care. Just as long as her friends don't gossip about it."

"Is that so. Well, did you ever ask her officially?"

"Not exactly. But, I know." He reached for the soap and lathered it under his armpits. Then he began to rub the soap over my shoulders, spreading it down my sides, my hips, and in between my thighs.

"Well, maybe, I'll call her and ask her how she feels," I said, testing him.

"Go ahead." He started to whistle and I shook my head.

"Do you have…like…a…"

"Conscience?" Caesar asked.

"Yeah. Like what the heck are you doing on this merry-go-round?" I should have directed the question at myself. But I didn't know the answer and Caesar was older than I was. Didn't he have more wisdom about life and love?

"I'm in an impossible situation. It's an impossible situation," he said.

"How ironic. That makes two of us then."

"Do you think people know?" I asked.

"God knows." He started to hum.

"God, who?" I asked.

"The universe, Angelina, the universe can feel it. That's what love does." He said, wrapping his arms around me from behind.

"What are you humming, anyway?" I asked. He turned me to face him and pulled me closer with two hands clasped around my lower back. We rocked from side to side. Caesar sang, *"the touch of your hand is like heaven….a heaven that I've never known….the blush on your cheek…whenever I speak….tells me that you are my own…"* I held him with my arms around his neck. We danced together in the shower, the steam forming like a cloud around us, and I began to sing the lyrics with him. It was John Coltrane's and Johnny Hartman's "My One and Only Love." My hands slid across his slippery body, soaping his thighs and calves. I bent down and washed his feet, running my fingers between his thin toes.

He turned the water off and held a towel open for me.

"How do you know that song?" He asked.

"My mother used to play that Hartman and Coltrane album. When I was small, I remember asking her to play that song over and over. It was a pretty strange request for a six-year-old," I said. "Does that sound strange to you?"

"It's certainly not normal. But, I ain't normal either. You and I…we ain't normal." He pulled on a pair of jeans rolled at the bottom and his torn blue t-shirt. I poked my finger in the hole, before collapsing back on the bed. I was naked, curled in a ball, with the towel sheltering me from the cool air.

"I hate this part," I said.

"What part?"

"The part when you just walk out the door. Because that means tomorrow comes. And, tomorrow I have to go into work and play pretend. And, it doesn't bother you one bit. You don't even care."

"I care. But men are different, I guess. In college, one girl had a boyfriend, but for months she used to come by my room at night to get laid. Then she'd go back to her boyfriend the next day." He laughed loudly and awkwardly. Why was that humorous? How could he have lived his whole life this way? I wanted to shake an emotion into him.

"So you've always just been some screw buddy, but in the end, the women didn't want you as a boyfriend. Don't you ever want a deeper connection? A relationship that reflects a mutual understanding and caring and respect…all the time?"

"Maybe, I don't need that," he said. Caesar's eyes glossed over. He reached for the lamp and clicked off the light.

"I think you're afraid."

"Maybe, I am," Caesar said, lying down on the bed.

"Caesar, can we go out together?" I knew the question was absurd.

"I'd love that. There's nothing more that I'd love. But. I can't. Because. Then, I'd have to lie. And, I don't like to lie."

I began to sob.

He curled up beside me and held me in his arms.

"Why? Why? Why?" I repeated.

"I don't know, Angelina. I don't know. "

"Don't cry. I don't want to cause you pain." He kissed my face all over, starting at my temples and then my cheek. With my knees to my chest, I tucked my head inside his rounded arm. He attempted to wipe my face dry with his palm, but the intensity of my tears increased, washing his hand with my pain. "I love you Angelina Moreau. You're my best friend," he said. I answered back with wheezes. And Caesar held me until I fell asleep.

Chapter Twelve

༄

The phone rang before the chickadees began to chirp. The alarm clock read 5:07 AM.

"Hello?"

"Angelina, I'm so glad you're awake."

"Mom, it's five in the morning. I'm not awake," I said, rubbing my eyes with my fists.

"Listen, your father is coming to see you."

"When?"

"Some time in the next two weeks."

"How did he get my address? Or my number, for that matter? Please tell me that you didn't give it to him."

"He called me. What was I supposed to do?"

"You were supposed to remember that a few years ago, when I testified against him, he told you that he wished I was never born. How do these things just slip your mind?"

"Oh, Angelina. Don't be so hard on him."

"Hard on him! Mom, he beat you for years."

"What's up, Gina-girl?" She sounded tired.

"The sky."

"And, the birds?"

"Yeah, Ma. And the damn birds."

"Don't use that word. It's not polite."

"Sorry."

"Anyway, your father is going to stop by that little restaurant you're working at, Mona Lisa's Solution."

"Seduction. Mona Lisa's Seduction," I said.

"That's an awful strange name for a little restaurant. Why is it named that?"

"Why do you always have to demean me and what I'm doing?" I asked.

"What has gotten into you?"

"It's not a *little* restaurant. I actually make quite a bit of money."

"Well, if you're happy that's the most important thing. Are you happy? You don't sound very happy."

"Are you happy?" I asked.

"Yesterday I was. My tomatoes are finally ripe. And, they aren't even mealy. Can you believe it! I finally grew tomatoes that aren't mealy."

"That's nice."

"I know. I know. It made me so happy. I think it was the new fertilizer," she said. "And I've been talking to them, because they say that is what you're supposed to do. Give them love to make them grow. Actually, it was your father that said that once when we were younger. He had his own garden then. Do you remember?"

"Why is he coming to see me? To offer his theological advice about love? Because, frankly, I can do without the hypocrisy. It's great daddy knew how to love tomatoes. But, really, mom. What about you? Or Neely?"

"Please. Be nice to him. He is still your father. He's coming because he loves you."

"Mom, the man hasn't spoken to me in years!"

"These things happen. He's gotten a lot of help in those years."

"Alright. For your sake, I'll be pleasant. But, that's the most I

can offer right now. I have my own problems now."
"Problems? What happened?"
"Nothing happened."
"Something must have happened. You don't sound well."
"I'm fine."
"Are you in some kind of trouble?"
"No, Mom. It's okay. I think I'm going to get going. I'll call you tomorrow."
"I spoke with John you know. He still really loves you, Gina. And, he's such a nice boy."
"Ma..."
"I'm just saying...maybe, you should—"
"—how's Neely?" I asked.
"She's here, getting ready for work. Hold on," she said, shouting, "Neely! Pick up the phone. It's your sister!"
"Okay, Mom! I got it!" Neely yelled, hearing her smoky voice, I smiled.
"Hi, Neely. How are you? I'm sorry it's been so long," I said.
"Hey, darlin.' I'm doing great. You're picking up some of the wild child slack for me. I appreciate it. Mom actual treats me like I'm normal now," she said, "Hey, Mom. Is it a criminal offense to listen in on a private conversation? I can hear your bracelets jingling." A receiver clicked.
"But as you can see, some things don't change," Neely said. I heard her light a cigarette and open a window.
"Has she figured out that you smoke?"
"If she did, she hasn't said anything. Although she asked me why I smell like Fabreeze all the time," Neely said and I laughed. "I'm moving to New York in a couple of weeks. Charlie got a job there and he asked me to come with him. I ended up landing a job as a legal assistant at a law firm. Can you believe that? I'm going to

have to wear button down shirts. I'm not sure how long that's going to last." Neely inhaled her cigarette. "What about you? Do you like it up there?"

"You'd love Provincetown, Neely. You should come to visit before you move."

"Dad's coming to visit you. You know?"

"Yeah. What's he like now?"

"He's like this walking infomercial for AA and he talks about Jesus a lot. But from what I can tell, he's really pulled it together," Neely said, adding, "People change."

I looked at the photograph on my nightstand, saying, "Neely, will you come here? Before Dad comes?"

"Of course. Today's my last day at work anyway. How about next weekend?"

"That's great. Thanks, Neely."

"No problem. Listen, I have to run. I'll put Mom back on." I waited for my mother to pick up the phone.

"Anyway, I think you should call John…"

"Ma, why do you think you always know what's best for me?"

"Because, I'm your mother. That's why."

"I wish you could have been that definitive when we were younger," I said, wishing immediately that I hadn't.

"I was definitive, Angelina. As definitive and as strong as I could have been then. But I wish I could have been stronger for you and Neely. Without your father, though, I would never have had you or Neely. Anyway, don't sleep too late. And be nice to your father," she said.

She still loved him, despite of the pain he had caused her. Even after he filed for a separation, and I heard from my friend, Molly, that he dated some woman he met in AA. He still checked in with my mother and she let him. I was sad for her then, all that

pain tangling up in love.
Was I reliving her mistake?
"I love you, Gina-girl."
"I love you too, Mom."

❧

Unable to go back to sleep, I got out of bed and stood by the sliding glass window. A sliver of golden light winked from the horizon and the chickadees chirped in chorus on the ledge of the patio. I put on jean cutoff shorts, a white tank-top, slipped on a pair of flip-flops, and grabbed my car keys. I decided to go for a drive.

Even with the windows rolled down, the air was sultry and stale. Around the bend of the west end of Commercial Street was an exquisite surprise. The breakwater—a long walkway made of boulders jutted out from the land, cutting into the calm blue sea and leading all the way to the lonely white lighthouse on a sand dune at the tip of Provincetown. I parked my car close to the curb and decided to take the rocky path across the water.

The white moon glowed like a thin layer of cellophane, not yet ready to say goodnight, even though the sun continued to push its way through the horizon. I began my trek, taking tiny hops like a ballerina from one rock to the other, leaping over the large cracks in between. The water swished against the breakwater from both sides, leaving a layer of whipped white foam at the base of the boulders. My eyes were fixed on the lighthouse, I was halfway there, but my destination seemed elusive.

The sun finally made its presence fully known, its orange edges vibrating like a mirage; the sky brightened into a pale baby blue and ascended into a spectrum of cobalt, sapphire, navy, and dark purple. My skin was damp along the back of my neck where beads of sweat ran down from my hairline. As land approached, I slipped my flip-flops off my feet; my toes squished into the dark chocolate sand, wet from the receding tide. I turned back to see how far I had come—nearly a half a mile.

I strolled along the sea's edge, the frigid water softly lapping against my ankles. A long dune covered in thin stalks of tall sea grass ran parallel with the shoreline. I picked up my pace until I broke into a quick jog, water splashing up to my kneecaps. Tiny crabs scrambled into holes and I hopped over large clumps of electric green seaweed that floated between the sea and the shore, moving with the push and pull of the tide. Finally, when I reached the lighthouse on the top of a dune, I collapsed on the dry sand. I swung my outstretched arms and legs back and forth, creating a sand angel; a light rain began to drizzle from the sky and I closed my eyes, relieved by the cool water against my hot skin.

I wanted to hide away on Long Point forever—or at least until my father had passed through. The day I took the stand at his trial, he looked helpless with his shoulders drooping and his fingers fidgeting in his lap, as if he were a twelve-year-old boy called into the principal's office. Many of his friends and people in the community occupied the benches in the courtroom, if not to show support, out of curiosity about my father's trial. After all, he was a good citizen, an extremely successful real estate investor, a family man. It was a battle between two boxers in a ring. In one corner, there was Mister Moreau, a generous community minded and wealthy man with the colorful and charismatic mask, and in the other, there was Daddy.

"I call Angelina Moreau to the stand." After years of intimidation, it is my turn to speak. When I place my right hand on the Bible, my father's eyes glisten with tears and he mouths, "I love you."

Neely tried to convince me that I shouldn't tell the truth. I expected this lecture from my mother, but not Neely. All her decisions had been based upon how far she could push my parents-from running away to the tattoo with her boyfriend's nickname "Ice," across her lower back. Once she learned that I planned to testify against my father, suddenly Neely began pleading with me, "You can't do that to Daddy. You can't send him away."

"So, what am I supposed to do. Just lie?" I asked.

"No. Just say, you don't remember what happened."

But, I did remember.

When the prosecutor asks me to explain the accident, when my drunken father just missed an oncoming SUV, driving through rose bushes, nailing a mailbox, and speeding away, I tell him all of it. I even tell him that when we returned home, I called the police to file a report while he passed out on the couch with a bloody nose.

"He flew off and hit her," I slip out in court. Whispers break out among the crowd and the Judge slams down her gavel to bring order to the court.

I look at Neely and my mother. They sit behind him in the front row, holding hands; my mother's long hair is pulled neatly into a bun. Neely's head is on my mother's shoulder, her lower lip quivers and I begin to cry. They both cry along with me and suddenly I don't feel as alone up there on the stand. I feel my father's piercing look of disgust.

When I step down from the stand, I walk past him and ask, "Why?" It is all I could get out, but an answer never comes.

Later that evening, Neely came in my bedroom to tell me the verdict. He was sentenced to an alcohol rehabilitation program and a hundred hours of community service. I left for Harvard and he returned to my mother after rehabilitation, only to insist on a legal separation two years later. My mother refused to offer him a divorce. We never discussed the matter any further and I stayed away from my home in Westport as much as possible, spending my summers off from college working in Boston.

My father was dead to me beginning that day of the trial, except for some reason, he was going to resurface in Provincetown.

On Long Point, the rain poured down and I ran to take shelter inside the lighthouse. I yanked the white painted steel door open with both hands. Inside a black spiral staircase led up to the top and I began climbing to a tiny platform. Crouched in the small space, my breath steamed up the windowpanes and I wiped away the fog with the front of my tank top. A seagull glided toward me, gracefully landing on the black rim that circled the outside of the lighthouse. I knocked lightly against the glass to send him away, but he turned toward me with peaceful ebony eyes and a carrot-colored beak curved slightly upward, an unassuming grin.

The rain dwindled and the sun's rays reflected a vibrant rainbow that arced over the mainland. I could see Mona Lisa's Seduction, shrunk to the size of a quarter, sitting insignificantly among fifty other miniature buildings. From the other side of the sea, Provincetown was nothing but a funnel turned upside down, the base of the triangle broad and expansive with the tip pointing toward itself. The image generated a similar view of how it felt inside the rainbow's arc, where the focal point of Mona Lisa's Seduction and the small town itself, magnified the intensity of every personal dynamic.

The distance offered me perspective like a director of a film, I could see the grander vision, but the distance was only a fleeting respite from the confusion, because my heart was not detached from the actors inside Mona Lisa's Seduction. After all, propinquity instigated combat. And, once you have been close to someone, years of distance could not diminish the potential for another battle. Along with the history of intimacy between two people came the residue leftover, residue that under certain conditions could ignite another explosion, one of passion or destruction. All wars were kindled by two contradictory impulses, to unite and divide- provoking only an unfeasible resolution.

The seagull flew off the lighthouse, alone, toward the open sea.

Chapter Thirteen

That day at work, I found myself hardening the muscles in my face, approaching customers without enthusiasm. Cara noticed that something was wrong. I kept messing up on orders: forgetting to fire a burger into the computer system, ordering a steamed lobster instead of a lobster salad sandwich, adding cheddar cheese to a chicken sandwich when the woman specifically told me she was allergic to dairy products. I rang in a round of margaritas with salt for a party of twelve, but the men wanted a round of martinis straight up with a twist of lemon. Cara asked me if I wanted her to pick up an extra table from my station. The "old me" would have vehemently refused but the "old me" was missing. I allowed Cara to help out and I thanked her profusely throughout the day.

Dark clouds rolled in from the bay, creating an unusual vacancy along Commercial Street. This only made matters worse as the time slowed to an excruciating pace. I yearned to see Caesar. I wanted to feel my arms around him. To pass the time, I snuck away to the corner booth inside the restaurant, pulling a pen from my apron pocket and a slip of blank paper from underneath the hoststand. I sketched a woman on Commercial Street, gripping an unopened umbrella, walking under a torrential rain shower. I escaped into this world, inside the space between my hand and the ink.

I heard my name and looked up. Cara stood at the bar with Lisa and Dylan; she smiled in my direction and went back to her conversation. Lisa shouted, "Oh, my God!" With my pen to the paper, I strained to hear their discussion.

Dylan moved toward me and slid into the booth.

"What are doing?" he asked.

"Nothing really. Just drawing."

"Can I see?"

"Sure," I turned the page over and waited for his reaction.

"Whoah. How long have you been an artist?"

"I'm not really. It's something I used to do."

"Well, I think it's something you need to do. That's amazing," he said.

"What were you talking about over there?"

"You really want to know?" Dylan asked and I nodded.

"Well, Cara called you Mrs. Riva. She seems to think you're involved with Caesar." Dylan said, watching me for a flicker of a reaction.

"Oh," I said, calmly.

"'Oh?' It's true? Or, 'oh,' it's not true?"

"Oh, if only my life were as exciting as everyone makes it out to be," I repeated a line that Dylan had once used with me regarding Ava.

"I was thinking that we should hang out sometime. Like in the daylight and without drinking tequila," Dylan said.

"That would be nice. We might even break a Provincetown record," I said, and Dylan laughed, scooting out of the booth.

"Well, I better get back to work," he said, leaving me alone with my drawing. I completed another two sketches before the end of my shift. Although, I had been sitting for most of the workday, an incredible fatigue set in. I was exhausted. Finally, the clock struck quarter of five, time to leave.

On my last table of the afternoon, I dropped a porcelain bowl of steamer clams onto the lap of a man in black dress pants and a button up Polo shirt. Apologizing profusely, I leaned over him with napkins trying to soak up the raunchy scent of clam juice. He stood up, shaking his head, and yelling profanities. I told him I would pay for the meal and brought he and his wife another bottle of eighty dollar Chardonnay and a mango crème brule for dessert. Cara said, "You're totally wacko to do that. He was such an asshole. Everyone makes mistakes." But, the whole afternoon felt like a mistake and I wanted to do something right.

Caesar never showed up at work. At the end of my shift, I called him from the restaurant phone. I needed to hear his voice, instead, I settled on his answering machine. I even dialed his number again just to hear his voice saying, "Hello, I'm not available right now." I hung up without leaving a message. Why hadn't Caesar shown up for work? It was a Thursday. Caesar always worked on Thursday nights.

As I headed up Commercial Street, I felt a hand on my shoulder. It was Dylan. His gesture was his way of saying, "Sorry you are having such a rotten day." "Hey, I forgot to ask you. Do you have my blue windbreaker?"

"Yeah, I think I saw it in the apartment," I said, remembering then how he had told me at the Pixie that he had been involved in something. "I found something interesting that morning."

"Really. What's that?" Dylan seemed nervous, biting the corner of his thumbnail.

"A rose," I said.

"With thorns or without?"

"With."

"Wow. That's nuts." Dylan said.

Cara peeked out of the restaurant's front door and shouted,

"Tony just dumped a bowl of alfredo sauce over Chris's head and now Chris is chasing him with a fork!"

"Well, I have to go play peace ambassador," he said, pushing his sleeves up to his elbows.

A brisk breeze cut the air and I pulled my hooded sweatshirt from my bag. I had been wearing it quite a bit, lately, more often than I ever had when I attended Harvard. Suddenly, it seemed, I was trying to remember where I came from.

※

My clogs crunched against the broken shells on the driveway. To my surprise, the front door was unlocked. Maybe Cara had forgotten to lock it in the morning. Before I reached the last step of the wooden staircase that led to our apartment I saw the light glowing through the crack of the open door. Someone had broken in.

I stepped out of my clogs and carefully placed them outside the door. I dropped my bag and softly pushed the door open with my fingertips. The Great Danes scrambled from the back hallway with their toenails scraping against the hard floor, jumped up to my shoulders and barked vigorously. They returned to the closed door of my bedroom, leading me to the intruder.

I took a hold of a fake crystal lamp, yanking the cord from the electrical socket, and inching toward the door. I allowed the dogs to bark for another minute or so, granting the intruder plenty of time to get away. Perhaps the intruder would rush out through my sliding glass door onto the deck and leave by the back entrance.

Where did my courage come from? I could have escaped out the front door, I could have called the police. With the lamp raised over my head, I stepped into the room. The dogs charged to the closet door. Besides their vicious barking, I heard shuffling inside the closet.

The doors pulled open from the inside. I screamed.

"Caesar!"

"Surprise!" he said. "I'm sorry, Sugar. I didn't mean to scare you." We collapsed onto the bed, laughing. The Great Danes licked his shiny black dress shoes.

"What are you doing here? And, for heaven's sake. What the heck were you doing in the closet? You scared me half to death."

"So, you were surprised."

"Yeah. I was a little surprised." I looked at the closet. "Caesar, I have to show you something," I said, leading him there. I pushed the clothes over and swung the small door open. "What do you know about this?" I untied a plastic garbage bag.

"Whoah. Honey. This ain't good," Caesar said, eyeing the cocaine and all the bags.

"Yeah. I know. What do I do about it?"

"Forget about it," he said.

"Caesar, it's in my bedroom. How do I forget about it? Shouldn't I ask Cara? What if the police bust her? Maybe, we can talk her out of whatever it is that she's involved with."

"Honey, the thing about people is they do what they want to do. The universe takes care of the rest. You can't change it," he said.

"We could try."

"Yeah, we could, but she'd lie. She'd say it has nothing to do with her. Then we'd have an intervention. Drag her to AA. She'd say she doesn't need to be there. Maybe, she'd go along with it. But, she'd find ways to sneak around. We'd go crazy trying to help her," he said. "Let's get out of here. This is creepy." I tied the plastic bag and we left.

"So, I really just forget it? Deny what I've found?"

"You can't fix people, Angelina."

"Hey, what are you doing here anyway? Hanging out in my closet for fun?"

"I'm taking you out."

"What?"

"I'm asking you on a date. I mean if you want…"

I linked my finger with his. "I couldn't think of anything else that I could possibly want," I said, kissing him.

"Good. Get ready then. We don't have much time." Caesar reached under the pillow on the bed and pulled out a rose, tickling my neck with the petals.

"It was you that cleaned the cuts on my feet that night? And you who left me the rose under my pillow? But, that was before anything…" Caesar pulled out his chapstick from his black pants pocket, and ran one stroke over each lip.

"But, why?" I asked.

"Why not?"

"Caesar, what happened that night?"

"Nothing happened between us. If that's what you mean."

"We left the Pixie together, after we danced?"

"No. I found you sitting on a chair on the patio at the restaurant."

"Why did I go there? That means I walked past my apartment."

"I don't like to ask too many questions. You said you couldn't leave until you found the Summer Triangle. Then, you asked me if I was your swan," he said.

I felt my cheeks flush with embarrassment.

"I told you, looks like it," he said, checking his watch. "You better get ready. We'll talk more on the way up."

"Where are we going?" I asked.

"I ain't going to ruin the whole surprise."

We were finally going out together. But he was married. We had no business going out on a date. But, one night wouldn't hurt, right? What had made him change his mind? I sniffed the rose.

"You fascinate me, Mister Riva."

"I'm not that fascinating really. I'm just a restaurant owner," he said, shrugging his shoulders.

❦

An hour later, we were on the road, burning up Route 6 in the passing lane with Provincetown basking in the sun behind us. The water from Cape Cod Bay waved and the wind whipped through my wild hair, rippling my shin length white cotton skirt. John Coltrane's saxophone wailed into the summertime air. Caesar tightly clenched the stick shift, but when I rested my hand on top of his, his grip relaxed.

"Hey," he said.

"Hey, what?"

"Where have you been all my life anyway?" he asked. I lifted his hand to kiss it, gently placing it back on the stick shift, and pulled my own hands into the safety of my lap but Caesar reached over and put my hand on top of his, focusing on the highway ahead.

Two gray hairs peeked through the opening of his shirt, at the base of his throat, and I didn't like it. Caesar had lived almost three decades longer than I had. Why hadn't we met under simple circumstances?

"Will you do me a favor?" I asked.

"Anything for you," he said.

"After you die, will you wait a couple of years before you come back down here? You know, just hang out in heaven for awhile. Wait for me. I'll find you on a cloud with your sexy chain hanging down your thigh next to a harem of angels. I'll tap you on the shoulder. And, we'll come back down together. As a team," I said and Caesar shook his head, smiling.

"What?" I asked.

"Nothing," he said.

"C'mon. Tell me what you're thinking."

"It's just, in the story of my life, Angelina, you're the curve ball."

We drove the rest of the ride in comfortable silence, without the awkward tension I had experienced with all the men in my past. The yellow sun shined brightly, reflecting against the windshield and blinding my view of the horizon. Caesar flipped down the visor.

"We're almost there," he said. Without signaling, Caesar coasted off the double lane highway, taking a right at the exit. We drove along a back road to Sandwich, passing a green Cape with a large front porch converted into a general store; an American flag waved from the rooftop. A cluster of elderly couples sipped coffee in ceramic mugs on wooden benches; a woman in her mid-thirties pushed an empty stroller as her husband carried their newborn baby swaddled in a pale pink blanket.

We continued driving down the two lane road, past a few family-style restaurants and old homes with vast yards filled with large oak trees. Gray squirrels leapt from branch to branch, and a Siamese cat rolled on its back in the grass in front of a field of yellow daffodils. Considering New England's industrious past, Cape Cod was suspiciously pure. The "Burger Kings," "Dunkin Donuts," "McDonalds," and "Starbucks" existed, somewhere, but you had to search for them. Capital enterprises did not blatantly scar the landscape.

We turned onto a dusty dirt road, large enough for one vehicle at a time; a mosaic sign "Venezia's" marked a street that otherwise would have been easily missed. Caesar steered the car speedily along, dodging potholes in the bumpy road that bounced me up off the leather seat.

We came to the end. A couple of cars were parked in a pebble lot. A little less than a quarter mile across, a kettle pond spread out before us, Caesar opened the car door and I followed him to the small wooden dock with seven canoes roped around poles cemented in shallow water. A man wearing a Red Sox's visor, placed his book on the dock, and stood up from his beach chair to greet us.

"Going to Venezia's?" The man yelled, pulling up his visor and wiping the sweat from his forehead.

"Yeah, man. How's the ride over there?" Caesar asked, nodding to a tiny blue cottage across the pond. I cupped my hand around my eyes and squinted—another wooden dock jutted out into the dark water on the other side. Two people in a canoe rowed toward us.

"On a day like this. Not bad at all. Takes about ten minutes. But, weather says it's gonna' rain later. So, I'm not supposed to let any more customers go over."

Caesar turned to me, "Sugar, you don't melt in the rain. Do ya?"

I shook my head, "But with me, you never know what you could be getting yourself into."

"You ain't kidding," Caesar said, brushing a strand of hair from of my eye.

He reached into his pocket and pulled out a silver money clip filled with one hundred dollar bills. He surfed through the stack of money, handing the man a twenty. The man held out two life preservers while Caesar stepped into the canoe. I took the orange jackets, tossing them into the boat, and waited for Caesar's hand. He offered it to me and I cautiously stepped into the shaky canoe, using his shoulder to balance. We sat down on the wooden seats with our backs facing our destination. The man untied the rope from the dock and Caesar, taking a hold of the oars, started to row.

"Hey! You better put on those jackets!" The man shouted.

I turned to look at Caesar. The blue vein at his temple pulsed as he pushed against the weight of the water. Before I had a chance to speak, Caesar had read my mind.

"I don't need no life jacket," he said.

"But, Caesar…" I looped my arms through the open holes and clicked the latches of the vest, covering my white halter-top.

"Look, we're almost there," he said, pointing to the dock.

"No we aren't. We're not even halfway. What if you have a heart attack or something. Then what?" I asked.

"I trust you'll save me," he said.

I swung around to face him. Leaning against the side of the canoe, I dipped my fingers into the cool water, trailing ripples along the surface.

"Be careful," he said.

"Of what?"

"Pond sharks."

"Pond sharks?"

"Yeah. They can smell a sexy female from miles away. Once they get a hold of your fingers, they can pull you right overboard," he said.

"The only shark I'm worried about is you." It was a joke and Caesar chuckled, but I couldn't help wonder about Caesar's history with women.

"You've done this before," I said. He thrust his arms forward, pulling back in a long stroke.

"No. But, I've always wanted to check out this restaurant. Just never had a reason to go. Until you, darling."

"No. I mean, an affair. Affairs. Plural."

Caesar looked over my head toward the shoreline. "No. It's not."

"How many?"

"Three."

"Including me?"

"Including you."

"Well…" he said, looking at me, "There were a few one night stands too…when I travel."

"Uh-huh," I said, feeling nauseous at his confession and knowing I couldn't love him for what he was not. "And Carol? Does she know?" I fiddled with the bottom latch on my vest.

"She knew about Laura."

Upon hearing her name, I unlocked the latch. Laura. The mistress before me. That was worse than hearing his wife's name. Laura meant that I was just Angelina, someone who floated through his life like an autumn leaf. The seasons would turn. The leave would fall and decay, and a new one would fill my place.

"How long? With Laura?"

"Five years."

My jaw dropped. Five years. That was a lot of years to be there for a man that could never fully be there for you. "Why did it end?" I asked.

"She…she…died from an aneurysm." He spit out the words like a watermelon seed. Caesar's eyes glistened with tears. "I rather not talk about it," he said. A gust of wind blew against my shoulders and I hugged my arms around my shivering body.

"Do you want my jacket?" Caesar stopped rowing, removed his black jacket and draped it over my shoulders. He picked up the oars and continued rowing with greater intensity, as if taking his grief out on the pond.

"Can I just ask one more thing?" I burned with curiosity to know him better, to understand him without judgment.

"Well, you're going to ask it anyway. Right?"

"Yeah. I am."

"Go ahead. You always speak what's on your mind. Don't you?"

"I guess. Since I met you, anyway," I said. "Why are you married then? I mean, why isn't Carol sitting in this boat with you?"

"She don't want to be here. I care for her. Like a sister. Maybe that's the way I always cared for her. We met in college. And we were friends. She got pregnant. I married her. I thought it was the right thing to do. At the time. But time changes things."

"You have an older child right?"

"Yeah. She would have been twenty-seven this year," he said.

"What do you mean? Would have been?"

"Isabella died in a car accident. High school." He barely got the words out. A large black crow cawed as its wings furiously flapped overhead, a reply came from somewhere inside the branches of a tall pine tree on the other side of the pond. Across the gray sky, thick charcoal clouds moved in and swallowed the sun.

"I think about it once in awhile. My marriage, I mean. I fantasize a lot about a life with you. You are smart and sexy and we enjoy the same things. And I can talk to you. And, I think, what the hell is my problem? But, I have this responsibility. This responsibility. I don't want to break up the marriage until my children are grown up. My kids need me. I'm like the stable force. I got to finish what I started. My parent's divorced but I was already twenty-five at the time. I don't know. I don't know. It's just where I came from. How I came programmed. You know?" Caesar said. And, I did know.

"But, why do something that will hurt?" I asked.

"We aren't hurting anybody, Angelina. Life was meant to be lived."

My toes curled inside my tan sandals. Looking down, I saw water was spurting through a small crack underneath the seat. "Caesar! There's a leak," I shouted, searching for a bucket. The water began creeping up my ankles.

"Well, ain't that perfect."

"What's that?" I tossed a half a bucket of water from the canoe. I bent over, refilling the bucket, keeping my eye on the shore. We were close. No need to worry.

"You know what you do when there's a leak in the canoe?" He said, keeping a steady rhythm to his rowing. "You keep going forward. Or else you sink."

I didn't argue or explain that there were other options. He could work to patch up the canoe. Or he could abandon the boat and swim to shore. He could row a boat that wasn't broken.

The canoe bumped against the wooden dock. We had made it across the kettle pond to a small blue cottage, bordered by a mosaic of flowers made from sea glass. A woman in a long skirt waited with menus tightly held against her chest, and an elderly man with a white mustache caught the rope Caesar threw from the canoe.

"This day must be a very lucky for you. We will close the restaurant early tonight. A cause of the storm coming." The man spoke with a European accent as he wound the rope in a figure eight around a wood piling.

"She brings good luck," Caesar said to the man as he stepped out of the canoe. Holding me by my wrists and pulling me out. The man smiled.

"*Sì, una bella donna. Che fortuna, Señor.*" He said, and having studied Italian, I was flattered by his compliment.

"*Grazie, Señor. Da dove viene?*" I asked him where he was from.

"*Un paese vincino Firenze. Sei italiana?*"

"*Cinquanta per cento,*" I said and the man turned to Caesar.

"You. Are a very lucky *Señor.* Truly. An Italian woman always has passion in her veins. But, be careful. *Stai attenta.* Once you have felt her love, you never can go back to another. Very dangerous." I laughed. We thanked the man and Caesar tipped him a twenty.

The woman holding the leather-bound menus led us through a small dirt path and up a hill toward the restaurant. I walked in front of Caesar. When we approached a garden of scarlet roses, white butterflies rose up from the red petals and then fluttered toward the gray sky. I stopped to look up and watch them fly away. Caesar encircled me in his arms, his chest pressed against my back, his lips lightly brushing my neck.

The woman held the oak door open for us and when we entered Venezia's, we were transported into a tavern with dark green ivy hanging from aqua ceramic shelves that were bolted against brick walls. The room was faintly lit by oil lanterns and perfumed with sautéed garlic and roasted espresso beans that steamed from a cappuccino machine. She led us to a hand carved wooden table, to the right of a platform on which a man played a grand piano, and another musician strummed the strings of a mandolin.

Caesar ordered a bottle of vintage Bordeaux. That was just like him, I thought, to request a French wine in an Italian restaurant. We sipped on the expensive wine, the bouquet of plums and spices moving down the back of the throat like an emotion. Starting with paper thin proscuitto and sweet melon—and garden tomatoes with fresh basil and mozzarella cheese drizzled in aged balsamic vinegar, we both occasionally let out a "Hmmm" or "Wow" in between bites. I chewed homemade pumpkin ravioli while Caesar turned his fork around tagliatelle drenched in a creamy mascarpone sauce with a hint of nutmeg.

"How is it?" I asked.

"Delicious. But it doesn't taste as delicious as you," he said, with a devilish grin.

I slid my foot across his ankle and Caesar began stroking my wrist. At a table to our left two middle-aged women looked at us with sharp darting glances and spoke loud enough for us to hear. "Same old story," one woman said, "a man with a mid-life crisis and a girl with a daddy complex."

I released Caesar's grip on my hand. After all, I was a psychology major at Harvard. I had studied Freudian theories. That's what people thought when they saw us together? A cliché?

"Is that what we are?" I asked.

"What?"

"What those women just said."

Caesar looked over at the two women, sitting parallel to our table. The woman with the short frosted hair and a jade necklace said with surprise, "Hello Caesar. I didn't recognize you. You look great." She eyed me, saying, "What's your secret?"

"Hey, Kathy," Caesar said.

"Enjoying dinner?" she asked.

"It is delicious, thank you."

"Well, take care."

"You too."

The woman leaned toward her dinner companion and continued talking in a soft voice. Caesar reached for the Bordeaux and filled up my glass before emptying the bottle into his.

"Who was that?" I asked, attempting to mask my jealousy.

"Who?" Caesar asked.

"The woman you were just speaking to."

"Oh. That's Carol's sister."

"Your wife's sister? That doesn't bother you?" I whispered.

"Why would it? It's no one's business, Angelina." Caesar said, not dropping the volume of his voice and turning his attention to the mandolin player. "I love this song. 'Tea for two'," he said.

"Is it true for you? What she said?"

"What did she say?"

"That you're in the midst of a mid-life crisis and I have a daddy complex?"

"Well, Sugar, I already had my mid-life crisis four years ago. I bought a Harley and a leather jacket. Got it all out of my system. But you certainly are the youngest woman I've ever been involved with. It's not an age thing. But I ain't gonna lie, it doesn't hurt."

"Well, you're the oldest. And I hate it."

"Hate what?" Caesar asked, nervously.

"I don't want to end up a statistic. I want to be with you, Caesar."

"You are with me," he said, reaching across the table.

"No. I mean. Fully. Be with you."

He was silent. The mandolin strings plucked away, gracefully, like the flapping of little wings. I waited. His eyes widened and he looked at me with his head tilted to one side.

"Would you really want that? To be with me? Maybe, I'm too old for you." He said, vulnerably. What did I really want? To share a life with Caesar? He established a life in Provincetown. He could never change that. How much time would we have together? And how long would it take before he cheated on me? But now that I had met Caesar, I could never imagine my life without him in it. We had too much to learn together.

"I'm certain. Almost," I said.

"Almost certain?"

"What in life is a one hundred percent guarantee?" I asked.

"Angelina. We're not practical."

"Love isn't practical. It's not a business negotiation."

"Responsibilities. I have responsibilities."

"I'm not asking you to abandon them."

"Look at you. I must be crazy. Why can't I…why can't I just?"

"You must not really feel love for me," I said. If he truly saw me, the way I saw him, he wouldn't let me go.

"That's not true! I just don't know. I don't know."

"Maybe you're afraid to change your circumstances. But circumstances change. You're afraid, Caesar Riva."

"You're right."

"Well, what about truth?! What about all our endless conversations about politicians? Those that manipulate and sneak around the truth? How are we any different? All our talking and talking about contradictions in government and religion. But what about us? We're a hypocrisy," I said, "You speak the rhetoric of these concepts and you can even cry about people dying in countries miles away. But, why do you avoid dealing with what's close to you?"

"I'm not that deep," he said.

"Don't you tell me that. Don't you dare say that. We are all the same. We are like onions. And only by feeling can we slowly peel back to the raw truth. It stings, sometimes. And it's not convenient. But, without the will to change…to grow…to act…then what was it all for?" I stood up, pressing my palms against the table and my wooden chair pushed back.

"We're on different wavelengths, I guess." Caesar's arms were crossed tightly against his chest. I stared him down, furious with his dismissive attitude. Caesar was limited, and, I was causing a "scene," perhaps to fully unleash that which he never would.

"That's such an easy out for you, Caesar. 'We're on different wavelengths.' Then, tell me about yourself. Get real. Tell me what wavelength you're on. I want to know. Can't you see that? I'm here. Wanting to know you."

"I make sure that I don't get out of control in love," Caesar stated, flatly.

"That's your wavelength?"

"That's my wavelength."

"Then, you're right. You need a woman that will keep it in control for you, Caesar. And that woman is not me, quite frankly. You already have her. Your wife. Someone on your wavelength. That's why you have your one night stands and your affairs…just another way to maintain control. You're a closeted fascist." I turned from the table. There was nothing left to say. My sandals clicked across the floor as the musician fiercely plucked the strings of the mandolin. After only a few steps, I felt his cold hand on my elbow; he turned me around to face him, and holding my face in his hands, kissed me. When I opened my eyes, Carol's sister was glaring at us. He kissed me again, his arms around my waist, and pecked the side of my neck, whispering into my ear, "There. Do you get it, yet, Angelina?"

૭

On the way home, driving down Route 6A, Caesar and I didn't speak—there was a layer of cellophane between us. We passed a blue Bentley with black tinted windows. I thought about the accident, the venom in my father's eyes. My evening with Caesar had diverted me from thinking about the impending reunion with my father. I needed more time. I needed a script and I needed to stick to it. I searched inside my purse for my cell phone. Unable to find it, I asked Caesar to borrow his. I wanted to call Cara to check in, to see if my father had phoned.

"Hey, Cara. It's Gina."

"What's up? I've been trying to call your cell. Like a trillion times. Where are you?"

"I'm taking a walk. What are you doing? Going out tonight?" I asked.

"No. I'm staying in."

"You're staying in?"

"Yeah. Can you believe it? When are you coming home?"

"I'll be there in a bit."

"Come home soon. Okay? It's too quiet around here."

"Did I get any messages?"

"Nope."

I sighed, with relief. Maybe, my father changed his mind. We ended the conversation and I looked at Caesar. "That was Cara. She's home," I said.

"Well that's good. I've been thinking about that room and I'm worried about her. If she's not careful, she'll end up like her mother."

"What do you mean?" I asked.

"Her mom was a coke addict."

"Cara didn't mention that."

"Well. It was all so long ago. Man, I can't even recognize myself from those days. It was a different life."

"What do you mean?"

"I was a coke addict too," he said.

The phone dropped from my hands to the floor.

"When Cara's mom took off, something broke in Cara. She never did fix it. But she's got time. She's still young."

"What about you? Did you ever fix what was broken?" I asked.

"I'm sober. Been sober for eighteen years," he said.

"Yeah. But, I mean, did you ever figure out why you chose that for yourself?"

"I didn't need it. It was just available. I think that humans are hardwired for addiction. I had to addict myself to positive things."

"Like chapstick?"

"Yeah," Caesar smiled. "And, you. I'm addicted to you."

Drawing my hand into his, Caesar interlocked his fingers with mine.

"Your hands are hot," I said.

"Yeah, Sugar. And, yours are ice cold. You know what they say about that?"

"What do they say about that, Caesar?"

"Cold hands, warm heart. Hot hands…"

"Cold heart," I said. Small droplets of rain began sprinkling the windshield, but Caesar let them pile up before turning on the wipers.

"So, where are we going to go?" I asked.

"Maybe I should take you home."

"Maybe you're right."

As we approached the line between Wellfleet and Truro, I felt my stomach twist.

"Carol and the kids are away," Caesar said.

"Really?"

"We could go to my house. But it's probably not a good idea."

"Yeah. It's probably not," I said. The wipers scraped against the windshield.

"Or, we could," he said.

"Yeah, we could."

"Do you want to?"

"What do you think?"

Caesar answered me by pulling a u-turn on the highway and drove back toward Wellfleet. "I don't want to make us crazy, Angelina," Caesar said. I didn't say that it was too late for that or that Einstein once said, "Insanity is doing the same thing over and over again and expecting different results." Albert Einstein was a very smart man.

Mona Lisa's Seduction

❧

The car climbed a steep hill, turned onto a dirt road, climbing even higher, digging deeper into overgrown brush and pine on either side of the narrow path. Clouds moved steadily across the white half-moon, allowing slivers of light to sporadically peek through.

We stopped in front of a closed gate. Caesar reached in the fold of the sun visor above my head and pressed the button of a garage door opener. The black steel gate opened, automatically swinging back and locking behind us. Street lamps lined up on either side of the pebble driveway, and two gardens—rows of vegetation and wild flowers stretched fifty-yards to the east and west. We entered a five-car garage, inside which were two motorcycles, a Harley, a 1940's mint green Vespa, a large Chevy pickup truck with a bumper sticker that read 'DemocracyNow.org,' and a SUV. Beach toys, plastic shovels, buckets, and a bicycle with training wheels were piled around the van. I walked quickly out of the garage.

Reaching for my hand, Caesar said, "This way." I followed him down a small wooden staircase, the lilac bushes perfuming the air with their sweet scent. An owl hooted in a tree nearby and a mosquito hummed loudly near my ear. I shouldn't have come here, I thought, but I immediately squashed it, because this was where I wanted to be, brushing the mosquito from my earlobe.

The two-story house was lit by black lampposts that encircled it and looked more like an Italian villa than a traditional Cape Cod home. The salmon stucco structure was covered by tall, narrow windows that arched on the tops, and large columns held a second-floor balcony in place across the full width of house. A square cupola rose from the flat ceramic tile roof.

"Wow. You live inside a dream, don't you? It's like a postcard."

I said as fireflies blinked on the top of the wet grass. When their light disappeared, another group answered back in two quick flashes.

"I guess. All depends on where you're standing," Caesar said. The rain began to pour down in thick nickel size drops and Caesar ran toward the house, taking shelter under the portico over the front doorway, but I stood out under the cold, wet shower. My white cotton skirt and top soaked in the water and clung to my body. Thunder rumbled in the distance. I moved my hips to the music. I raised my arms above my head, and like a Spanish Flamenco dance, snapped my fingers.

"You're crazier than I thought," Caesar yelled, shaking his head.

"Well, I have to be," I shouted out, my arms swaying like the tree branches.

"Why is that?"

"I love you. Don't I?" I said and Caesar laughed. The thunder began to growl angrily, lightening burst a flash of light into the sky and I ran, taking shelter under the portico.

Inside, I slipped out of my sandals, leaving them on the tile floor, next to a straw doormat. We walked through a narrow hallway, leading to the living room. He pressed a knob, turning on a ceiling light. A crystal chandelier cast rainbow triangles on more than fifty paintings, which hung salon-style along the white walls. A watercolor of Provincetown's harbor sat beside a charcoal sketch of a nude woman sprawled on a chaise lounge; an oil painting of yellow daisies in a gold fish bowl had been placed next to a five-foot canvas covered in indigo blue with a small scarlet heart turned upside down in the middle. In another painting, an elderly black woman was dancing. In another, a Macintosh apple was jammed in the hole of a gold saxophone. Hanging above that was a black background splattered by forest green and bright orange. At first glance, the chaos of colors and subject matter of all the paintings did not make sense. But after carefully taking in each one as if reading chapters of a book, I saw the rich, complex, and unified whole of it.

"Are you coming, kid?" Caesar called from somewhere in the house, his voice carrying through the rooms.

"Yeah, Sir. I'm coming." I walked from the living room to the back of the house into a glass solarium filled with lush floor plants and tall bamboo. Ferns and spider plants hung from hooks in the ceiling, their overgrown leaves brushed against my forehead. White orchids were mixed throughout the jungle of green and I could smell a combination of mint and rosemary in the air while the rain was beating against the glass ceiling.

"Sir?" Caesar's voice trailed down a black spiral staircase.

"Kid?" I called back as I ran up stairs to the second floor. A crimson Oriental rug ran along the hallway, leading to a room at the end. A light shone underneath the door. It opened a crack, through which Caesar stretched out his arm and waved his tee-shirt like a flag.

"I'm calling a truce," he said.

"I don't know, I might have to call a UN Summit meeting," I said, and he opened the door.

"Ooooh. I love our peace-making meetings." Caesar kissed me on both cheeks. The messiness of Caesar's bedroom shocked me—it was such a stark contrast to his disciplined nature. His clothes were strewn about the hardwood floor. Papers and half-full ceramic mugs covered the oak desk in the middle of which was his laptop computer. A double mattress lay on the ground with a white feather comforter clumped in a ball in the middle. African artwork crookedly hung on pink painted walls. There were no framed photographs of his family in this room, or anywhere in the house. However, there was one photograph of Caesar behind a chef's line, scrubbing the grill, his hair thick and dark, and his skin tan; he must have been twenty-six or twenty-seven. His crooked lips held a flirtatious smile, his eyebrows were drawn tight and tense as he focused on the grill; the essence of Caesar hadn't changed in twenty years. A mandolin, guitar, and a large bongo rested on top a pile of jeans and silk shirts.

"Your walls are pink," I said.

"Yeah." He sat on the bed, opened the top drawer to his nightstand covered with bills and notes, and pulled out a joint.

"Is there something you're not telling me about your sexual orientation?" I asked.

"I'm a lesbian. You didn't know that either?"

I laughed and he lit the joint, inhaling as he leaned back onto a stack of pillows.

"Well, my little lesbian, I'm going to get out of these clothes. I'm soaked," I said.

"Hmm. Good idea."

In the bathroom, I stripped off my white halter top, drenched cotton skirt, and underwear, and dropped them on the blue fuzzy bathmat. I pulled Caesar's white tee shirt over my head; it hung past my kneecaps. Shaved facial hairs stuck to gobs of toothpaste inside the sink and a note stuck to the mirror read: Bank deposits, Get Donations for August Charity, Little League Game, Call Punchy about Speeding Ticket, Angelina! I ran a plastic comb through my hair, slicking it back into a tight bun at the base of my neck.

"You look beautiful," he said and I laughed nervously.

"Yeah. I bet."

"Absolutely beautiful, Angelina." I smiled shyly at him.

Caesar reached from underneath the covers for the switch on the stereo by the side of his bed. Louis Armstrong sang "La Vie En Rose."

"Underneath it all, you're really a romantic, aren't you?" I said, laying down beside him on top of the comforter and reaching for the joint.

"Yeah, I have to be," he said.

"Why is that?"

"Because it keeps me going. Someday, I will be with you. You know," he said. Maybe it was the wine from dinner. Or the marijuana. Or the rainy evening. I wasn't sure why he had told me. But I knew. He would be with me. Someday.

"I can't think of the last time I've had a woman in my bed. This way," Caesar said.

"What about Carol?"

"She sleeps downstairs. In her room."

"Oh," I said, "What about all those other women?"

"Well, everyone is special in their own way. But I already told you. You're my curve ball."

"What does that mean?"

"Just what I said," Caesar stroked my cheek. I closed my eyes. The smoke dissipated in the room and he put the joint out in an empty glass ashtray. I tucked my head inside the nook of his shoulder.

As we drifted off to sleep, I heard him say, "I miss you, already."

❦

I awoke every half hour; my conscience did not allow me to sleep. At some point during the night, I had made my way under the feather comforter, spooning into Caesar's embrace. His knees bent, neatly fitting behind mine and my feet lay flat across his.

Startled by a loud bang, I nudged Caesar with my elbow. "Did you hear that?"

With his eyes closed, he groggily whispered, "It's nothing. Just a tree branch."

I strained to listen, and waited. It was as if something was scurrying inside the house.

"Caesar, I heard it again. It's inside."

Half-asleep, Caesar rose from the bed and reached for his guitar. Grabbing the instrument from his hand, I said, "What are you going to do? Play the robber a song?" I handed him a baseball bat I retrieved from the corner of the room.

"I guess, I'll ask him to play a couple of innings of ball, instead," he whispered back. Something shattered downstairs, sounding as if it came from the living room. Caesar's eyes widened with panic.

He quietly walked to the top of the stairs, peering over the edge of the banister. He crept down the spiral staircase and I followed with my fingers clawing into his back. We slid against the wall of the solarium and entered the living room. The light switched on.

I held my breath as I studied her, her dark ponytail pulled loosely back in an elastic, her slightly crooked nose and high cheekbones, her milky skin. A gray skirt clung to her slim hips and a white dress shirt fit snugly against her small breasts. I couldn't help but recognize the physical similarities between us; she was an older version of me. Carol Riva was bent down, picking up pieces of shattered glass of a vase that she must have knocked over; red roses were on the floor and their petals drowning in the water.

I looked at Caesar. He looked at her. She looked at me. I had to escape, but my limbs were hardened in place, the white wall holding me up. Carol casually walked to the leather couch and sat down, saying, "Lydia's bringing the girls in. Marcus is at my parents for the night." She fumbled in her Louis Vuitton purse, pulling out a cigarette and a lighter.

"Honey, you can't smoke in here."

Carol lit the cigarette, inhaled deeply, and exhaled the smoke toward Caesar. She looked at me, saying, "Can you believe that? The man actually has the audacity to tell me I can't smoke. That's Caesar Riva for you."

I jolted. The five foot painting fell from the wall, hitting me on the back of the head and knocking me to the floor. Caesar ran over to me and lifted the painting off my body. He walked away, positioning himself halfway between me and Carol, his face revealing nothing. Carol smoked her cigarette and I searched her face for an emotion. Why didn't she walk over here and slap me across the face? Why didn't she burst into tears? How could she just sit there—blasé and hollow? As perverse as it seems, I wanted to hug her then.

"Nothing's going on here," he said, telling the lie as if he believed it. Caesar appeared vacant, empty, inhuman.

I stared at Caesar and Carol's eyes suddenly burned with similar vengeance. "Do not treat me like a moron. And don't treat Gina that way. Take responsibility, Caesar," she said, looking at me, "Cara told me about you." I placed one foot on top of the other, pulling the fabric of the tee-shirt down.

The door opened.

"Daddy, we're home!" The young girl shouted, but upon seeing me, fell immediately silent. I walked toward the door. Caesar stepped forward, with a plea in his eyes, asking me to understand. I looked at his daughter, and then back at him. Carol walked out of the living room, dragging her suitcase behind her, saying, "Make sure they brush their teeth. And pick up the glass." As I reached for the doorknob, the young girl took a hold of Caesar's hand.

Outside, I saw Lydia by the garage, carrying Caesar's other daughter in her arms, heading toward the house. She glanced at me, without judgment as if she had already read this chapter before. I sat on the bumper of Caesar's Porsche with my head in my hands.

The lights shut off in the living room and Lydia came out. She unlocked the car door for me and I climbed in. We drove back to Provincetown without a word between us, until I said, simply "I live with Cara." As I opened the car door, she reached over and took hold of my arm.

"He's a lovely man," she said. "He does so much for the community. Really. He's got a lovely heart about a lot of things. But, in the world of Caesar, Caesar always comes first, ninety-five percent of the time. Don't keep yourself in the middle of all this for five percent. Some people don't change."

I nodded. I thought tears would follow, but they didn't.

In my apartment, I listened to the message he had left on my cell phone. "I love you, Angelina," he said, despair in his voice. And I began to cry.

Mona Lisa's Seduction

The next morning, I asked Cara if she would cover my shift at the restaurant. I couldn't go there. I tacked a black tee-shirt above the skylight and hung a blanket over the rod to cover the sliding glass doors. I returned to bed, still wearing Caesar's white tee-shirt and I went back to sleep.

My phone rang. It was 11:30 PM.

"Honey, are you alright?"

"I'm not feeling very well."

"Do you want me to bring you something?"

"Could you find a way to get my shifts covered for a couple of days?"

"Whatever you need."

"A week."

"A week!"

"Yeah."

"Okay. No problem, Sugar," he said, "I'll call you tomorrow."

"I think I need some time alone. Could you not call me?"

"I hate the idea but I'll do whatever you want."

"Thank you, Caesar."

"So you don't want me to call?"

"No."

"Okay…okay."

I put my head back down on the pillow.

I slept.

Mona Lisa's Seduction

The next day when I woke up, I was no longer tired. I heard a knock on my door. I didn't feel like talking. I didn't feel like eating. I didn't feel like showering. I didn't feel. I slept.

On the third day, I turned on the lamp beside my bed. I scrutinized the painting that leaned against the wall. The sullen girl on the curb stared back at me. I placed my bare feet on the cold floor. I grabbed the beginner's book to painting from the plastic bag and returned to my bed. I read it all the way through. I turned off the light. I went to sleep.

Mona Lisa's Seduction

I woke up at 7 AM. I opened my bedroom door, went to the kitchen, poured Cheerios and milk in a bowl, and brought it back to my room. After I finished eating, I stood on my bed pulled down the tee-shirt from the skylight. I walked to the glass doors and ripped down the blanket, squinting until I readjusted to the sunlight. I crouched down to my knees in my white tee-shirt, my red hair falling over my breasts, and dumped the painting materials from the plastic bag to the ground. My teeth tore open the package of canvasses and paintbrushes. I began from the inside, turning it all out. Squeezing the tubes of colors into the palette cups, dipping into the paint, reacquainting myself with the girl I had left behind, the girl that hid her dreams under a bed frame years ago because it wasn't practical. The fine tipped brush caressed the blank canvas with a long scarlet stroke.

By the fourth day, I had finished my second painting. I was hungry. I ate three bowls of Cheerios and two grilled cheese sandwiches. I put my John Coltrane and Johnny Hartman CD in my stereo. I started on my third painting. I checked my phone. Caesar hadn't called. I started on my fourth painting. Dylan phoned that evening. I didn't pick up.

Mona Lisa's Seduction

The following morning, I made scrambled eggs, bacon, and toast. After eating my breakfast in the living room, I rubbed Big Fred's belly for awhile. I returned to my bedroom and shut the door. I saw the postcard Caesar had given me, tucked in the frame of the mirror over the bureau. The Bangs Street Gallery Art Opening. It was tomorrow night. I opened the sliding glass door. The warm wind blew into my room, blowing the lace curtain in the air. I walked onto the balcony, and gazed at the long, barren sandbars, stretching for miles. The tide was dead low. I brought my paints and a fresh canvas onto the balcony. I painted. I ate a turkey sandwich for lunch. I painted. I cooked macaroni and cheese for dinner. I painted until the tide had fully turned, until the sea came entirely back to shore.

I saw something round pop up from underneath the water. It was a seal, its slick brown coat shimmering under the sunlight. She gracefully dove down and I waited until she returned for another breath of air. Finally, she did. And I smiled.

Chapter Fourteen

The next afternoon, I heard knocking against the apartment door and I opened it, only wearing the tee-shirt.

"Jesus, Mary, and Joseph!" She said, throwing her arms around my neck.

"I like your haircut," I said.

"What the hell is going on?" Neely asked.

"I'm kind of in a rut."

"Kind of? Darlin' do you have a mirror in here?" She entered the apartment and sat down onto the couch, slapping the seat twice, she said, "Come here." I sat down beside her, tearing up. Neely embraced me, rocking me in her arms.

"I don't know where to start," I said.

"A shower. Gina you stink. Granted, I know I was into the whole 'grunge punk-rock look' a couple of years back. But you're taking it to a whole new level," she said and I laughed. "Good. Laughing. Start with laughing."

"How long can you stay?"

"Just the night. I thought you'd be busy working and I have so much to do before I leave for New York," she said, spinning a gold bracelet around her wrist. "John's here too."

"What!" I said, feeling an emotion return to me for the first time in days. Anger?

"He's at the motel checking us in. He dropped me off here. He found out I was coming to see you. The kid said he was just going to follow me here so I might as well save on gas money."

"Sounds like John."

"What happened to your hands?" She asked and I looked down at them. They were splattered in violet, scarlet, and yellow paint. I led her to my bedroom to show her my paintings.

"Holy crap, Gina!"

"You like them?"

"They're amazing," she said, studying them. "Intense. Where the heck did this come from?"

"I have no idea." It was a half-truth. I didn't know where my ability to paint came from but I knew why they were intense. I couldn't tell her about Caesar. "There's actually an art opening I was planning on going to tonight."

"Cool," she said, "are you planning on wearing that lovely ensemble?" She flicked her hand at my tee-shirt, covered in crusted streaks of paint.

"I think a shower is a brilliant idea."

"Good. I knew you were in there, somewhere," she said. "While you take a shower, I'm going to call John to tell him to meet us. Why don't we eat dinner at the restaurant you work at?"

"Uh…I rather not. Just tell him to meet us at the Town Hall," I said, turning on the faucet. I peeled off the tee-shirt and stepped under the water.

෨

We sat on the park benches outside Town Hall, waiting for John. Wearing a tight purple dress, Ella was singing, "New York, New York" in her husky voice, scissor-kicking her legs like a Rockette. A crowd had gathered around her; a mother handed her child a dollar and the boy dropped it in a basket in front of Ella.

"Are you watching this?" Neely said. "This place is unreal."

"That's what I said when I got here. She's here everyday. Sixty-eight, can you believe that?"

"I hope I look that good. I can't even kick my leg that high now." Neely said and I laughed. She seemed happy that she had brought a smile to my face.

"Are you nervous about seeing John?"

"Not really," I said, running my hands along the front of my strapless, green, silk dress.

"Well, you look smoking hot," she said, scanning her eyes over me. "Actually, I've never seen you look so beautiful, Gina."

"Remember, you're comparing me to four hours ago when I hadn't showered in a week."

"No. There's something else." She paused, mulling something over. "You're in love."

"Where is John anyway? He's never late." I looked at the street, buzzing with people. I saw him, wearing khaki pants with perfectly ironed creases, brown loafers, and a pink Lacoste shirt.

As he approached us, he said, "Sorry about the attire. I left my black leather pants at home." He scratched the cleft in his chin. "Hi Gina. It's good to see you." We leaned in for a quick hug, awkwardly patting each other's backs. I smelled tequila on his breath.

"Why the heck are you so late?" Neely asked.

"I stopped in the Crown and Anchor," he said, running his hands through his dark hair. "The people were pretty nice. One guy even bought me a drink."

Neely and I locked eyes and started giggling.

"What's so funny?"

"John, that was a gay bar," I said.

His ears turned red. "I don't look gay. Do I?"
"Well, you were always very neat," I said, teasingly.
"Great. And I wore pink. It's supposed to be in. I need to find a store. Where do I buy a shirt around here?"
"Don't be such a homo-phobe. You can't tell if people are gay, John. When were you born, anyways? 1922?" Neely said, lightly slapping him on the back of the head.
I began skipping up Commercial Street, saying, "C'mon. Let's use John as bait to get free drinks."
"Very funny," John said, putting his hands in his pockets. Neely ran to catch up with me, looping her arm through mine and we skipped together.
"Where are we going anyway?" He asked.
"An art opening," Neely and I said, simultaneously.
"Oh, no." He stopped walking. "I'm not wearing a pink shirt and going to some artsy-fartsy opening."
"Stop being a jerk." Neely gave him a sharp look.
"Fine. But I'm stopping at a bar to get a drink first." He said, pointing at The Claw. "You don't mind? Do you Gina?"
"Not at all," I said and it was the truth.

᠅

People stood outside the gallery on a brick patio, holding champagne glasses and talking, some were smoking cigarettes. We squeezed through the crowd into the building the size of a summer cottage. As a man passed, Neely took two champagne glasses off a tray and handed one to me.
"Cheers," she said and we clicked our glasses together. We moved along the edges of the walls, looking at the watercolor paintings, mostly inspired by Provincetown's ocean landscapes.

"Yours are better," she said aloud.

"Shhh!" I said, nudging her with my elbow. "You're not just saying that?"

Neely raised her eyebrows at me. Of course she was telling the truth. It was Neely. Scanning the paintings again, I felt a surge of optimism. I could paint. Perhaps I could even have a future as an artist?

"Why is that man staring at you?" Neely said, raising her glass to her lips.

"What man?"

"Across the room. Between those two couples. He can't keep his eyes off you."

I saw Caesar and we locked eyes. He smiled subtly and I returned the gesture until I found myself smiling too radiantly. I looked back at Neely, saying, "That's my boss. From the restaurant."

"Uh-huh." Neely said, placing her hand on her hip. "And?"

"And. Nothing."

"Right."

"Hi, Angelina." He put his hand on my bare shoulder, sending a shiver through my body.

"Hi. Caesar this is my sister. Neely." As they shook hands, I examined Caesar's unshaven jaw and wrinkled carrot shirt.

"How are you feeling?" He asked.

"Better." I wanted to hug him.

"You look exquisite."

"Thank you." I wanted to kiss him.

"Whoah! Free drinks!" I heard John's voice. Neely waved him over. John made his way toward us, holding his glass on a tilt, spilling his champagne from side to side as he walked.

"Caesar this is…"

"John," he said, extending his hand. "I'm the ex-boyfriend.

E-X. No more S in the equation."

"John!" I said.

"She broke up with me in a bar. 'We can't date, anymore.' That's what she said. That's it," he said, looking at Caesar and turning back to me. "Why did you break up with me anyway?"

"John, please not here," I said, pleadingly. Caesar placed his hand on my lower back.

"Here? What's wrong with here?"

"Excuse me. I have to use the restroom," I said, walking toward the back of the gallery. I felt Caesar, following me. As we walked down a small hallway, Caesar opened a door and pulled me into a dusty storage closet.

"Why is your ex-boyfriend here?"

"Do not start. Jealousy is not an option for you." A glimmer of moonlight shined through a small window, casting a bluish glow on his face.

"I don't like it."

"Where's Carol?"

"I think about you all the time."

"Why haven't you called me then?"

Caesar pulled me to him, inhaling the smell of me. "You told me not to. Trust me. It wasn't easy," he said, running his hands across my collarbones. "That kid's not good for you."

"Really, Caesar. Can you even hear what you're saying?"

"He's not."

"Well, I'm not getting back together with him," I said, feeling my desire for Caesar begin to ache. I took a step back. "I need to find Neely."

He hooked his arm around my waist and reeled me to him. Pressed tightly together, I felt him hard against my thigh.

"I'm not getting back together with you either."

"You're not?" He said. "See, you're a lot more rational than you realize."

"No. I'm not," I said. My body began to grind against his, but I stopped myself.

"What else is going on?" He asked.

"You want to talk?"

"I miss talking with you."

"I started painting. Neely said they are amazing."

"I bet they are. You know, I'm on the Board of Directors for the Fine Arts Work Center. An art director from a program in France is coming to Provincetown to evaluate work. I could get you an appointment," he said. I watched his lips move. I wanted to fuse into him, to forget he existed. "I'm so glad you started. Before you become famous you better make sure you—"

"—oh, Caesar, just shut up and kiss me."

He rushed to my mouth, hungrily at first, and I dug my fingers into his back, but after our initial taste, we began to move in a fragile rhythm, as if ours tongues were licking the blade of a knife.

I pushed him back. I needed to find Neely. As I carefully exited the room, I saw John in the corner, holding two glasses of champagne.

"Hey, where's Neely?" I asked.

"Mad at me. Like you."

"I'm not mad at you, John."

"She told me I wasn't supposed to upset you while I was here and she stormed outside," he said, gulping the champagne.

"John, why do you drink so much?"

"I don't drink that much," he said, looking at me sharply. "Why did you break up with me?"

"Because you drink too much."

"Oh," he said, "well, you were mistaken. I don't drink too much,

Gina. Some people smoke dope. Some people snort coke. Some people eat. Some people screw. Some people smoke cigarettes. Some people work eighty hours a week. Most people drink," he said, finishing one glass and setting it down on the table beside him. "You know what your problem is? You've always been too perfect."

Caesar approached us, his eyes seeming more pained than jealous. I hated seeing that look in his eyes and it confused me. Why did he become sensitive and compassionate only when I pushed him away? When I was closest to him, Caesar's emotions ranged from apathy to apathy. I shook my head and he left the gallery.

"Not anymore," I said.

"Oh, yes you are." As John continued to pick an argument, I looked him over, wondering why he felt like a stranger. "You're still your perfect little self. Well, good luck finding someone just as perfect—"

"John," I said, placing my hand on his upper arm. "Let's not do this."

"Do what?"

"Bomb each other with hateful words. It's easier to do that right now. But it's not going to change what's going on between us."

He placed his half full champagne glass down on the table, saying, "See. I don't need to finish it." He put his hands in his pockets. "If you had a problem with my drinking, why didn't you ever say anything?"

"Because, I'm not perfect. And I never was," I said, kissing him on the cheek. "I'm going to find Neely. Will you be alright for a little bit?"

"Uh." He scanned the room. "I'll give you some time with Neely."

"Where will you be?"

"The Claw, I guess," he said, "Not because I want to drink...it's just...more my scene."

I found Neely outside on a bench, pulling off petals of a daisy she had plucked from a wheelbarrow planted with flowers. I sat down beside her, dropping my head to her shoulder.
"How did it go with Jose Cuervo?"
"Alright. I think in time we'll be friends."
"You can't wait for it to go away, you know."
"What do you mean?"
"The love."
I picked my head up from her shoulder. "Neely..."
"You don't have to lie to me," she said. "He sat down beside me when he left here. I said, 'you love me sister.' He said 'yes.' I asked, 'and you're married?' He nodded."

I crossed my legs and folded my hands in my lap, staring at a carpenter ant crawling over a brick and carrying a large crumb on its back, and waiting for Neely to yell at me. She grabbed my hand and pulled me up. "C'mon. Let's go for a walk."

We strolled mutely up Commercial Street, holding hands. Neely's fingers were cold. People in the street moved slowly, some stopped to browse a high end clothing boutique called Silk and Feathers and a jewelry shop named Spank the Monkey, and others surrounded menus hung in restaurant windows. A handsome middle aged man gave another a peck on the cheek, a young Asian girl sat on his shoulders and her ankles locked around his neck. She tugged the string of her red helium balloon, watching it bobble in the air. A drag-queen cut through the crowd on a purple scooter, yelling, "Tonight. The show of your lives. Crown and Anchor. 8 o'clock. Come one and come all. And, remember if you're not protected it's better not to come at all." She tossed handfuls of packaged condoms and candy from a Penny Patch bag into the air. Neely bent down to the pavement, scrambling with four ten-year-olds for the treats. She snatched two pieces before one had a chance to take them. She looked at the brown-haired boy and said, "Sorry, kid, it's a tough world." I picked up two Starbursts and handed them to the boy. His eyes brightened and he ran to catch up with his friends.

"What did you do that for? I was teaching the kid a lesson of a lifetime," she said.

"Yeah, maybe. But it's a lesson we learned too young."

"Here," she said, handing me an Atomic Fire Ball. "For old times sake."

I popped the plastic, putting the candy in my mouth and tucking it inside my cheek.

"Let's go down here." I followed Neely down a street toward the bayside.

A bunch of teenagers were waiting in line at a Mexican take-out stand and holding drinks in paper bags. We passed a bar called the Sandbar; people were squeezed on a deck connected to the building, shouting above a cover band, playing "Hard to Handle" by the Black Crowes.

"How's the fire ball treating you?" I said.

"Not nearly as bad as it used to be," she said, eyeing me. "It's crazy, isn't it? Humans can condition themselves to anything."

As we walked further away from the Sandbar, I started to hear waves lapping against the shoreline. We stepped onto a wharf, streetlamps ran the length it. Commercial fishing boats were docked along one side of the pier and Whale Watching boats sat on the other—small motor and sailboats were sprinkled throughout and bobbed on the sea's surface. The wind rippled my green satin dress. When we reached the end of the wharf, Neely and I sat down on a wooden plank and dangled our legs over the edge. Neely attempted to light a cigarette, but the wind was persistent. I cupped my hands around hers, until it caught the flame. I watched the red ember of her cigarette burn.

"So, when are you going to stop seeing him?" Neely said, breaking our silence. I was thankful Neely hadn't used words like "affair" or "mistress."

"I wish I never started it," I said.

"Yeah. Wisdom can be a pain in the ass. I've been learning too late for years now," Neely said, exhaling smoke into the air. "But you have to quit him. Cold turkey. If there is anyone in this world that can do it, it's you. Just put your mind to it, like you did everything else." I knew she was right, but I realized then, I had never thought about quitting. I had only thought about fixing it, unclogging his heart.

"Neely, I can't not see him," I said, leaning carefully over the edge and glancing down at the inky sea fifty-yards below. "Don't you want to tell me I'm morally bankrupt? I mean, how could I do something like this? Especially with all that mom's been through with dad dating that woman."

Neely flicked her cigarette over the edge. As it fell through the black night, the ember glowed until it disappeared into the water.

"I don't judge you, Angel. It's not my style," she said. "But you need to know that your love isn't going to dwindle out. You can't keep waiting for someday in the future, when you don't love him anymore. This isn't like John. It's a different kind of love and you're going to have to walk away with your heart still wide open. Whether you do it now, twenty years from now, or some day in between, that's your choice. I hate to say this to you, but I have to…have you ever thought if he really loved you, he would never have put you in that situation to begin with?"

"It's not that simple, Neely," I said. "He has a good heart. He's done so much charity work. He helps a lot of people. But he's always been too busy to look at certain things. He just has trouble relating at a deeper level."

"You sound like someone I know. Someone, we both know," she said, placing her arm around me. "How long are you going to make excuses for him? Because, you and I know, Mom's made a lifetime out of it."

"He loves me."

"He loves what's reflected through you. He loves the love in your eyes, Angel."

I scraped my teeth over my bottom lip.

"Remember when you were ten and Mom took us to the Animal Rescue League? You wanted a dog for your birthday," she said, "you passed by a litter of cute puppies, toward an old mutt in its own cage. It was barking like crazy. A woman told us that it had probably been abused. That's the dog you picked."

"Peaceful."

"Yeah, you named the darn thing Peaceful. He would snap at us when we tried to pet him. But you were so patient. You laid out a trail of biscuits, training him to trust you. Eventually, he started following you around and sleeping in your bed," Neely said, spinning her yin-yang ring around her finger. "One day, when you were playing outside, he attacked you. Bit into your ankle and you had to go the hospital to get stitches."

I extended my right leg, looking at the mark above my ankle. The scar formed two parentheses. "Yeah, but it wasn't his fault. We were playing catch. He meant to go for the stick."

"You know what happened to that dog?"

"Mom and Dad gave Peaceful away."

"Yeah. They explained the situation and an elderly couple took him in," she said, "three weeks later, when their grand-daughter was visiting, Peaceful bit into her face. The girl had to get skin grafts. They attempted to sue Mom and Dad, but they settled out of court. They put Peaceful to sleep."

"Why didn't anyone tell me?"

"I don't know," she said, "but, it's always been your way. You see something a little broken. You love the life right into it. You only see the goodness. Even when it hurts you."

I looked out to the lighthouse, its green light flickering on and off in steady five second intervals. "Neely, do you think people can change?"

"Of course they can. But the question is completely inconsequential."

"What do you mean?"

"Remember how I used to yell at Mom and Dad? Do everything possible to make them change?" She said and I nodded. "Well, they never changed because of me. They only reacted to my behavior. And my actions didn't really help me all that much. I have an 'Ice' tattoo across my back for God's sake. I didn't feel good inside. Eventually I stopped worrying about them changing and I realized that I could change so I did. Now, look. I have a great boyfriend. I'm going to New York to start a good job. I don't smoke dope anymore. My life's not perfect. But I'm not chasing my own tail."

"Why haven't you told me all this before?"

"I don't know. I guess, I always felt embarrassed. I was the big sister and I didn't set the most shining example," Neely said, pulling her hair into a low pony-tail. "I couldn't talk to you this way. I couldn't protect you." Neely dropped her head in her hands and began to cry.

"Shhh…" I rubbed her back. "It's okay Neely. We were doing what we had to do. We were surviving."

She rubbed her eyes. I wiped a tear from the tiny black freckle above her lip.

"What about Dad? You really think he has changed?" I said.

"All I know is that I've forgiven him. He doesn't beat mom. He doesn't drink at all." She sniffled, collecting herself. "And I don't think it's going to get any better than that."

"Hey, c'mon. It's time." I swung my legs around the ledge and stood, pulling Neely up.

"Time for what?"

"Smiling," I said, linking my arm through hers. "Can you believe I really named that beastly dog, Peaceful?" Neely laughed and I patted her hand.

As we walked back toward the street, I heard shouting from a motorboat anchored twenty yards past a large fishing boat. "Just stop. Stop seeing her, man. Forget she exists!" I recognized the voice. I squinted at two men, facing off in the shadows.

"Sorry. Can't do that. Business is business. You of all people should know that." The other man said, bending down to pick up something off the boat's deck. When he stood, the other man punched him in the face. Crack. There were sounds that made me nauseous. A child in pain. An animal whimpering. A lover's withdrawn silence. But flesh smacking against flesh was a sound that forced me to gag—and I did, tasting the bile in the back of my throat. I bent over, putting my palms on my knees.

Neely grabbed my hand and we began to run.

ೕ

"Get a loud of this," Neely said, pointing to a small stage.

We found John at The Claw, singing karaoke to the Clash's "Should I Stay or Should I Go" with a beer in one hand, and four

Mona Lisa's Seduction

college girls in cut-off jean shorts were dancing around him. The people whistled and hollered as the song waned, but John wouldn't let go of the microphone.

"Excuse me, ladies and gentleman," he said and the microphone squealed, forcing a few people to cover their ears. "Testing. One. Two. Three."

"Pull it away from your mouth, you moron!" A man screamed and John adjusted the microphone.

"I would like to direct your attention to the back room," John said, pointing at me. "That's the girl I'm going to marry." Their heads turned and I wiggled my fingers, forcing a smile. They clapped and a man shouted, "Nice going dude. She's hot." When John was stepping down from the stage, his foot tangled in the microphone cord and he fell in a belly flop to the floor. I gasped and a few men bent down to pick him up while the crowd fell silent. John leaned the microphone-stand down to him, saying, "Just as soon as I complete AA." He held up his beer bottle, foaming over the top and pouring over his hand, and smiled in a half-grin to reveal one dimple. People started to laugh.

"He still knows how to charm the crowd," I said.

"Addicts always do." Neely replied.

John didn't put up much of a fight when we told him it was time to go home. I suggested they stay at my apartment instead of walking all the way to the hotel. When we arrived, Neely went into my bedroom and John flopped down on the couch. I slipped off his loafers and placed a blanket over him. John began to sing off-key: *"Just call her Angel in the morning...just touch her cheek before she leaves me, ba-by...and if morning said we sinned...then it was what I want-ed now...and if we're meant to be victims of the night then I promise you I won't be blinded by the light...just call her An-gel..."*

He had slaughtered the lyrics of "Angel of the Morning," but a thick, black smoke had built in my throat. The irony was a bit too much to take at the moment; it was as if I could hear life laughing at me. I kissed John's forehead and he closed his eyes. I moved toward my bedroom.

"I never really saw you. Did I, Angel?"

"Sweet dreams, John," I said, snapping off the light.

Neely was already snoring gently when I crawled into bed. I put my arm over her and snuggled closely beside her, and without waking, she laced her fingers through mine.

I awoke in the middle of the night and tip-toed toward the bathroom. When I heard rustling from the living room, I peeked around the wall to check on John. I saw her naked body outlined by the moonlight. Cara pulled the blanket over her shoulders and pressed down on top of him. John grunted. I jolted like a needle entering skin. It was instinctual. I ran into the bathroom, sat down on the shut toilet seat, and stared at a lightening bolt shaped crack in a tile on the floor. My shock quickly turned to indifference. I understood then why Carol Riva hadn't shouted or cried when she had found me in her house.

Chapter Fifteen

In the morning, I woke up to the smell of onions and brewing coffee. Neely was already up, sitting on the edge of my bed and surveying my paintings.

"Hey, what are you doing?" I said.

"Promise me something."

"What's that?"

"Don't just stuff these away. Get some art professional to check them out," Neely said, turning to me. With her strong jaw line and electric blue eyes, staring intensely, she looked just like my father. "I mean, I know I'm not smart like you. But I'm a different kind of smart. Intuition smart."

"I'll trade you my book smarts for your intuition."

"I'm not joking, Gina. Pinky swear promise me," she said, hooking her pinky through mine.

"Pinky swear," I said. "Let's see what's cooking in the kitchen. I'm starving."

"No wonder why you can't flip an egg. You can't do it with a spoon," John said, teasingly and Cara giggled, softly slapping him on his arm. When we entered the kitchen, Cara stepped back from John's side and they both eyed me nervously. She was wearing John's pink shirt.

"Hey guys," I said.

"We're cooking breakfast for everyone," John said, scratching his bare stomach.

"Wow, John. I think I can see two chest hairs from here. You're becoming a man," Neely said.

John looked at Cara, saying, "That's Gina's sister, Neely. As you can tell, she's the wise-ass of the family."

Cara extended her hand, "It's really nice to meet you. I hope you're not here to steal Gina back."

"Nope. Just passing through," Neely said, pouring coffee into two mugs. "She has some business to take care of first."

"What business?" John handed me a plate with two eggs, bacon, and two slices of toast.

"Top secret," I said, biting the toast and sitting down at the kitchen table with Neely.

"We made Bloody Marys. Want some?" Cara asked. Neely and I shook our heads.

Cara and John joined us at the table, both taking a sip of their Bloody Marys. Cara held a piece of bacon with her hand and crunched into it. John adjusted the silverware on his placemat, straightening them before picking up his fork. Throughout breakfast, Cara laughed exuberantly at Neely's jokes and giggled at John's responses, and I noticed she didn't speak, her boldness was stifled in the company of strangers.

When we finished eating I began clearing the plates and placing them in the sink.

"I better take a shower," Cara said, curling a piece of hair around her finger. While looking at John she asked, "Will you guys still be here when I get out?"

"Probably not," Neely said.

"Oh," Cara said, disappointedly.

"Why don't you take my number," John said, "just in case you're ever passing through Connecticut and you have an emergency." Cara's eyes brightened and I watched John follow her into her bedroom.

I turned on the sink faucet and began washing the dishes, handing them to Neely to dry.

"Don't you want to kill them?"

"No."

"Well I know you're over him. But still, it's an unwritten rule. Your friends don't make out with ex-boyfriends," Neely said, grabbing a plate from my hand. "I would want to rip his eyeballs out. How come you're so calm?"

"People break rules. And they have their reasons, even if it doesn't make sense to the outside world," I said. "Please, Neely, you're talking to me. The walking Hawthorne novel."

"What?"

"*The Scarlet Letter.*"

"I don't get it."

"The affair."

John entered, wearing his pink shirt. "The affair?" The water began to run in the bathroom.

"Yeah, the affair…it's a woman problem I've been dealing with," Neely said.

"Sounds kinky," John said, folding down the collar of his shirt.

"No, it's a gynecologist issue."

John covered his hands over his ears, "New topic, please," and Neely lightly jabbed me in my side.

"Well, I guess we're finished," I said, wiping my hands dry on a dishrag.

Neely looked at me. "I'm not a fan of good-byes. So…" She threw her arms around me, squeezing me tightly. "I'm going to wait outside."

"I love you, Neely."

"Ditto, darlin'," she said, walking out of the room.

"I hope that wasn't too weird. About Cara," he said, leaning against the counter top and crossing one foot over the other.

"Well it's life and life is weird."

"Yeah. But I sort of feel guilty."

"Don't."

"It was nice to see you, Gina," he said diplomatically, and leaned in for a hug. "Don't be a stranger." He smoothed his palms across the sides of his hair.

"John, I have to ask you something before you go."

"What's that?"

"Did you ever cheat on me when we were together?"

He looked up at the ceiling, scratching his nose. "No. Absolutely not."

I squeezed his hand, saying, "Take care of yourself." John dodged my gaze, walked out of the room, and left the apartment.

I finally knew my answer. John had clearly lied to me. I flicked the wind chime that hung over the kitchen sink, the thin metal bars clanged loudly and slowly settled to fleeting tinkles. My intuition was sharper than I realized. I just had to get my emotions out of the way.

෨

That afternoon, I approached Mona Lisa's with trepidation. It was my first day back and I imagined the other workers had gossiped extensively about my absence. I saw him at the entrance, clutching a stack of green menus and sitting, slouched on a black stool. Thick clouds gathered in the sky, rolling out to the sea like tumbleweeds. Caesar whistled to himself as he watched the crowd wandering along Commercial Street. When he saw me, his eyes widened and he smiled broadly. During our relationship, he seemed to grow more delighted by my presence, as if each encounter were a surprise gift. Usually, I greeted him with equal eagerness and exhilaration, but now I skirted his gaze and hurried toward the work station on the side that was hidden from the customers' view. I tied my apron on and when I reappeared on the patio, he stood up from the stool. I began clearing glasses from an empty table and he appeared, helping me collect dishes—something I hadn't seen him do before, for me or any server. I focused on the white table and on Caesar's small, almost feminine hands. He clumsily piled the dishes into his arms, a place I yearned to be.

We had existed like deep sea divers charting a foreign terrain of vibrant coral reefs, moon snails, and electric yellow and black striped fish, but all we discovered below the surface evaporated when we came up for air. Why couldn't we surrender to our mind's confusion and our heart's clarity? In love, Caesar and I still had so much to learn.

I collected a tray of glasses and walked away, dropping them inside a large plastic tub. The restaurant became busier and Lisa sat three tables in my station with customers.

"Excuse me," Caesar said softly from behind my shoulder. I stepped away from him. "Angelina?" He spoke my name inquisitively as if he didn't recognize me.

"Yes?" I looked into his hazel eyes that seemed to innocently beg for the return of my affection.

"You need something?" Caesar asked. His pruned a strand of hair from my shirt. I opened my mouth to say something and then shut it when Dylan tugged on my shirtsleeve. Caesar walked away, clasping his hands behind his back, and returned to his post on the stool.

"I'm glad you came back. You gave me plenty of time to think about something we could do," Dylan said.

"Really?"

"Yeah. You interested?" I glanced at Caesar, and looked away, focusing on three tables of customers with closed menus, waiting for me to take their orders.

"Sure," I said.

"Well, I was thinking that you haven't been to the top of the Provincetown Monument yet. And, it's a really beautiful view. I haven't been in awhile, but you don't have to go with me. If you don't want to. I mean if you're too busy or something." Dylan buried his hands in jean pockets, jiggling the loose change inside. From his perch on the stool, Caesar watched us. When he caught my eyes, he flicked a penny into the air, caught it, and flipped it over onto the back of his hand. He checked to see what side the penny had landed and fixed me with a silly grin, trying to get me to laugh.

"Sure, Dylan." I agreed.

"Great. Do you want to go tomorrow morning? Around eleven?"

"That's perfect," I said. Dylan spotted Cara riding a bike up to the restaurant. He rubbed his chin and I noticed a dark purple bruise across his knuckles.

"Dylan! What happened to your hand?"

He put it in his pocket, saying, "Nothing. Just knocked it against the grill."

"Hey! Are you coming or what? We don't have much time, baby. Besides, the ground is burning holes into my toes. It's smokin' hot." Cara called across the patio to Dylan, yanking on her white tube top and shifting her weight from one bare foot to the other.

"I better go. Duty calls." Dylan joined Cara, straddled the bike, gripping the handles and standing up with his feet on the pedals.

Cara sat on the seat wrapping her bronzed arms around his waist, and pressing her chest against his back.

"Bye, Gina," Cara said, waving.

I thought about Dylan's bruise and remembered last night's incident on the pier. It was Dylan's voice that had sounded so familiar. Dylan had punched the man on the boat.

"What was that all about?" Caesar had walked up next to me.

"Nothing."

"It sure looked like something."

"What if it was something? It's not anything. But, even if it were…"

"You know, honey, you should be a little more cautious of Dylan," Caesar said.

"Is that right? I find that interesting."

"What?" Caesar asked.

"First you tell me, John's not good for me. Now, you warn me about Dylan. I mean, really…"

"So, you are going out with him. Man, I can't believe it." He shook his head.

"Why not? It's not like you and I are ever going anywhere."

"That's not true. I thought of taking a trip to France in the fall and I wanted to ask you to go with me. But—"

"—But, you have a wife."

Caesar laughed loudly and like a driver obnoxiously holding down a horn, making me feel foolish. "Your ears are turning red," he said. He reached out to touch them, but I pulled away.

"Hello! Did you hear me? Your wife. Remember? The love of your life," I said through gritted teeth.

Caesar laughed even more fervently. "Yeah. That's it. She's the love of my life," he said. He pulled out his chapstick from his back pocket.

"That's it? You have nothing else to say to me?" I asked.

Caesar's lips parted and I waited for him to speak, but he clamped his jaw. I heard the murmur of customers chatting, dishes clanging against glasses in the bus pans, a small poodle yapping, chickadees chirping above in the locust tree, and the sustained ring of a bell from an annoyed bicyclist trying to get through the throng of tourists on Commercial Street.

"Angel!" The voice of my father came at me like an asteroid. Caesar turned around to look, I hid behind his body.

"Angel. It's me." I peeked out from behind Caesar, there was no escape. There he was. His blonde hair was covered in gray and his blue eyes sparkled; his arms sprung open wide to embrace me.

"Who's that guy?" Caesar said.

"That guy is a disaster." I said in a low voice. My father stood still, his arms open, waiting for me to come to him.

"Aren't you going to give the old man a hug?"

I moved obediently toward him. He closed his arms around me, firmly locking me inside. My arms hung flat against the sides of my body like the edges of razor clams and I waited for it to be over.

"I know what you're thinking," he said, resting his hands firmly on my shoulders as I wriggled free from his grasp.

"What am I thinking, Dad?"

"You're thinking, how could I still look so young?"

"Dad…"

"What can I say? AA turned me around. Big time."

"Dad…"

"Really, Angel. I'm a new man."

"Dad!" I shouted and a family of five at a nearby table broke from their conversation to stare at us.

"Cool down, Angel. You don't have to scream. I'm not deaf."

He chuckled, rubbing his hand through his thinning hair.

"Dad, I'm in the middle of work right now. Can we meet during my break?"

"I haven't seen you in almost four years and you can't make time for me?"

"Sure. I can make time for you, Dad. I'm just saying—"

"—Maybe, I shouldn't have bothered coming if you don't really want me here," he said, smiling faintly. "But, it was worth it. Just to look at you. You're breathtaking. I always knew my little angel would become quite a woman." He took a few steps back.

"Dad, I don't want you to go."

"Well, that is the greatest news I've heard all year. Why don't we go talk over there?" He pointed to the pier that extended into the sea.

"Okay. You go ahead. I'll just ask someone to watch over my tables."

My father walked toward the gazebo. He limped, slightly dragging his right loafer along the pavement.

With my father out of sight, I unleashed a tear. Caesar took a hold of my hand. I let Caesar hold my hand and gently stroke it with his rounded thumb.

"Go ahead, Angelina, I'll get someone to watch your tables," he said. "Are you alright?"

I shook my head and ran toward the side station, covering my mouth with one hand, gripping onto my stomach with the other. Caesar followed me. He began to rub my back softly.

"Maybe, you should go home. You're really pale, Sugar."

"I'm fine. I'm fine. Thank you, Caesar," I said.

I made my way across the wooden walkway toward the gazebo. My father sat underneath the Mona Lisa with his right leg bobbing up and down. I took a seat beside him, holding onto the edge of the bench, like a child gripping the string of a helium balloon. I fixed my gaze on a squirrel, hanging low in a tree branch, balancing before he leapt. I was nauseous and my throat had swelled, as if I was having an allergic reaction.

"I'm really a changed man, Angel."

"Uh. Uh."

"In rehab, I was forced to think about things. Work the steps of the program. You know?"

"Yep."

"And, I'm clean now. I'm happy now. It's just your mother and I, we were too young. We should never have gotten married."

"Thanks a lot," I said.

"I've forgiven you and I hope you will forgive me too. I love you, Angel." My feet crossed at the ankles and I swung them, back and forth, like I was on a swing set.

I saw Caesar, perched on his stool. He was flirting with an eighteen-year-old Jamaican waitress, tickling her cheek with his fingertips. She giggled like a wind up doll. The rush came flooding back to my insides, making feel like I needed something.

"You know that. Don't you, Angel. How much I love you?" I almost responded on auto-pilot, I love you too. But if I had come to Provincetown to put my past behind me, then the past had followed me like a ferocious tiger hunting a gazelle in the African wilderness. The beast hadn't let up, nor would it. After all, it was a natural cycle. The way a predator pursues the prey. My moment for evolution had arrived.

"Can I just ask what exactly have you forgiven me for, Dad?"

"Well, calling the police. Testifying against me in court. I mean, families should stick up for one another. Right? But, it's okay. I understand. You were young. Impressionable." I stood up from the bench.

"But, you did it. You drove off the road and slammed into the mailbox," I said.

"It was the alcohol. I'm not an alcoholic anymore."

"Just like it was alcohol that forced you to beat on Mom?"

"Oh, Angel, there weren't that many beatings."

"One! Dad! One beating is *too* many beatings!" I shouted.

"I've found God now. I've been regularly attending AA. I haven't mentioned this to Neely, but I've spoken to a minister about seminary school."

"What? You're Catholic."

"Well, I don't think celibacy is right for me."

"So, you switched religions and now you're going to become a minister?"

"I can help people this way. I've been going to church five days a week with Monica. She sings in the church choir and she told me…"

"You do realize that you still haven't divorced Mom?"

"You would really love Monica," he said, "she's good for me."

"Okay. Let me get this straight. You quit the booze but now you're addicted to church. How long will it last?"

"Your mother and I were just a bad combination."

I sat back down, feeling defeated. "Do you have any clue? What it was like for us?" I dug my fingernails into my thighs. "I used to hide in the back of the closet and just wait…wait for you to stop whacking her…and all the times, I picked you up from the bar in between my algebra homework. Do you understand that? How terrifying it felt to be your daughter?" I asked, with my arms crossed over my chest.

"Wow. That's awful," he said, shaking his head. He spoke as if I had narrated a story about someone else's life. How could he have possibly changed if he had never realized who he was? I stared at his face, the slight bump at the bridge of his nose—just like mine. Over the years, I had made friends and lovers out of strangers. How did I come to make a stranger out of the man who gave me life? Staring into his eyes and taking notice of the similarities between us only spread the chasm, for what I wanted us to be, was not what we were. I wasn't sure if I wanted to go back to the start or if I wanted to start fresh. Extend my right hand and politely state, "Hello. I'm Angelina Moreau. Nice to meet you."

I stood back up. A dozen sailboats fluttered along the surface of Cape Cod Bay, like a school of striped bass. The orange, yellow, and red sails shuddered with the slight breeze. A stray grass green and white striped sailboat anchored across the way on Long Point.

My father pushed one arm against the bench, grunting as he slowly stood, and I noticed then how much he aged. I remembered him as a strong and powerful creature, like a Grizzly bear, but the bear had shrunken; his hair had thinned at the back, showing a patch of scalp. He placed both hands on my shoulders and coughed.

"I meant what I said Angel. I've really changed. I don't know what I have to do to prove it. But, if you could just give me another chance. Just trust me."

"Well, what about..."

"Hey! Remember those days?" He asked, pointing to a young girl in a bright yellow bathing suit playing in the water with her father. "Don't you remember all those times together at the beach? You used to love the water. Like a little mermaid. I'd stay in with you for hours." He smiled and I did too, watching the young girl with dark hair, attempting to float on her back. The man's hands were tucked under her and he slowly stepped back. "Daddy?" She called out. "I'm right here," he said. She relaxed and floated on her own until her enthusiasm or her fear set in. She began kicking her stubby legs and her father was immediately there to pull her close to him. "I did it all by myself! Did you see that, Daddy?"

"There were good times. You know," he said, pinching my cheek.

"Do you remember leaving early? Do you remember the fighting?"

"Everyone argues, Angel."

"Really, Dad? So, when that little girl goes home, she's going to watch her Dad throw a half a bottle of whiskey down the hatch and more than likely beat her mother? Is that how it goes?"

"What's gotten into you? I don't know what you want me to say."

"How about just…I'm sorry?" I said, hearing the desperation in my voice.

His eyes became watery, I thought he was on the verge of an apology, he said, "You know. You weren't all that perfect either. I mean, you really didn't let me in. You weren't easy to love."

"I need to get back to work. My break is over," I said.

"Well, I'm glad we had this talk. It's about time we settled our differences," he said, pulling me toward him for a hug. "C'mon. Give me a real firm hug." When he let go, I jogged down the walkway toward the restaurant.

"Angel." My father had caught up to me. He knelt down on his knees. The sun reflected the gray in his hair and tenderness in his eyes. "May I have the pleasure of your company tomorrow, your highness?" I hesitated. "Please, my lady," he begged. Maybe he wasn't all that bad. There had been good times. He wasn't drinking anymore. Maybe there would be better times, if only I gave him a chance.

"Sure, Dad," I said. "I'll meet you tomorrow at Town Hall. 5 o'clock." He slowly rose from the ground, brushing the dirt from his knees. He placed one hand on his lower back, grunting.

"Are you okay Dad?"

"Not really," he said, limping. I locked my elbow with his.

"What happened to your leg?"

"I was sleep-walking and I forgot there were fives steps. I took one giant step down the whole staircase," he said, laughing and pulling a pant leg up.

"Dad, you should probably have it looked at. It's swollen."

"Nah. It's a great babe magnet. Sort of like a cute dog. An accessory."

"I'm not so sure it will be such a great babe magnet if you have to get your leg amputated."

"C'mon. What's more sexy than an old guy with a prosthetic leg?" He joked, continuing, "Hey. Speaking of old guys. Who's that?" My father nodded toward the stool.

"Caesar Riva. He's my boss."

"Why was he looking at you funny before, when I came in?"

"He wasn't looking at me funny."

"Angel, the guy was looking at you. And, I didn't like it," he said. I looked at Caesar; his black Ray Bans shielded his eyes.

"Stay away from that guy, Angel," he said, chuckling. "I used to be that guy."

"Okay. Well, I guess, just give me a call tomorrow."

"Great. And, one last thing."

"What's that?" I asked.

"You know how much I love you, right?"

I nodded. My chest tightened. I was dizzy and nauseated from love, like riding the Twirl-a-Whirl so many times in a row that the amusement park ride lost its pleasure. The alchemy of love entangled with a demoralizing ache. There was no distinction. Love was pain and pain was love.

"Hey, girl. Smile. Would ya'?" My father said. And, I did. "That's my Angel." He walked toward Commercial Street with his hands tucked in his pants' pockets. I straightened my crooked waitress apron and went back to work.

"Hey, honey. You okay to come back?" Caesar asked. I eyed the girl carrying a bus tub of dishes and when she passed she puckered her lips, smacking them in the air like a kiss at Caesar. He looked at her desirably.

"You know what, honey," I angrily accentuated the endearment. "This love is a total farce. I'm hunger and you're greed. You'll never grow." The corners of Caesar's lips dropped and his face flattened out, as if I'd slapped him. I untied my apron and draped it over his shoulder. I tore the black kitchen buzzer from the elastic in my skirt and dropped it into his hand.

"I'm done," I said.

"Angelina!" he called out and I turned around. Caesar stared at me, pleadingly. I waited for him to speak. When he didn't, I shrugged and began walking.

I pushed my way through the web of strangers on Commercial Street. A man on a bicycle repeatedly rang a bell, not slowing down as he pedaled toward me. He had no intention of swerving his bike and he forced me into a store glass window. With my body tightly pressed against it, I yelled, "Hello! I'm a person!" He raised his arm in the air, extending his middle finger.

Across the street, I saw a red neon sign that read: Spirit Ice Cream. I purchased a banana split with five scoops of chocolate chip, caramel and hot fudge sauces, whipped cream, M&Ms, and extra cherries. I pulled open a door at the back of the store and walked into an outside garden. A young couple was arguing on a picnic bench. I sat down across from them and plunged a large spoonful into my mouth.

"I just don't know how you could say that to me?" The woman said, crossing her legs.

"You asked me! You asked me who was the most attractive woman I ever photographed, so I told you!"

"Well, you photographed me."

"Yeah, I did. And, I'm engaged to you," he said, gripping the sides of his hair. "God, get over it." I furiously attacked my sundae, piling it into the spoon before I had even swallowed the bite in my mouth. The man looked at me, saying, "You can't be back here."

"This is not a good time to start with me," I said with my mouth open.

"We're in the middle of something. Can you move?"

There was only one picnic table.

"Apparently, not."

"What's your problem?"

I placed my spoon upright in a scoop of ice-cream and stared at him. "Look, I'm really sorry you're having a conflict here. Your fiancé's upset because you told her some other woman is sexier than her. Instead of telling her, she's being stupid, just give her a hug and tell her you love her…"

"That's obvious. I'm marrying her."

"She just needs to hear it," I said. "As for my problem…my alcoholic, domestically abusive father who I haven't spoken to in years, came into town. He has a girlfriend, even though he hasn't officially divorced my mother and apparently he's no longer an alcoholic and he's switched religions to become a minister. He says he's changed. But he's still a world class manipulator and I still fall for it. I just broke up with a man and he's married and we were having an affair and I've said a lot of awful things, trying to convince myself that I hate him. Because I have to let him go even though I'm going to love him until I die." I popped a cherry in my mouth.

"That sucks," he said, reaching for his fiancé's hand. "Do you want to go see that movie?" She nodded, they left, and I ate until I was so full I felt numb.

༄

By the time I reached the apartment, I knew Caesar was not the man to whom I meant to say those harsh words. A woman passed, pushing her screeching baby in a stroller. She stopped, reached into the carriage, and gently pulled him out. She pressed his head to her breast and rocked him until he quieted. I thought about turning around and walking back to the restaurant, but didn't.

I was disappointed Cara was not home; I wanted company. I pulled my suitcases from underneath my bed and began packing underwear and socks from the top drawer in my dresser. I had to get out of there. I didn't know where I was going, but I couldn't get out of there quickly enough. The phone rang, but I didn't answer.

"Hi, it's me. Um. Guess you're not there. Okay. I love you." Click. Caesar's voice was soft and tender; I played the message again. I reached for the receiver. I wanted to call and act like an adult, but I felt more like a five-year-old, so I tossed the suitcases to the floor and collapsed on top of my bed.

When I woke the sky had blackened over, a thick layer of dark gray clouds covered the moon, and not even a sliver of light leaked into my bedroom. My arm carefully fumbled in the air, searching for the switch to the lamp on my nightstand; I clicked the switch over with my thumb, but the light didn't come on. Distant thunder grumbled through the screen window like buffalo with hooves beating against the open range, hurriedly approaching my camp. The power was out.

I blindly moved toward the bathroom, my fingers leading the

way, sliding against the smooth walls, one step at a time. Inside the bathroom, I opened the medicine cabinet, pulled out a book of matches, and lit three cranberry scented candles. I drew the bath water and dropped my clothes to the mat. A boom of thunder cut through the silence, and a breeze fanned the candle flames, casting slender shadows against the white tile walls. I stepped into the bath, the searing water almost too hot to bear, but then I let go, collapsing into it.

A flash of lightening illuminated the sky outside the window, like day into the night; it disappeared as quickly as it came. The thunder rumbled more boldly than before, roaring into the blackened sky like an airplane ready for take off.

I closed my eyes and pulled my knees to my chest, the bubbles foaming peaks on my knee caps.

"I've been moving to remember…been moving to forget…" The strumming of a guitar accompanied his voice, which came through the screen window like a welcome intruder. *"Moving through rainy days, moving through sunshine too…"* A lightening bolt cracked the sky. *"I wove this web through and through…"* A heavy rain came down. *"And, now, Sugar, you've moved me. So, I'm stuck in a web of you."*

The wood door swung open, and Caesar stood there, his guitar strapped on his back, his silk shirt stuck to his chest, wrinkled and ruined. Droplets of rain clung to the tip of his broad nose. I knew I should send him away.

He unbuttoned his soaked shirt, removed his black shoes and pants and slid into the bathtub. I rested the back of my head on his chest and he cupped my breasts with his hands. I studied them; I wanted to remember every crevice, every fine line, the lonely brown freckle on top his right wrist bone. The gold wedding band shimmered in the candlelight, so I placed his finger into my mouth and slid the ring off, putting it on the edge of the bathtub.

He held me until the candles burned down to the wicks, the wax dripping down the cabinet door and onto the cold tile floor. I watched water form into a droplet around the bottom edge of the faucet, hanging on until it couldn't fight gravity any longer; it dropped and pinged against the bath water, creating a ring across the surface, expanding slowly until it finally vanished. Our fingertips wrinkled like golden raisins, as if erasing the years between us.

"Caesar?"

"Hm?" He replied.

"Never mind."

※

Caesar stayed at the apartment until six in the morning; we had fallen asleep on my bed, lulled by the symphony of the stormy weather. Cara's high heels cracked like fireworks against the wood floors and woke us. Caesar's arm was draped heavily over my hip. We had become careless, or perhaps, more bold. He dressed. As he bent down to tie a shoelace, I remembered the ring on the bathtub edge.

"Just give it to me later. No one is going to notice. And, I don't care if they do." As he got up to leave, he saw my paintings. "Wow! When did you do all these?"

"Last week."

"I have a board meeting today at the Fine Arts Work Center. The art director will be there. Why don't you pick out the best one, so I can show him."

"You pick."

He immediately reached for the painting of two bodies underwater. The man and woman were naked and painted in sap, viridian, and emerald green, entwined like two clumps of seaweed. Her legs clutched the man's waist, his hands clasped around her back in a prayer. An open oyster shell was dug into the sand, a pearl emitting light and floating to the surface. Caesar tucked the painting under his arm. He kissed me goodbye, barely brushing my lips, and then disappeared like a puffy milkweed blown into the breeze. I heard him say hello to Cara as he walked out the front door.

Cara barged into my room without knocking, dressed from the night before in a short jean skirt and pink tank top.

"Caesar just left here," she said.

"Yep," I replied.

"It's true," Cara said. Her expression softened. "Wow. I can't believe it. I thought it was just a rumor. I really can't believe it." She sat down on the corner of my bed and I scooted over under the sheet.

"You know, Cara. I really can't believe it either." I said and tears ran down my cheeks, but I was smiling.

Cara rubbed my back. "Why are you crying?" she asked.

"For everything that ever was. For everything that can not be. Because it all hurts so much." I thought about the version of me, before I had come to Provincetown. I had never cried in front of people. Suddenly, I was 'Ms. Water Works.' I broke into hysterical laughter.

"You need a Valium or something? Why are you laughing, now?"

"Love."

"Totally over-rated."

"No. It's life's litmus test."

"For what?"

"To see who you are. And who you want to become."

"You've really lost it."

"Oh, trust me, I know. My freak flag is waving loud and proud."

"What are you going to do about it?"

"Let if fly until the wind dies down."

She rested her head on the pillow by my side and before I drifted into sleep, I heard her say, "I'm really sorry, Angelina."

When I woke up again, she was gone. The telephone rang. It was Dylan.

"You still want to meet up?" He asked.

"I'll be there in fifteen minutes," I said, grabbing Dylan's blue windbreaker from the chair. I slid on a white tank top and cut-off jean shorts, and headed out the door into the daylight.

Chapter Sixteen

With fatigued legs, I climbed the steep hill toward the monument; my quadriceps quivering with each slight step. The pallid sun reflected off the black pavement and the heat cooked through the soles of my thin rubber flip-flops. It was a summer day when sitting still produced sweat and each breath was a battle. Even the chickadees on the branches were too exhausted to chirp. I tied my white tank top, soaked with perspiration, into a knot.

As I neared the top of the hill, I saw the monument's granite crown peaking through luscious green treetops; archway windows were carved on each of the four sides of the structure. The tower was a campanile, the design inspired after the Torre del Mangia in Siena, Italy. I had read that the monument was a tribute to the Pilgrims first landing of the Mayflower on the tip of America in 1620. It was in Provincetown that the Pilgrims had signed the Mayflower Compact. I could not help but smile at the contradiction between the Pilgrims who sought a New World to escape England and the antiquated architecture of the monument which had been derived from an old world country. Just as the structure seemed peculiar in Provincetown, I too felt misplaced. Yet, like the Pilgrims, I had been seeking a New World, as well– and I had found what I was looking for.

Finally, I had climbed to the peak of the hill, but after purchasing my ticket at the booth, and entering the monument courtyard, I realized the true climb had not yet begun. Dylan waved from a park bench in the shade at the base of the tower and tapped his watch.

"I thought you were standing me up," he said and stood to greet me, puckering his lips. I turned my cheek and his kiss landed there. I handed him his blue windbreaker.

"Thanks for returning it," he said.

"You know, that morning, I found a lot of interesting things in my room," I said, hoping to lead Dylan into a discussion about the contents of the storage room.

"Oh, really. Like what?" he asked. I had remembered what Caesar said: I should forget about it. It wasn't really my business. So I changed the topic.

"Sorry, I'm late. You didn't warn me that I'd be climbing Mount Kill-a-man-jaro in this heat."

"Just wait. It's going to be worth it. Trust me. It's an amazing view up there."

"Great." I wiped the perspiration from my forehead with the knot of my tank top.

"There's an elevator right?" I asked and Dylan chuckled.

"Nope. But, if she made it. It's safe to say, you can make it." Dylan pointed at a petite elderly woman with long white hair. She walked out of the monument, supported by a wooden cane and the silly smile of a young girl riding a roller coaster.

"It's splendid, dear," she said, addressing me. "What are you waiting for down here? Go get 'em." She was right. What was I waiting for?

"Are you ready?" Dylan asked.

I gave him a sneaky grin, and using the phrase I had stolen from Neely years ago, I shouted, "See ya', wouldn't want to be ya'!"

and ran through the arched doorway, leaving Dylan behind.

"Hey!" he yelled.

"I'm going to beat you to the top." I shouted back.

"No fair. You got a head start." Dylan said, his voice echoing inside the tower.

"C'mon, man. Are you going to let a girl beat you?" I yelled back.

Dylan's sneakers squeaked against the granite ramps at every turn, but I didn't look back. I charged up the stairs, with my left arm extended to help me make the sharp turns and to prevent me from slamming into the stone. The cement steps alternated with smooth inclined ramps, giving my calves a break and kicking my quadriceps into fifth gear.

The inside of the monument was like a medieval fortress, damp and darkly lit by orange tinted torch-lights; occasionally, I passed by a plaque engraved with the founding year and name of a Cape Cod town. My hurried steps blurred the information, one plaque undistinguishable from another.

"Angel!" Dylan's shout resonated off the granite walls. My toes were barely touching the ground. I was flying.

"Please, Angel, would you just stop for a second?"

I halted, peeking over the chipped white railing. "Just for a second," I said, resting my arms against the cold cement ledge, and dropping my chin on top of my hands; my chest was heaving up and down. I searched for the top of Dylan's sandy colored hair, but he was not in view. He was further behind than I thought.

"Dylan?" I asked.

No reply.

"Dylan Duncan. Hello?"

"Dylan, you're making me nervous. If you're having a heart attack, please, say help or something." I waited, my heartbeat reverberating inside my chest.

"Help!" he shouted, and I screamed as he grabbed my hips.

"You're a cheat!" I shouted, immediately shifting back into a full sprint; I continued up the tower with longer strides and a deeper determination. Dylan and I ran neck and neck. We were close. I could feel the summer heat beaming through the doorway at the top. When we rounded the last turn, I sharply leaned in, cutting Dylan off like a racecar driver around the track. I crossed the threshold and raised my closed-fisted arms in the air. But I lost the motivation to taunt Dylan with my victory.

The view humbled me.

"Oh, my God," I said, grasping a hold of the steel bars under one of the large archway windows. Dylan joined me. Inside of the crown of the monument, I could look out over the miniature world below.

"There's Commercial Street," Dylan said. Tiny white buildings ran in two parallel lines like the edges of toast, containing the hearty substance of a sandwich; the people, smaller than bumblebees, swarmed inside the street. Their faces were indistinguishable, but their colorful clothes: cobalt, magenta, orange, scarlet, and lemon-yellow, were like the bright colors of an enormous fruit basket.

A snow-white seagull launched from the top of the bell tower on Town Hall. He set out toward the horizon; his gray-tipped wings gracefully flapping through the stale air and over Cape Cod Bay. I wondered how the seagull traveled with such resolute and reverent trust in the universe.

"Come with me," Dylan walked to the opposite side of the monument and I followed. "I bet you didn't expect this." And, he was right. I hadn't.

At the tip of the horizon, a blue strip of the Atlantic Ocean vigorously pounded against the sandy shore and dunes rolled like Scottish hills along a barren and pristine section of land. Closer to the monument, in the foreground, a hilly green field was covered in yellow dandelions and white gravestones, some hidden by moss and lined up, like a grid, across the earth. With so much activity on Commercial Street, I was astonished to see the flip side. The cemetery. Provincetown had different life energies emerging on either side of the peninsula. Yet, there was an inherent balance inside both regions. There was seclusion in the mania of Commercial Street and connectedness in the solitude of the graveyard, rolling dunes, and immense Atlantic. There was a whole inside each part. And, perhaps, that was how the seagull flew with complete trust throughout the universe. Nothing was ever missing.

I stretched my arms out to the sides and began to run slowly, gracefully moving my arms up and down like wings. I looped around the tower, keeping my eyes on the horizon in each direction. A slight warm breeze blew against my back as I returned to Dylan. His hands clenched the steel bars, vertically lined against a window and he stared at the pavement directly below.

"I got to tell you something," he said.

"What?" I asked.

"I'm in a lot of trouble."

"The room?"

"You know?"

"I stumbled upon it," I said.

"The thing is….I came here so young and angry….and it was so easy. But, it's gotten out of control. And, Cara…..she's really got a problem with the coke. It's my fault." Dylan sat down on the cement, placing his elbows on his knees and dropping his head.

I sat down beside him, leaning back against the sharp edges of a granite block. "Have you talked to her about it?"

"Yeah. A billion times, but she says she doesn't have a problem," he said, "I was selling drugs in P-town long before I was with Cara. Eventually we started dating and partying. Soon we were snorting lines—here and there. She teamed up with me and started selling too. I wanted to keep her out of it, but she told me she needed to make money so she could get out of Provincetown. I thought it made sense and I was helping her. How twisted is that? When I became the head-chef at Mona Lisa's, I pulled myself together."

"You stopped selling?"

"No. I stopped using the junk. Cara didn't. And she was in on the deals, so I couldn't really stop her. She was out of control. She'd be passed out in bar bathrooms. I'd have to put her to bed. It's getting worse and worse." Dylan crumpled his windbreaker in a tight ball. "I cheated on her with Ava. Cara loved me so much. I thought if she was going to lose me, she'd just stop. Pretty dumb, huh?"

I placed my hand on top of his, trailing my fingers over his dark purple bruise.

Dylan looked at me, saying, "I didn't knock my hand on the grill."

"I know. You were on the boat. You punched that guy. I was on the wharf that night."

"He's now the main supplier. I decided to stop selling a year ago. I got out of the game," he said, "Cara was so angry about Ava and me. She said it was more business for her. I've been asking him to stop seeing Cara, but he won't. I just want her to stop hurting herself. Why can't I fix it?"

The Town Hall bell rang, startling me. I stared out at the rolling sand dunes as I counted twelve reverberating gongs. I could make out a split in the pine trees, a path to the dunes.

"Is Cara working today?" I asked.

"Yeah, why?"

"And this supplier…how dangerous is this guy? I mean, as far as drug dealer's go."

"Snuggles just wants his money."

"Snuggles? How does a drug-dealer get the nickname 'Snuggles'?"

"He grew up here. He used to bring his blanket to school, up until the fifth grade."

"Do you have a Jeep or SUV?"

"No."

I thought about where we could get one and I remembered the pick-up truck in Caesar's garage.

"Caesar has one," I said. "Call this Snuggles character. Tell him to follow our tracks on the dunes." I pointed to the area.

"What are we going to do?"

"We're going to give the man what he wants."

When I phoned Caesar, he was on his way to the Fine Arts Work Center for the meeting. He told me the keys were in the truck and of course I could borrow it. Caesar hadn't asked 'what for?' And for the first time, I was glad he didn't have the ability to dig any deeper. Dylan retrieved the truck from Caesar's home. After making arrangements with Snuggles, we piled the trash bags into the truck's bed and set off for the sand dunes.

"She's going to hate me," he said, eyeing the speedometer.

"Maybe for awhile, but she'll forgive you."

"No, she'll hate me forever."

"Well, would you rather have Cara hate you for doing something out of pure love or love you for allowing her to continue to hate herself?" I looked in the side mirror; the plastic bags were rippling in the wind. "You're doing the right thing."

"I know," he said, scratching his arm, "but, the right thing is so against my nature."

A police car pulled out of the Cumberland Farms.

"There's a cop behind us."

Dylan pressed the brake at the stop sign and put on the blinker. We turned onto the highway and the blue and red lights began flashing. Dylan pulled over. A series of cars whipped past us as we waited for the police officer to make his way toward the truck. I sucked in a long breath of air, holding it and attempting to kill my anxiety. Dylan stared at the orange traffic light fifty-yards ahead, a trail of sweat running from his temple.

"Well, well, what do we have here?" The pudgy cop stepped up to the window, patting one of the bags. He spit out a sunflower seed and leaned his head down to look into the truck. "Dylan?"

"Hey, Punchy!" Dylan said, and I exhaled the air gratefully.

"What's going on?" he said. "You know why I stopped you?"

"We're going to the dump."

"Yeah, man, I can see that," he said, "but, I can't let you get off so quick. It's been a long time coming." Dylan nodded, his fingers jingling the keys hanging from the ignition. I could tell he was thinking about speeding off.

I opened the glove compartment and handed Dylan the registration. "Here, don't you need this?"

"Thanks doll-face," the cop said, taking the document. He walked back to his car, with his thumbs tucked in the loops of his pants.

Dylan was biting his fingernails, his eyes filled with fear.

"Let me guess. Punchy used to be a big fighter in high school?" I said, hoping to lighten the tension.

"What are the chances that I finally get caught when I'm trying to end it?" He said, looking in the rearview mirror. "I guess you can't run forever."

A tiny spider dangled from a thread of a web connected to the ceiling; it swayed gently back and forth, hanging in mid-air. I blew at the web and watched the spider quickly retrace its steps to gain footing on the windshield.

"You're going to have to do me a favor," Punchy said, handing Dylan the registration and a ticket. "I had to stop you because you got a brake light out. I stopped Caesar twice already and he still hasn't paid the tickets. Give this to him. Tell him next time I'm going to have to seize the vehicle."

"Oh," Dylan said, smiling widely. "Thanks Punchy."

"Well, that's a first. No one thanks me for getting a ticket," he said, walking away. Dylan waited for him to pull onto the highway; a cloud of dirt surrounded us as he sped off, and just like that our bad luck had flipped. Dylan merged onto the highway and we drove through a green traffic light.

Dylan turned up a narrow dirt road in between a forest of pine trees. When we approached the sand dunes, Dylan stopped the truck to let the air out of the tires. The sun beat against the black seat and the backs of my thighs stuck against the leather. I stretched my arm outside the window, fanning my fingers to feel the air blow through them. The truck met the sand and we drove into the depths of the stark land, spreading in all directions like a desert and without any evidence of life. Yet I sensed the arid region harbored its share of sinful secrets. We climbed up a small dune and descended down to park the truck in the valley. We got out, sitting down on the hot sand and staring at the tire tracks. The pale yellow sun scorched my skin and a greenhead fly buzzed around my feet, searching for a spot to settle. From behind my back, I could hear the Atlantic waves roaring in the distance as we waited for Snuggles to appear.

"What if this doesn't work?" Dylan said, brushing a fly off his knee. "Cara could still find another dealer. People can't change just like that."

I saw the bumper of a red SUV reach the crest of the dune. "If it doesn't work, you let it go knowing you did all that you could. And that's more than most people would ever attempt."

We stood and I followed Dylan to the back of the truck. The SUV pulled up beside us and Snuggles got out, placing aviator sunglasses over his eyes. He was shorter than I was, but built with muscles too big for his frame, and his head appeared to sit on his shoulders. I could see blue veins protrude from his forearms and I was surprised he hadn't beaten Dylan to a pulp that night on the wharf.

"Alright, dude. Let's do this," he said, with a high pitched voice. "I hate it out here."

"Before we do," Dylan said, "how do I know you won't still see Cara?"

"Look dude, I have plenty of business in town. You of all people should know that." He laughed, putting his hands on his hips. "But I've also known Cara since high school and she's going to keep herself in the game. I can't promise she'll be out for good. But you got my word. I won't be dealing with her." He eyed the bags. "Not after our deal."

Dylan began pulling bags from the truck and dumping them to the ground.

Snuggles picked up a bag, saying, "You know, Dylan, it wasn't cool to bring your girlfriend here. Not cool at all."

"I'm not his girlfriend," I said, dragging a bag to his SUV.

"Well, whoever you are, you better be cool," he said, tossing a bag in the back of his car. "She better be cool, Dylan!"

"She's cool as long as you're cool."

"What the hell, dude? Are you trying to get yourself killed, Dylan?"

Dylan had finished clearing out the truck and he carried over a couple of bags. "The thing is Snuggles…I don't trust you."

"I'm offended…you taught me everything I know."

"And, my friend is an insurance policy. She's not from around here. She's heading out of town," he said, staring him down. "If you don't uphold your end of the bargain…I'm going to turn myself in and I'm turning you in too. And, if anything happens to me or Cara…" Dylan pointed at me, saying, "She's going to turn you in to the cops alone."

"Dude, you need to chill out."

"Are we clear?" Dylan asked.

"Yeah, man. It's all clear."

We dragged the remaining bags to the SUV, they shook hands, and I returned to the truck to wait for Dylan. I pulled up my tank top to dry the sweat off my face.

"I can't believe he didn't knock you out," I said as Dylan started the engine.

"He wouldn't have done that," Dylan said. "He used to work for me. When I stopped dealing, all the business went to him and Cara." Dylan turned the truck around and honked the horn. Snuggles flashed two fingers in a peace sign as we left him in the dunes.

"Why did you tell him I was leaving town?"

"Because you will be," Dylan sighed. "You have to let go. Don't stay through the winter or you'll get addicted."

"To what?" I asked, thinking of Caesar.

"Provincetown."

We sped up the highway, passing a field of dead grass. I wondered how long it had taken for the green to turn brittle and brown. I wondered how many people even noticed. I thought about what Dylan had said. Letting go. Maybe it wasn't about letting go of relationships, environments, jobs, or behaviors. They were not possessions I purchased and owned forever. They were experiences I rented on my own free will. However when what I chose no longer served my growth, it was time to invest anew. It was about letting in the power to love myself enough to invite change in the face of fear. Letting in. That's what love really meant. Letting in the faith that although I didn't know what was to become of me, I was committed to the creation of a more authentically aware, compassionate, and complete version. Moment by moment. Lesson by lesson. Letting in, I realized, was a solitary journey but the only way to fight against living in a dead pasture.

༄

I raced up the steps to my apartment. I didn't have time to change clothes. It was nearly five and I was supposed to meet my Dad at Town Hall. In the bathroom, I splashed cold water on my face, and when reaching for the hand towel I saw Caesar's wedding ring on the edge of the tub. I tucked it in my back pocket. When I entered my bedroom, I found a large manila envelope on top of my bed. I grabbed it, along with my cell phone, and made my way onto Commercial Street, sprinting all the way to Town Hall.

As the tower bell rang, I scanned the benches for my father, still panting for air. The seats were filled—families eating ice cream cones, elderly women gossiping, and couples holding hands. I couldn't find him. I walked toward the Town Hall building, sat down on the bottom step, and set the envelope beside me. Ella was there, as usual, and wearing a bright yellow skirt and halter top. A white silk scarf tied around her shoulders with black images of saxophones and dancers. I squinted, but couldn't make out the gray cursive writing. She swayed, clutching the microphone in both hands, and crooning "That's Life" in her deep, smoky voice. A toddler shook from side to side, looking up at Ella and letting out delightful squeals, enticing a few people to laugh from the benches. Her mother crouched down to take a photograph and the young girl began clapping her hands, her smile exposing her two top baby teeth.

After an hour had passed, I began to worry. What had happened to my dad? The sun had moved its way across Commercial Street, leaving a lilac afterglow in the sky above, and a cool breeze blew in from the bay. I picked up my cell phone.

"Hi, I was just going to call you," he said. "Where are you?"

"Town Hall."

"I'll be there in a half hour."

I pushed end on my cell phone and picked up the envelope by my side, sliding out a catalogue. My fingers trailed over the words: *Studio Escalier*. I turned the cover and began to read:

> *Located in Argenton-Chateau in France, we are an international point of contact for professionals, emerging artists, and beginning art students. Studio Escalier is an intensive studio art school and international residency program designed by master practitioners dedicated to the contemporary classical studio of drawing and painting from life.*

I pulled out a postcard tucked between the pages. There was a hand written note from the art director of the Studio. He was impressed by my piece and was extremely interested in viewing more of my work. I should come by 24 Pearl Street to the Fine Arts Works Center to meet with him. I turned the postcard over and there she was—the Mona Lisa. I felt my lips turn upward, ever so slightly.

As the time passed, the majority of people on the benches slowly began to disperse, joining the strolling crowd along Commercial Street, but I remained on the bottom step and waited in the twilight. The orange moon was swollen, hanging low in the starless sky.

Ella moved toward me with her purse tucked under her arm. She took a long swig of water from a bottle.

"I like your scarf," I said.

"Oh, thank you dear," she said, putting the water bottle on the step and pulling her shoulder length brown hair in a ponytail.

"What does the gray writing say?"

"Je ne sais quoi," she said, wiggling her fingers over her bright blue eyes and saying, "It's a French expression. It means…a certain something."

"How long have you been singing here?"

She sat down on the step beside me and crossed her legs, saying, "I came to P-town when I was sixty, so I guess it's been eight years already. Wow. I can't believe eight years have flied by. It took me so painfully long to get here." Ella picked a piece of lint off her skirt and folded her hands in her lap. "I wasted so much time."

"I heard you used to be a minister."

"That's true. My whole life I tried to fit in," she said, staring at the people sluggishly moving through the street. "Even though when I was six, I knew I was supposed to be something else. While the boys on my block took karate class, I begged my momma to take me to ballet. People can't understand it. I know. I couldn't even understand it, darling. God just made me this way. But, it was a feeling of being trapped and unable to get out. Like a clam being born in a lobster shell. That's probably why I went to seminary school. I thought God could fix it. I married. I had a lovely home in the suburbs. The years passed and I became a respected minister in the community. I couldn't help but return to the Gospel of John. *'If you hold to my teachings, you are really my disciples. Then you will know the truth and the truth will set you free.'* I wasn't living the truth. I was living a well-crafted image and I kept myself busy, but in still moments alone, I felt my hollowness. I began researching about transgender and I started the transition right after my fiftieth birthday."

"Weren't you afraid of leaving everything behind?"

"Oh, darling. I was terrified," she said. "My father still refuses to speak with me, but, my mother secretly comes to visit me here. And, once in awhile I'll chat on the phone with my ex-wife. I didn't change because I thought it would be easier. I've had my share of people pointing and laughing. I've been hit by rocks. But I smile back at them because they know not what they do." Ella pulled out a compact mirror from her purse and examined her reflection. She applied pink lipstick over her lips, smacking them together. Her gaze lingered in the mirror as if she was alone, and suddenly she smiled widely.

"You never wanted to retaliate?"

"Of course." She closed the compact and placed it in her purse. "But, I always ask myself this question: will my words or actions spread light or cast darkness? For what you shed upon the world, you shed upon yourself. It's divine law." Ella looked at her microphone-stand and stood, saying, "Most people have never spoken to me about this."

"Most people wouldn't have been able to respond so honestly."

Her kind eyes looked down upon me. She untied the silk scarf around her shoulders, handing it to me. "Here, dear."

I saw the Hermès label, saying, "I can't take this. It's much too generous."

"No, you will take it. This world is made up of many defensive people, darling. But you must remain this way. You must always speak from the heart and not from the tongue. I want you to do something for me."

"What's that?"

"When you are among those that have not yet learned to speak from the heart, remember this moment," she said, placing her hand on her hip and snapping her fingers. "And, you'll say, *je ne sais quoi*, and leave it at that."

Ella blew me a kiss in the air and walked back to her microphone-stand, picking up a packet of sheet music from the ground and flipping through the pages. I moved to take a seat on an empty bench, closer to her, and looked down at my postcard of the Mona Lisa.

"Hey, beautiful," he said, leaning down to kiss me on the space between my eyebrows.

"Caesar. Thanks for meeting me."

He sat down, sliding closer to me. "So, you got the package." I nodded. "He couldn't believe you didn't have any professional training. I'm not sure how much the program costs, but I will help you pay for it if you need me to." Caesar handed me a small black velvet box, saying, "Here."

"What's this?"

"It's from your dad."

"What?"

"He stopped by the restaurant this afternoon."

"Oh," I whispered, "he was supposed to meet me here."

"Yeah, that's what he said," Caesar said, "but, he had to go home. Something about Monica needing him. He said you would understand and to call him when you get back."

"Oh," I said, feeling my throat clog with pain. Caesar put his arm around me and I flipped open the jewelry box. It was a diamond heart-shaped necklace, just like the one he had given to my mother years ago.

"That's nice," he said.

I closed the cover. Caesar was right. It was nice. But it wasn't enough and it never would be—not for me, at least.

"You know, Caesar. You were wrong on two accounts."

"What's that?"

"We did go somewhere and we won't talk forever."

"I'll always be your friend."

"Then why does it hurt so badly?" I looked into his eyes, searchingly. They glowed brightly into mine with adoration.

"Because, I love you," he said, "and you know it."

Caesar stood and made his way to Ella to whisper something in her ear. She nodded and bent down to her sound system. Caesar returned to me with his arm reaching for me and the music began to play—*La Vie En Rose*. I moved into him and we began to dance. When he pulled me closer, I held my distance.

"Caesar, do you know how hurtful an affair is?" I asked calmly and I felt his body tense.

"We didn't do anything wrong. We didn't hurt anybody, Angelina," he said flatly and his face revealing nothing.

I rested my head on his heart, listening to the heavy beat of it, saying, *"Je ne sais quoi."*

"I don't get it."

I held his jaw and smoothed my thumb across his cheek. "I know. You don't."

We continued to sway to the music, closely pressed together; Caesar guided me in one large and slow loop back to where we started. Before Ella finished the lyrics of *La Vie En Rose*, I moved to the bench to collect my belongings. I needed to head to Pearl

Street to meet with the art director. I pulled Caesar's wedding ring from my back pocket and handed it to him.

"Good-bye, Caesar Riva," I said boldly and teasingly. The way I did, before we began. I felt my lashes wet with tears but I smiled lovingly.

Caesar reached for my hand and firmly kissed the back, letting his lips linger there while his eyes fixed me with tenderness. He cleared his throat and then replied equally as bold, "Good-bye, Angelina Moreau."

As I passed Ella, I twirled around, spinning the silk scarf in the air above my head, and then I stepped down from the curb to join the large crowd of strangers on the street. After a few steps, I thought about turning around to look at Caesar, walking in the opposite direction. But I didn't. I kept moving, moving forward and with my eyes set upon a bright bluish star in the sky.

Epilogue

From time to time a series of questions run through my mind. Was Cara intentionally antagonistic or a heartbroken and insecure woman? Was Dylan a ruthless womanizer or a man afraid to commit to love he could lose? Was Caesar Riva a selfish married man who used other women at his convenience or a lonely man committed to sticking out what he started with his wife, for the sake of his children? And, what am I? The Harvard graduate, All-American soccer player with a list of outstanding accomplishments or a reckless adulteress?

Like Mona Lisa's sly smile, these enigmatic questions have no tangible replies. I may never know. But what I do know is we are all in this together with the Mona Lisa's unflinching gaze following us all. There is a saint and a sinner, a creator and a victim, a lover and a hater inside all of us. And the Mona Lisa's slightly upturned lips are here to ask—what one do you want to be? For that is the power of her seduction. The peaceful comfort of sitting still among the contradictions. Even within herself. For whatever has happened or will happen, she knows that she is a piece in a mystic puzzle and her part creates an indelible impression. When I look at her, she reminds me that in life's large game of hide-and-go-seek, it's safe to come out. Listen closely and you will hear.

Olly, olly, oxen free!

"To change skins, evolve into new cycles,
I feel one has to learn to discard.
If one changes internally, one should not continue
to live with the same objects.
They reflect one's mind and psyche of yesterday.
I throw away what has no dynamic use."

—Anaïs Nin

ACKNOWLEDGMENTS

Without love this creation would not have been born. I thank my two big brothers (Billy and Charlie) for showing me mental and physical strength with the lives that you lead. You are each one wing, helping me learn how to fly. Without the support of Dawn Henrique, in the early days, this mission would not have come to fruition. Thank you for your consistent care, patience, and support. Your soul is an eloquent song with an endurance that plays on like the ocean waves. And, to the late Mister Sweet Johnny Coltrane. "Dear Lord." Your reverence flows through me. Your saxophone has the power to awaken sleeping hearts. I thank Ms. Oprah Winfrey. When I wanted to give up, you were consistently there at four PM, sending your message to commit to giving back to the world, the best way I know how. Kristy Love Troup thanks for taking a cut on the rent, for my sake, back in 2002. For generously helping me as a struggling writer and encouraging me to continue to follow my dreams, even though I was eating oatmeal twice a day. Your middle name personifies who you are. And to Joe Murray, thank you, for generously helping me to not eat oatmeal twice a day. Susy Garcia, Lauren McDonnell, Courtney Hurst, Bethany McDonald, Laura Franz, Susan Shore Gotham…the words, the love, the encouragement, the smiles, and the laughs. Thank you all, from the top to bottom and left to right of my whole being. Marzia, Maurizio,

Patrizia, and Massimo Sesini: Ti volgia bene. Grazie Mille. Ying, thanks for being one of my biggest fans from afar. "You and I, we ain't normal." I adore that quote. Thanks for being 'not normal' with me. Don't be afraid to keep evolving. Love, Yang. Becky Kinel, thanks for breaking it down with me. You're a beautiful person and I greatly appreciate that you put up with my neurosis along this journey. Thanks for being the kind of person that pushes me to keep evolving.

Pamela Mandell, my editor, thank you for the work you put into my manuscript. You did it with an abundance of love and I thank you for teaching me to trust myself. Jerid O'Connell, I thank you for selflessly assisting me with the visual details of this project. I will not forget your random act of kindness, I pinky swear. Also of Fuel Digital Inc., Candice Prizer, and John Kohler, I appreciate all your technical help and kind-hearted support along the way.

Lastly, Ann Rogers. You are a pearl. I've always known it. And, I'm glad you've finally opened your shell to the world. You taught me courage and to change in the face of fear. I love you, Mom. You are the most successful human being that I ever met. And, what a privilege it is for me to say that I came from you.

"b'Evolutionary"
with love and peace,
Kim Rogers

www.kimrogers.org
www.kimrogers.blogspot.com